Kiss Me If You Can
A Spicy + Unconventional Romantic Comedy
Cheryl Terra

Bang It Out Writing

Author's Note

This is the first book of the If You Can series, but a spicy prequel novella called **The Boy Next Door** covers some events mentioned in this book. Kiss Me If You Can can be read and enjoyed without having read The Boy Next Door, but the prequel gives more insight into the relationship between Nellie and JP, as well as Nellie's family situation.

If you haven't read the prequel or would like a reminder of the events, you can find a basic synopsis on the next page.

There is also a character summary **at the back of the book** featuring names and basic descriptions of important characters.

Please note that this books is written in Canadian English, which has rules and spellings from both UK and US English. It also contains phrases and words specifically from Québécois French. Translations of those can be found **at the end of the book**.

Content Warnings: Full content warnings can be found on my website, but please note that the If You Can series contains characters who engage in casual relationships with characters not involved in the main relationship dynamic. This will not include adultery of any kind between the MCs.

This book contains a large age gap teacher/student relationship, toxic parenting and family situations, slut shaming, references to non-consensual activity, and multiple explicit scenes.

The Road So Far

A Summary of Previous Events in the If You Can Series

The Boy Next Door

- Nellie's best friend Anne-Marie has an older brother named JP that Nellie insists she doesn't have a crush on.

- After telling him about a high school boyfriend who spread nasty rumours about her, JP tells Nellie it's okay to want sex but not want a relationship.

- JP and Nellie secretly hook up. Nellie doesn't initially tell him she's a virgin.

- When they're done, Nellie asks him not to tell anyone what they did and rushes away. She's afraid of her religious, conservative businessman father finding out.

- Kiss Me If You Can starts about three years after the events of The Boy Next Door

Want the full story? Get your copy of The Boy Next Door here: **geni.us/bndct**

Prologue

Here There Be Dragons

THERE WEREN'T MANY PEOPLE who could convince me to be a princess instead of a dragon, but Anne-Marie Marchand was one of them.

It wasn't that I didn't like princesses. I did, very much. I just also wanted to fly and breathe fire. But Anne-Marie said she was having a Disney princess party and none of the princesses were dragons, so I couldn't be a dragon princess. And I agreed, but only because she was my best friend *and* it was her birthday.

And because she said I could dress like *my* favourite princess for the day, as long as that princess wasn't Ariel because that was her favourite princess and no one else could show up as Ariel.

Well, except the *actual* Ariel, who her parents said was a close personal friend because seven-year-olds didn't understand how hiring children's entertainers worked.

So instead of running around an elegantly decorated backyard that looked more like a wedding reception than a child's birthday party and roaring at people while pretending to breathe fire, I was clad in a fancy yellow party dress and insisting I got to be Belle for everything.

Which was causing some problems.

"But I don't want to be Cinderella!" a girl named Emilie protested as Anne-Marie tried to shove a blue foam crown into her hands. "I wanna be *Belle*."

"Nellie already claimed Belle," Anne-Marie said. "She said before the party."

"That's not fair," argued another girl named Yasmine. "It doesn't count if you said it *before* the party."

"Yes it does," I said. "Anne-Marie said I could."

"That's not *fair*!" Emilie repeated, batting the blue foam crown away from her. "We weren't even here yet."

"I know," I said. "That's why I said it before the party. So no one else could get it."

"Why don't you just rock-paper-scissors for it?" said someone else. I looked over to see Anne-Marie's eleven-year-old brother standing nearby with a bored look on his face.

Ugh.

JP.

"Because that's stupid," I said. "I claimed it."

"It's not stupid," JP said. "It's fair."

"Why are you even here?" I asked.

"My mom said I have to be," he said. "Otherwise I'd be literally anywhere else."

"Jean-Paul," said another new voice, and all of us turned to see Anne-Marie's dad, Mr. Marchand, walking up to us. Behind him, my dad walked stiffly, his lips pressed in a flat line. Not too far behind them, my and Anne-Marie's moms were sitting at a white-clothed table. Anne-Marie's mom was wearing her normal expression of polite interest, but she was very determinedly not looking at my mom, who had her arms folded and a deep frown on her face.

"You are here because you love your sister," Mr. Marchand scolded his son.

JP sighed. "I am here because I love my sister."

"Good." Mr. Marchand looked at me, then at Emilie. "Girls, what is going on over here?"

"Nellie is not being fair," Emilie said to my dad, her voice shaking as she pointed at me.

My mouth dropped open and my cheeks went red with anger. "That's not true!"

"Yes it *is*! You said—"

"No!" I stomped my foot. "It's *not*. It's not even a *little* true."

"Nellie, you do not interrupt people when they are speaking," my dad said, his voice clipped.

"I wasn't! She—"

"Nellie," he said again, his voice impatient. "You are being rude."

"Daddy, I'm just—"

"They both want to be the same princess for the mermaid race," JP interrupted from where he was standing. "Nellie says she called it before the party, Emilie says that's not fair, and neither of them realize it doesn't matter."

"It does too matter," I said. "And stop being rude. I was speaking."

"Eleanor, enough," my dad said.

I looked up at him, hurt. "But you just said—"

"Alright, alright," Mr. Marchand said. "Well, if you will not *roche-papier-ciseaux* to choose, why don't you each tell me why you think you should be Belle and I'll decide?"

Even from a distance, I saw Anne-Marie's mom's polite expression falter into a wince. Beside her, my mom's face was nearly purple.

"Okay," Emilie said, folding her arms. "Well, I want to be Belle because she's my favourite and I like to read. Nellie can't even read."

"Hey!" I protested. "I can too."

"She can't read *well*," Emilie said. "And I can sing better, *and* I'm French like Belle is."

"I'm French too," I said.

"You don't even speak French at home," Emilie said.

"I take it at school!"

"I learned it when I was a *baby*!"

"Yeah, well, I'm *more* like Belle." I looked up at Mr. Marchand, determination on my face, and lifted my hand to count on my fingers. "One, my name is *Nell*-ie. Like *Belle*. Two, Anne-Marie said we have to be princesses today and Belle is the only princess I like so she said I could be Belle because I'm not allowed to be a dragon."

"There aren't any dragons in any of the movies," Anne-Marie said with a sigh.

"There is in *Sleeping Beauty*," I said, then turned back to Mr. Marchand. "Three, I have brown eyes like Belle does—"

"Emilie has brown hair, though," JP said.

"*Four*," I said loudly. "I don't let *rude* and *primeval* boys interrupt me."

"Primeval?" JP repeated, amused.

"And I've watched the movie a billion times so I know what primeval is because that's what she says Gaston is," I finished, folding my arms. "And also Anne-Marie said I could be Belle, so that means I should automatically be Belle."

Mr. Marchand looked at me for a moment, then chuckled and glanced at my dad. "It almost looks like you've got a little lawyer in the making here, Max."

My dad nodded. "A parent's dream."

I looked from Mr. Marchand to my dad, confused. "What's a lawyer?"

Behind me, JP burst out laughing. "Seriously?"

I glared over my shoulder at him. "What's so funny?"

"My dad is a lawyer," he said. "It's a job."

"A very good job, Nellie," my dad said.

"But what kind of job?" I said.

"Well, there are many types of lawyers," Mr. Marchand said. "But overall, it means helping people know the law so they don't get in trouble."

"You'd love it," JP said. "They argue all day."

I looked at him, horrified. "I don't want to do that."

"Why not? You love to argue."

"I do *not* love to argue," I argued, and I would've probably argued more, but I was distracted by a woman with long, dreamy, bright red hair held back by a purple shell clip floating up to us.

She had arrived wearing a sparkly green mermaid tail and purple seashell top, but moments after greeting Anne-Marie, she'd spun around and the whole thing transformed into the beautiful turquoise ball gown she was wearing now. She smiled, first at my dad and Mr. Marchand, then at Anne-Marie, then at the rest of us.

"What seems to be the problem over here, princesses?" Ariel asked in a tinkling, sing-song voice, then caught sight of JP. "And prince?"

I assumed JP would tell her like he'd told his dad, but even though he always had something to say about everything, JP was oddly quiet and his cheeks went pink.

"We're having a minor disagreement about who gets to be Belle," Mr. Marchand said, his voice almost reluctant.

Ariel reached out, taking the blue foam crown from Anne-Marie and picking up the yellow foam crown that was still on the table beside her. "How about this: you can *both* be Belle, but one of you will be Belle with the yellow crown and the other will be Belle with a blue crown. Like how Belle sometimes wears her blue-and-white dress and other times she wears her yellow dress?"

Emilie and I exchanged glances, silently agreed that we *had* to do what Ariel told us to, then looked back at her and held out our hands.

"Okay," we said in unison.

Ariel smiled. My dad and Mr. Marchand looked simultaneously annoyed and relieved. JP's face was still pink.

"Who else still needs a crown?" Ariel asked, turning back to Anne-Marie. "Once everyone has one, we can get the mermaid race started."

"What's a mermaid race?" Mr. Marchand asked.

"It's similar to what humans would call a three-legged race," Ariel said cheerfully. "And you know..." She hummed softly, then looked over where the boys at the party were smacking each other with their foam crowns while they waited at the start line. "We have six princesses who are going to race, but only five Prince Charmings to pair them with. Perhaps Princess Anne-Marie's brother could help us out and join the mermaid race?"

"Me?" JP asked.

"Well, duh," I said. "Marc-Andre can barely walk."

"Yeah," Anne-Marie said. "He would get hurt."

"Yeah," I said, even though I'd definitely been more concerned about being the person with the potential disadvantage of dragging a toddler across the yard to the finish line.

"It would be so very helpful, Prince JP," Ariel said. "As a favour to me?"

"Well... okay," JP said, much to everyone's surprise, although I think he regretted it after Ariel wrangled us over to the start line and handed him the last unclaimed crown.

"Okay, princesses and princes!" Ariel said, clapping her hands together. "Find the person with the same colour crown as you! That's your partner for the mermaid race."

I looked at JP.

JP looked at me, then at Ariel, then at the yellow crown in his hands. He looked up at Ariel again, then drew in a breath and let it out before resignedly putting the crown on his head.

"Come on, Nellie," he said. "Let's get lined up."

I fidgeted, picking at the skin by my thumbnail as I considered asking Emilie if she'd switch crowns with me, but her mom was already tying her to her partner. Then I considered saying I didn't want to run the race, but even at that age, I couldn't bring myself to back away from a challenge.

"Just so you know, we better win," I said, joining JP at the start line and pushing my skirt out of the way to line my leg up next to his.

"I always win," JP said.

I rolled my eyes, but didn't say anything else as JP's mom came over and helped tie our legs together. She said something to him that I couldn't hear before heading back to her table. JP shrugged, then awkwardly put his arm around my shoulders. Given that he was four years older than me, JP was much taller than I was, so it was easier for me to hold onto the back of his shirt.

"Take your first step with the leg tied to mine, okay?" he said as we staggered up to the start line.

I nodded. Both of us watched as Ariel moved to the edge of the start line, then brought her hand up in the air.

"Okay, princesses and princes!" she called. "On your mark—"

JP bent his leg. I didn't because we would've probably fallen down.

"—get set—"

"Ready?" he asked.

"I was born ready," I said.

He snorted.

"—*go!*"

And yeah, maybe JP was annoying and rude, but I couldn't deny he wanted to win as badly as I did. Both of us were dead set on coming in first, and even though JP's legs were longer than mine, we barely stumbled as we rushed towards the finish line.

Which, of course, meant Emilie screeched it wasn't fair that I got paired with JP, since he was bigger than everyone else and that meant he was faster. And her partner agreed, which made one of the other pairs agree.

So of course, I had to argue that JP being taller than everyone else was actually a bad thing because our knees didn't even bend in the same place. And that it didn't make us faster because he had to match how fast I could run since my legs were shorter. And that his gigantic head meant that we were more likely to fall over, so the fact that we kept our balance at all was amazing.

And of course, Anne-Marie was on my side because we were best friends, which meant Emilie started crying, and Ariel tried to cheer her up while JP and I stood to the side, our legs still tied together because neither of our parents had come over to help us. His mom was with Anne-Marie and his dad was on the other side of the yard, directing someone on where to put a gigantic three-tiered ocean-themed cake. My parents were at the same table they'd been at before, my mom with her arms folded and one leg crossed over the other while my dad leaned towards her and said something. His face was so calm and collected that to anyone else, he probably looked like he was commenting on something as trivial as the shade of white the Marchands had selected for the tablecloths.

But given the way my mom's mouth tightened and twisted, it was not that.

I twisted my mouth to the side, then reached down and tried to find the end of the strap tying us together to see if I could undo it myself.

"Don't mess with it," JP said.

"Don't tell me what to do."

"You'll get it knotted," JP said. "Then you're gonna be stuck with me tied to you forever."

I immediately stopped playing with the strap and straightened up. JP jostled me as he laughed.

"Just wait for your parents to help," he said.

I sighed, looking at the table. "Yeah, but they're arguing again."

JP followed my gaze. "Again? How often do they argue?"

"Probably more than lawyers," I said.

My dad finished saying whatever he was saying to my mom. Neither of them spoke for a moment, then my mom stood and started marching towards the Marchands' house. My dad's eyes followed her until she was about halfway across the yard. He stood and, without so much as a glance towards me, walked in the opposite direction to join Mr. Marchand near the cake table. Without thinking, I brought my thumb to my mouth, sticking the tip between my teeth and biting down.

"I'll try to get it undone," JP said.

"No!" I said. "You said you'd knot it and I'd get stuck to you."

"No, I said *you* would knot it and get stuck to me," he said, twisting and reaching down to fiddle with the strap. "I'm older than you, so I can untie it better."

"Being older doesn't make you smarter," I grumbled.

He chuckled. "You know, you really should think about being a lawyer. Considering you argue about *everything*, you'll be a pro at it by the time you're old enough."

"I don't argue about everything!"

"Sure you don't."

"I don't," I said. "And even if I did, it doesn't sound very fun."

"It's what I'm gonna be when I grow up," he said. "Like my dad."

"Well, that's *definitely* not what I'm gonna be," I said.

"What are you gonna be?"

"A dragon," I said.

"I mean as a job."

I folded my arms. "Dragon."

"You can't be a dragon when you grow up."

I was getting very tired of people telling me I couldn't be a dragon. "Why not?"

"Because you're a human and humans can't be dragons," he said.

"Yes, they can."

"No, they can't."

"Yeah, they can!"

He laughed. "Trust me, I'm right. You can't be a dragon, and you're gonna be a lawyer one day."

And maybe I didn't know what I wanted to work as when I grew up yet.

But after JP got the strap loose and I scurried away to join my best friend for the rest of her party, there were two things I knew I'd never be: the person who allowed JP Marchand to be right about anything, and a lawyer.

Chapter One
It's Not Me, It's You

OF ALL THE HEARTS I'd broken in my life, there were only three I regretted.

The first heart belonged to Bodhi and he was in love with me. In his eyes, I was a goddess, something beyond ethereal, something that defied his understanding of the mortal plane comprising our existence.

We spent every single day together that summer between eleventh and twelfth grade. He would have done—and did do—anything for me.

Then he found out I was being paid to hang out with him.

I'd never felt guilt the way I did when he locked himself in his bedroom. I pounded on the door, begging him to open it, and was almost ready to climb the side of the house and break in through his window when his parents got home.

"I'm so sorry," I'd said to his mom as she joined me at his bedroom door. "I didn't know. I really, really didn't know."

She'd been kind about it, but I think both of us had shattered a bit when Bodhi's dad finally jimmied the lock on the door and opened it to reveal Bodhi lying on his bed, face buried in his pillow and a knockoff Tigger plushie I'd won for him at Canada's Wonderland a few days earlier clutched in his arms.

"I'm sure she still likes you, sweetheart," his mom had said as she tried to console him.

"I do," I'd said from the doorway, where I was hovering.

"But not like *that*!" he'd wept.

Which was absolutely true.

Although, it was a little surprising he even knew the distinction between liking someone and *liking* someone since Bodhi was six years old and I was his almost-eighteen-year-old babysitter. But even though his mom and I managed to convince him that I could still be his best bud even though I was also being paid to babysit him, I never quite got over the guilt of making him cry like that. His parents assured me it was okay, that I couldn't have done anything differently, but I just...

He didn't deserve me hurting him like that, even if it wasn't my fault.

The second heart I regretted breaking was my own, but that was much later and much more complicated.

And the third heart? That was Shawn's.

No, wait. Sheldon's.

No... it was...

Oh, right. *Shane's.* The third heart was Shane's.

"Look, Shane—"

"It's Scott."

I frowned as I stopped at an intersection, waiting for the light-up man to appear and let me know it was theoretically safe to cross. "Really? Not Shane? Did you change it?"

He half-laughed. "Nope. It's always been Scott. Scott Humprey."

"Hmm." The light changed and I started forward, cradling my phone against my shoulder in case I slipped on any of the slushy patches lining the crosswalk, since I was carrying a twelve-pack of beer in my left hand and obviously I wouldn't be sacrificing that if I fell. "Whatever. Look, Scott. It's not me. It's you."

"Just what every guy likes to hear," he said dryly. "'*You're* not the problem, Scott. It's *me.*'"

"You misheard me," I said. "I said it's you. Not me."

He was silent for a moment. "Wait, what?"

"It. Is. Not. Me," I said, loudly and clearly and packing all the annoyance I could into it, although in fairness to Sonny, part of that annoyance was because it was a bone-chillingly cold February day in Ottawa and I was *not* dressed for the weather. "It's. You."

"It's me," he repeated. "I'm the problem? *You're* the one breaking up with me, Nellie!"

"Breaking up with you would require us to have been dating in the first place," I said. "And we absolutely weren't."

"We slept together *five times*," Snyder said. "You led me on and—"

"Hold it right there," I said. "I didn't lead you anywhere. I was *very* clear with you when we hooked up at the frat party that I was straight-up fulfilling a fantasy of getting railed in a toga."

He made a disgusted noise. "So you remember how we first fucked but not my name?"

"I'd take that as a compliment if I were you. How many guys can say the girl they slept with couldn't remember their name, but never forgot how good they were in bed?"

"I can't believe this," he said. "Yeah, and then we fucked *again* at the tailgate party."

"Mm-hmm, and at the Halloween party," I said wistfully. "You looked so cute in your sexy postal worker costume."

"At some point, you knew I was gonna think it was serious," he said. "People don't just fuck the same person over and over without assuming it's going somewhere."

"Okay, first of all, Steve—"

"You're doing this on purpose, aren't you?"

"You're smart for a frat boy," I said. "Especially one who misunderstood the nature of our situation for an entire semester, apparently. So let me make this clear for you one more time, okay? First of all, yes, people do fuck the same person over and over again without it being serious. They're called fuck buddies. Friends with bennies. People that are hangin' and bangin'. Benafriends, if you will, although I'd say we should probably go with the hangin' and bangin' title since you and I are *not* friends."

"I can't believe you're—"

"Next, we are not together," I continued. "We never *were* together. I don't do relationships. I don't do serious. I would have thought that was clear given I not only outright told you I didn't want anything serious, but every single one of our hookups involved a party and we never, not once, saw each other outside of those contexts."

"Yeah, but—"

"But nothing. We fucked in a closet at a party, Sterling. I had a selection of condoms for you to choose from and told you if you weren't cool with the fact I'd hooked up with that girl who ended up being your pledge's twin sister earlier that night, we should probably stop. What about any of this screams 'I'm a girl who's relationship material' to you?"

"People can change."

I ignored him. "I straight-up said to you, multiple times, that I think relationships are a way for one person to control another and I'd rather keep things physical and fun instead of committed and boring. That's why we always hooked up at parties."

"Not *every* hookup was at a party."

"Oh, *right*," I said. "Remind me again which time wasn't?"

He didn't respond.

"Simon? Wanna remind me about the time that wasn't at a party?"

"How was I supposed to take that?" he said. "You showed up saying we needed to stop hooking up because I was taking things the wrong way, then you spent the night. A normal person would assume you changed your mind."

"Maybe being so normal is why you're not the right guy for me, Stanley."

"Wow. *Wow*."

I switched the beer to my other hand and reached up, adjusting my phone so I didn't strain my neck. "What's so 'wow' about that? People can be not-right for each other."

"I guess I kinda just hoped I'd be enough for you."

"What's that supposed to mean?" I asked.

"You know." He chuckled, his voice taking on a mournful hint of self-loathing. "I'm the chubby nerd who isn't traditionally attractive and who just wants to be with someone so he can treat her right and make her happy. You're the super hot, curvy blonde girl with an incredibly warranted reputation for being a total goddess in bed. You've always been out of my league."

And ugh.

Ugh.

"First of all, fuck you," I said.

"Excuse me?!"

"For implying I'm that goddamn shallow. You know I'm into basically anyone. Short, tall, thin, fat, muscley, male, female, non-binary—"

"I get it. You'll fuck anything that moves."

"That's the spirit," I said cheerfully. "So what you look like makes no difference to me. Second of all, being chubby isn't a bad thing, dickwad. I mean, I'm chubby."

"You're not chubby," he said. "You're curvy. That's—"

"—a synonym." I rolled my eyes, even though he couldn't see me. "I don't give a shit. Life is too short not to get extra cheese and my weight's not gonna stop me from sitting on someone's face, as you well know."

"You're average sized."

"It doesn't matter what size I am, I'm still hot." Which was one-hundred percent accurate. "The point is, I'm not out of your league because of how either of us look. I'm out of your league because you're a dick."

"And so you waited until after Valentine's Day to call and break up with me? You're breaking up with me because I sent you *flowers*, Nellie."

"I didn't ask for them. And it's not like it was an engagement ring, Sullivan. And *again*, I'm not breaking up with you. We were never dating." I turned down the next block, shivering in the cold and flexing my fingers as they started going numb. "It is *not* my fault you assumed we had something that we didn't."

That was enough for him to finally move from self-loathing to anger. "I guess it serves me right for getting involved with the school slut."

I burst out laughing. "Like I haven't heard that before."

"Do you even *know* your body count anymore?"

"Of course I do."

He snorted. "Let me guess, you're one of those people who keeps a list. How many notebooks long is it now?"

"I made a spreadsheet, actually. Far more convenient and easier to access on my phone."

"You're joking."

"Maybe I am. Maybe I'm not. You'll never know, will you?"

He scoffed. "You know what? You're right."

"I'm glad you see it that way."

"You're the kind of person who's okay with sleeping around and breaking people's hearts because they have the fucking audacity to want to be around you. Clearly, I'm coming out on top here since I don't have to deal with you anymore."

"I dunno," I said. "I'm starting to feel pretty good about not having to deal with you, either."

"Yeah, but you have to deal with yourself. Everyone else can escape, but you're stuck with you."

I half-laughed. That stung more than expected, but I didn't want Skylar to know that. "At least I'll never be bored."

"I know you're trying to fuck the whole world, Nellie, but spreading your legs for everyone isn't going to make them like you."

I laughed again, louder that time. "You understand acknowledging that you knew I was a slut makes you extra stupid because not only did *I* warn you about me, you knew what you were getting into?"

"Fuck you."

"Again, thank you, but I'm no longer interested. You keep telling people I'm your girlfriend and that's making it hard for me to fuck other people because they think I'm cheating on you. And I might be a slut, but I'm *not* a cheater." I turned onto a sidewalk that led to an old-looking house with scraggly bushes in the front. "Look, thank you for the flowers, but we're not a couple. So stop sending me things. Now if you'll excuse me, I'm going to my friends' place for dinner and I want to check out early so I'm ready for my internship interview."

"The Forensic Analysis and Investigation internship? The one with the police department?"

I frowned. Seth wasn't in the Forensic Science department, and I was almost certain I'd never told him about the internship. I didn't usually talk about school while I had someone's dick in my mouth. Then again, it wasn't out of the ordinary for me to do something and then completely forget about it. "Yeah. I've got my last interview tomorrow."

"Right. Well, from the bottom of my heart, I hope you fail."

"I'd expect nothing less. I gotta go now. Catch ya later... Sailor."

I hung up, shoved my phone into my pocket as I hurried up the steps, and banged on the front door. It flung open barely a second later, a burst of warm air and golden light and loud conversation spilling out into the cold February air.

"*Ehhhh*!" shouted Calvin, who had warm brown skin and big, expressive eyes. "Nellie!"

"Hey!" Brandon, Calvin's roommate, joined us at the door, reaching out to take the beer from my hands. He was average height and had white skin tinged with red beneath a thick, unruly beard. "How's it going? I didn't think you were coming."

"Why wouldn't I?" I asked. "Coming is one of my favourite things to do."

Calvin cackled and threw an arm around my shoulders as he slammed the front door closed. "Yeah it is."

"I thought you have your interview tomorrow," Brandon said. "For that summer job?"

"The FAI internship," I said. "I do."

He eyed the twelve-pack I was carrying. "And you're gonna go hungover?"

"Of course not. Even though it's basically a formality at this point. I've rocked every other round of interviews and they hinted last time that I've already been shortlisted." I motioned at the beer. "That's for you guys."

"And this is why we love you," Calvin said, opening the case and helping himself to one of the beers. "C'mon. There's a ton of food and we're doing a buffet-style sorta thing. I made the siomai you liked last time."

"You know the way to my heart," I said, following him to the kitchen.

"And this is kinilaw," he said. "My mom's recipe."

"What's kinilaw?"

Brandon handed me a paper plate. "It's kinda like ceviche."

I shook my head. "Nope. No thanks."

"One bite," Calvin said, lifting a scoop of kinilaw from the bowl. "You said you didn't think you'd like the sisig last time but you did."

"Zero bite," I said. "Next time, okay? No offense to your cooking, but I can't risk food poisoning before my interview."

Calvin clutched his heart at the implication raw fish might make me sick, but if I'd known then that I'd already fucked up the interview, I would've just tried it. And had a beer. Or two. Or the entire case and not wasted my time waking up early, doing my makeup, and getting to the hotel they were holding the interviews at twenty minutes early.

But there was no way I could have known what would come from breaking Scott Humprey's heart.

Chapter Two
Stride of Pride

"So then he goes, 'Well, maybe if you let me put it in your butt,'" Sydney said.

I let out a surprised bark of laughter, easing off the brake just enough to roll the whole five feet traffic had moved forward before coming to a complete stop again. "And you said no?"

"What makes you think I said no?"

"Mainly that you're sitting comfortably in the front seat of my car and not complaining about how much your ass hurts," I said.

"Maybe he was really careful."

I snorted. "I have serious doubts that Tyler is the kind of guy who would be considerate and gentle with anal. He looks like the type who would think a drizzle of his chew-flavoured spit would be enough lube."

"He doesn't chew tobacco," Sydney said.

"He looks like he does."

"Tell me how you really feel."

"Like my super-hot best friend can do way better than *Tyler*."

"Well, yeah. But my options were limited last night. When I got back from my parents, Reid had that girl over again and I wasn't into sitting around listening to them fuck."

"You've fucked people for stupider reasons. So what'd he say after you said no anal?"

"Again, what makes you think I said no?"

I looked at Sydney, raising my eyebrows. She blinked her greenish-brown eyes at me innocently, a mischievous smirk hidden on her rosy pink lips. Syd was the kind of gorgeous that looked just as good in a baggy hoodie with no makeup as she did in full glam makeup and a ballgown. She was tall, standing at least three or four inches higher than my five-foot-three, and had long strawberry-blonde hair, smooth, fair white skin, and long athletic legs and toned arms.

We'd been best friends since our first year of university. I'd seen her around a few times because she lived in the same apartment building as me, but it wasn't until near the end of our first semester that we'd run into each other in a nightclub bathroom. And as everyone knows, the bonds forged in a women's bathroom are near unbreakable, so we'd decided to be each other's wing-women and skipped out of the bathroom arm-in-arm to try and get laid.

It worked, because of course it did, though I'd been a little sad when I woke up the next morning in some guy's bedroom and realized I hadn't gotten any contact information for my bathroom buddy. That sadness was short lived when I snuck down the hallway to the front door so I could leave and stumbled across Syd doing the same thing.

"Oh, sweet," I said. "We picked up roommates?"

"I guess so," she replied. "We live in the same building, right? Wanna grab a coffee while we walk-of-shame together?"

"Yes to the coffee, no to the walk-of-shame," I said. "That would imply I'm ashamed of this."

"But calling it a walk home sounds so boring."

"I know. That's why I call it a stride-of-pride."

We'd been best friends ever since, obviously. Which is why she was now sitting in my car, suffering in traffic with me as we made the drive to my dad's house in Montreal.

"Okay," I said. "So if you didn't say no to anal with Tyler, what did you actually say?"

"After you."

I frowned at her, glancing out the windshield and rolling the car forward almost six feet that time. "I didn't say shit. I wasn't there."

She burst out laughing. "No, that's what I said to him. 'After you.'"

My mouth dropped open. Not in shock, really, but in sudden, all-encompassing excitement. "Did he let you put something in his butt?!"

Syd shrugged and faked studying her conveniently short nails. "I might've blown his mind and his dick at the same time."

"By putting something in his butt?"

"Well... yes."

I hooted, slapping my thigh before inching another few feet across the St. Patrick Street bridge.

"What?" Sydney asked, her voice taking on that faux-innocence again. "I told Tyler it was only fair, you know? If he wanted me to take it in the ass, then he should be willing to take *something* in his."

"I can't believe he agreed to it."

"Me neither. Which is why I felt a little bad after we finished and I told him I had to go home."

"After all that, you didn't go through with it?"

She sipped her coffee. "There's a big difference between me slipping my finger in for a nice lil' prostate massage and taking an actual penis in the butthole. Which is what I told him. But that was a mistake on my part."

"Why?"

"Because I doubt he would've been able to get it up again anyway. Like, that dick was *spent*."

"Got every last drop out?"

"Enough that I didn't bother having a protein shake after going to the gym this morning."

I cackled again and Syd giggled.

"But like, really," she said when we finished laughing. "Who actually wants to take it in the ass?"

"I mean, I do."

She looked at me, surprised. "Really?"

I shrugged. "Why not? I wanna know if the whole 'intense anal orgasms' thing is a myth or not."

"I think it is for women," she said. "Guys at least have a prostate."

"Yeah, but I still think it'll feel at least a little good." I tilted my head to the side for what felt like the eightieth time, knowing that just like the previous seventy-nine times, I wouldn't be able to see what was holding traffic up so much. "It's not something I'm planning on doing anytime soon, though. Like, it's intimidating enough that I'm gonna be a little picky about who I do it with the first time."

"That's different for you."

"Well, I'd want someone who knows what they're doing."

"What about that guy you've seen a few times? The frat boy... What was his name again... Santino? No... Saul? Wait. Scott, right?"

Sydney was both a bad liar and a terrible actor. I rolled my eyes. "Scott Humprey. You can just ask what happened. Who told you?"

She didn't bother trying to deny it. "Brandon. He said you were laughing about it last night, but some of the stuff the guy said sounded pretty fucking heinous and he wanted me to check on you."

"I'm fine," I said. "It was nothing I haven't heard before. You know. I misled him, I'm a slut, no one will ever love me even if I let them put it in my butt. That sort of thing."

"Wait, he said the butt thing?"

"I may have exaggerated that last part, but I'm sure if he'd thought of it, he would've said it."

"You know that's not true, right?"

"Of course I do. I'm very lovable." I shot her a smile. "And it's not the burn he thinks it is to tell a girl who doesn't want a relationship that no one's going to want a relationship with her. Like, thank you? That's what I'm hoping for? It's not my fault he couldn't handle me."

"You think you were too much for him?" she asked.

"I'm too much for everyone. Scott knew what he was getting into. He just thought he was special enough that what I said wouldn't apply to him."

"I'm sure he's special in his way."

"Of course. Like a box of Cheerios in the cereal aisle."

She snorted. "So you're okay?"

"Of course I am. I was just oversharing with Brandon because that's who I am as a person."

"He doesn't get it," she said, sipping her coffee.

"Get what?"

"Why you don't want a relationship."

I sighed heavily. "This is going to be the longest drive to Montreal you've ever had if you're going to get into this with me again."

"I'm *not*," she said. "I'm just—"

"Your end game with hooking up with a ton of people might be to find the one you want to fuck for the rest of your life, but mine isn't. I don't want to do the relationship thing. Brandon knows that."

"I just think you'd be cute together," she said. "I know he isn't into casual hookups—"

"Which is why we're better as *friends*," I said pointedly.

"—but I just want to make sure sleeping around and partying is worth giving up what might be a good thing with Brandon."

"It's kind of bullshit that you're asking me that," I said. "Why is it that it's always the person who likes to fuck around and have fun who's expected to give up their scandalous ways for a life of commitment and monogamy? Why doesn't the commitment-lover ever give up their monogamous ways so they can slut around together for the rest of their lives?"

"Is that rhetorical? Because if not, it's because the typical societal expectation is that people settle down and end up with one other person."

"And that's a good enough reason for me to do it without question?"

"Just because that's the answer doesn't mean I agree with it. I know I want my forever-person eventually. If you don't, that's perfectly fine. But it's also my job as your best friend to make sure that's what you *actually* want and that it isn't just a result of your asshole high school boyfriend ruining relationships for you for the rest of your life."

"Well, it's not," I said.

Which was true.

Mostly.

I mean, it wasn't entirely Adrian's fault. There were plenty of people in my life who had ruined the concept of relationships for me. Hell, we were on our way to visit one of them.

Just one of them. Even though one of the other ones lived right next door. Although, I don't know if it was fair to say he "ruined" relationships for me. It was more that he'd shown me how good the non-relationship life could be.

Regardless, we weren't going to see *him*. Despite his efforts—not his best efforts, obviously, but they were efforts all the same—and aside from a couple of ill-timed notes left on my car, I'd avoided JP Marchand for the past three years the same way I'd avoided getting into a relationship in any way. I didn't have the time nor the capacity to deal with the drama. I was already taking a double-major honours degree in forensic science and anthropology; I didn't have time to deal with the double-major bullshit that was dramatic boyfriends and controlling relationships.

"Brandon is a great guy," I said as traffic started moving slightly faster than walking speed. "And that's the problem."

"Don't you dare give me some kind of 'he's too good for me' bullshit," Sydney said, her voice fierce. "I won't stand for anyone insulting my bestie like that, even if it's you."

"Not at all. We just want and need different things, Syd. I like the chase, you know? I like the part where we're flirting and dancing around things before finally getting to the hookup. I don't like all the boring cuddling-on-the-couch stuff that comes after. Which is what Brandon wants."

"You're against cuddling?" she asked.

"Not *against* it. But it's boring. I want the... you know." I twisted my wrist in the air. "I like things that are a little more adventurous. I like the challenge. The *journey* to it. Not the romance."

"If that's the case, why haven't you gone after Doctor Sexy yet?"

I groaned as Sydney giggled. "It's Ben. Or Professor Cameron. He doesn't like being called Doctor."

"Oh, right. Professor Took-Every-Class-He-Taught-Because-He's-So-Hot."

"I took all of his classes because he's good at what he does." I let the car inch forward, then braked harder than necessary. It made no difference because we were going approximately zero kilometers an hour. "Just like how I'm taking every single one of Dr. Spitzki's classes, even though he's a grumpy old asshole. He just happens to be a grumpy old asshole who knows everything about forensic pathology. Ben Cameron just *happens* to be panty-droppingly hot, probably because he's like, a legit certified genius who's one of the leading forensic psychologists in the country despite being twenty-some years younger than most of his colleagues."

"Forensic pathology is directly related to your degree, though," Sydney said. "You don't want to be a forensic psychologist."

"Yeah, but it's interesting. And the prof was hot."

She snorted. "But not hot enough for you to take up the challenge? Or is the student-teacher thing too much of an ick?"

"It would only be an ick if I was still in his classes or something. There are a lot of reasons I'll fuck someone, but for an A isn't one of them. But I took everything he teaches already." I tapped my fingers on the steering wheel, bouncing my knee as traffic stayed at a standstill. "Unfortunately. This semester would be a lot more interesting if I got to stare at his face three times a week like I did last semester."

"Yeah, but even if you're not in his classes, you still see him around campus and stuff."

"For now. But he's on sabbatical next year."

Sydney raised her eyebrows. "Wait, for real? So you could—"

"No. He said he's moving to California to do a study at Stanford or something." I sighed. "So I'll never get to fulfill my teacher/student fantasy."

"You have a teacher/student fantasy?"

"I might, if it was with him."

She snickered. "Maybe you'll meet a guy in Montreal who'll be willing to roleplay."

"Maybe. Though at this rate, we're never going to get out of Ottawa, let alone to Montreal," I said.

"You'd think you'd sound happier about that considering how much you've been dreading it."

"I just hate sitting in traffic," I muttered. "Trust me, I'd be more than happy to miss a father-mandated visit for an actual reason instead of some random bullshit I clearly made up."

"I dunno why," she said. "Frankly, I'm excited about it."

"Yeah, because you're not his kid."

"True, but maybe we can pull some kind of Parent Trap situation if this mansion you always complain about is decent. I'd absolutely dress up and go to fancy rich-people parties for free tuition and rent."

"And all you have to do is sell your soul," I said. I'm pretty sure he'd notice that we look nothing alike."

"Nothing a little hair dye can't fix."

"You're taller than me."

She shrugged. "I'll just make sure I stay sitting all the time."

I snorted. "You know that if I thought it would work, I'd take you up on this in a heartbeat. But we'll see what you say after this weekend."

She laughed and shook her head. "I'm sure it won't be that bad."

"You've never met my dad."

She laughed, but I didn't.

Chapter Three
Driving Lessons

WHEN WE REACHED THE source of the traffic congestion, Sydney winced.

"Shit," she said. "That sucks."

I nodded, twisting my mouth to the side. Blocking the left lane was a red Honda Civic, hazards flashing and hood up, the front passenger tire completely flat. On the sidewalk, a woman with a dark brown undercut and thick-rimmed glasses was juggling a toddler and her phone in one arm while she clutched the hand of the slightly older child beside her. She was trying to talk on the phone, but the toddler was grabbing at it, and even from a distance, I could see the glimmer of tears in her eyes.

"Why wouldn't she just stay in the car?" Sydney asked.

"In case someone doesn't stop and hits her." I brought my thumb to my mouth, biting down on my nail for a moment before I flicked my signal light on and pulled into the left lane in front of the red Civic.

"What are you doing?" Sydney asked.

"Nothing," I said, then put my hazards on and turned the car off before getting out.

"—three hours?!" I heard the woman say. "No, I'm blocking traffic on... I have two kids. Two young kids! Please, isn't there—"

"Is it just the tire?" I asked.

She glanced over at me, confusion on her face. "What?"

I motioned at the car. "Do you have a spare?"

She shook her head.

Fuck. I dug my fingernail into the side of my thumb. "What year is it?"

She frowned. "What?"

"Your car. What year is it?"

Twenty minutes later, I closed the trunk of my car, waved at my new friend Amy, gave four-year-old McKenna a high-five, and got back into my Honda Civic.

"Where'd you learn to change a tire?" Sydney asked as I turned the car back on.

"My mom," I said.

"I thought your mom didn't drive."

"She did until I got my driver's license and then she stopped. But the first thing she taught me about driving was how to change a tire."

Which was a lie.

The first thing she'd taught me about driving was to get the fuck out of my car if I broke down. Although, I guess she didn't *teach* me that so much as she reinforced it, since we'd both learned that lesson at the same time.

It was a few months after she'd left my dad. We were on the way to the Toronto airport so I could go see my dad for the weekend. Mom was driving a little Ford Escort that was older than I was at the time. Which I guess wasn't that old, but considering my mom had sold her year-old SUV almost as soon as we arrived in Toronto, it seemed old to me.

"This can't be happening," she'd been muttering as the engine sputtered pathetically each time she turned the key. "Not this, too. God, please help me out here and—"

And then there was a loud bang and we both jerked forward.

It was God's way of helping her out, if you believed in that sort of thing, and also thought God had the same sense of humour as one of those wishing monkey paws. The woman who rear-ended us didn't hit us very hard—neither of us were hurt—and she was driving a Lexus. So even though I missed the flight to Montreal, she paid for me to get on the next flight, and by the time I got back, she'd replaced my mom's Ford Escort with a slightly newer Ford Focus, even though my mom admitted the damage wasn't that bad.

"Why'd she do that?" I'd asked.

My mom's mouth twitched and she shook her head. "It doesn't matter. But one day, we'll be able to pay it forward."

"Okay," said Sydney, breaking me out of my thoughts. "But you just let that woman have your spare tire?"

"Don't look too much into it. The longer we take to get to Montreal, the less time I have to spend with my dad."

"Yeah, but what happens if you get a flat tire now?"

"We'll be stuck and won't have to go to Montreal at all, maybe," I said cheerfully.

Unfortunately, my tires held up for the rest of the drive and I reluctantly accepted that I had to spend the next two and a half days in Montreal. Thank God my dad had a business trip he couldn't get out of, since otherwise he would've expected me to be there for the whole week. But I'd agreed to go to some charity gala he wanted me to attend as part of my obligations to him for paying for my tuition and living expenses. And Syd had agreed to come with me so we could go out partying that night, since we'd never partied in Montreal together before.

Although, I realized when we got there, I may have forgotten to tell my dad that she was coming.

"Eleanor, *ma fille ange*!" my dad called as soon as we walked in the house. The sound of his voice speaking crisp, clipped French made me cringe more than I already had been.

"Please, Dad. It's Nellie," I responded in French that was much, much less crisp than his.

Polished shoes clacked against the tile in the foyer as he crossed it. He was the kind of person who looked like a tall, imposing man, especially in photos when no one of actual height was standing next to him. Up close, he was an inch or two shorter than average, though you would have never guessed given the way he carried himself. Nor would most people guess that he was in his mid-fifties; he had dark, thick black hair and olive-toned white skin that carried a few distinguished wrinkles in the corners of his eyes and around his mouth, but otherwise appeared smooth.

People also probably wouldn't guess that he and I were related, much less that he was my dad. Luckily for me, my mom's genes had apparently been much stronger. I had the same brown eyes and blonde hair as her—though hers was long and wavy and frizzy and I kept mine cut to my shoulders and straightened—and the same rosy white skin, though I shared my dad's straight nose and heart-shaped face.

"Hmph," he said. "Your accent has become even more atrocious, Eleanor."

I gritted my teeth. The insistence on calling me by my full name was meant to be an insult. As was the swap to English. "*Ce n'est* Eleanor *pas,*" I said in the most English-sounding accent I could manage. "*Mon nom est* Nellie, *s'il vous plait.*"

He chuckled patronizingly. "Oh, alright. *Nellie,* then. It sounds so juvenile, but if it makes you happy, I'll continue using it. Welcome home."

I tried not to shudder as my dad hugged me, lifting one listless arm to hug him back as my bag dropped to the floor with a clunk. Beside me, my dad's assistant, Pierre, scooped up the bag, then turned to Sydney, who was standing silently behind me.

"May I take your bag, Miss?" he asked in English.

Sydney, who was taking a linguistics degree with the intent of eventually working for the government as a translator or something, gave him an unimpressed look and responded in French so rapid that I didn't even understand it.

My dad, however, did.

"Nellie, who is this you've brought?" he asked, his voice steady but cold as he released me from his grip.

And that was when I realized I hadn't told him I was bringing a friend.

"This is my friend Sydney Amhurst," I said, stepping back so she could move forward and extend her hand. "We thought we'd go out and celebrate the end of term together."

"Pleasure to meet you, Mr. Belanger," Sydney said, slowing her words down since she wasn't showing off anymore. "Thank you for having me."

"No gratitude necessary," he said. "Seeing as I wasn't aware Elea—excuse me, *Nellie*—was bringing a guest. Had I known, I would have asked Pierre to prepare a room for you."

"It's okay," I said. "We'll share my room."

My dad's jaw tightened almost imperceptibly, his eyes stonier than usual. "You are not planning on bringing Ms. Amhurst as your date tomorrow evening."

It wasn't a question, but I pretended it was. "No. Anne-Marie set me up with her friend, Bruno. Syd's going to visit another one of her friends."

"Good," he said. "Regardless of the current trends, *ma fille ange*, you know I expect you to attend these events with a traditional date."

Sydney looked at me, a crease between her eyebrows betraying the surprise that I'd been telling her the truth about how my dad was.

"I can get a hotel, if it's an issue," she finally said, breaking the silence.

"It's not," my dad said. "However, Pierre will show you to Nellie's room and you may settle in while my daughter and I catch up, since I have not seen her since... Well now, since before Christmas. Nellie, please come to the kitchen with me. I have someone special I'd like you to meet."

Oh, fuck.

With everything else I had going on, I'd forgotten the other reason my dad had been so insistent about visiting before his business trip was because he wanted me to meet... her.

His new girlfriend.

Good old... uh... What's-Her-Name.

Chapter Four
The Gold Digger Cure

I F   G O O D   O L D   W H A T ' S - H E R - N A M E was anything like the previous girlfriends, she would be neither old nor good.

No, What's-Her-Name would be tall, slim, and at most a decade older than me. And she would be the kind of person who thought she'd scored the jackpot with the older rich guy who wasn't horrible to look at and was already picking out the twenty-four-carat diamond for her engagement ring.

But it wouldn't last.

There was a reason the new model of girlfriend never progressed to being his wife. They could have called my dad the cure for gold diggers: the man who made women realize that money wasn't everything. They kept flocking to him, each one younger and taller and skinnier, often blonde, often with expensive taste; each one determined to be the next wife of Maximillian Belanger until they actually tried it and realized no amount of money in the world was worth marrying my father.

But as I followed my dad through the house, silent as he made the kind of small talk that didn't require a response, I realized it actually had been a while since I'd met one of my dad's "special someones."

He'd broken up with Brayleigh, the woman he'd been dating the summer before I started university, the same day I'd left for university. Funnily enough, I'd thought it was sweet of him, since he'd broken up with her after she'd lied about asking me to stay out of the house all night because they were hosting a dinner party in an attempt to make me look like the spoiled brat she said I was.

In hindsight, he was probably just looking for an excuse to end things because he was tired of her.

The next time I'd gone to see him had been the week before Thanksgiving in October and I'd accidentally called the new girlfriend Stefani Rae because I hadn't realized he'd broken up with the woman he'd been telling me about three days earlier and started seeing Laralyn instead.

By Christmas, Laralyn was gone and I think the next one went by a normal-ish name. Zoey, maybe, but it was short for a multi-part name that featured at least two "lyns" in it. During my second semester, there had been two more, then another one over the summer, and then I stopped keeping track.

I couldn't remember the name of the last one I'd met, though in fairness, I don't think my dad ever introduced us. She'd clearly been a rebound from the one before *her*, Selena Grace. My dad would never admit what happened, of course, but Anne-Marie had told me everything, since her mom had been on the deck with some of her friends and had to subtly usher everyone back inside when she heard moaning coming from the pool house in my dad's backyard.

But when she was seeing her guests off about half an hour later, my dad's car pulled into the driveway. She watched him get out of the car as his assistant unloaded a suitcase from the trunk.

Ten minutes after that, Selena Grace got into her car and drove away, and no one had seen her again.

That had been in the summer, which meant it had been at *least* six months since I'd met "someone special," which had to be a record.

When we got to the kitchen, a room bright with white cabinets and wooden countertops and cobblestone-inspired floors in shades of terracotta and faded persimmon, my dad stopped and turned to me.

"Nellie, *ma fille ange*," he said. "This is my girlfriend, Kimberlee."

She wasn't blonde. Or my age. Or particularly thin, even.

She *was* tall, but her hair was long and straight and dark brown. Her frame was on the softer side of athletic: somewhat curvy, but a sleeveless cream-coloured top showed off toned arms and smooth, medium brown skin. She had large eyes and a soft smile on glossy lips tinted with maroon lipstick. And while she was still clearly younger than my dad, I would have guessed she was in her thirties.

Which had to be a record. The last woman he was with who was in her thirties was probably my mom, and that was only for the last couple of years of their marriage.

"It is so nice to finally meet you, Nellie," Kimberlee said.

"You, too," I said, like I knew anything about her aside from her name and definitely hadn't forgotten that.

"Come," my dad said. "Let's have a seat and a drink as we catch up. Pierre made up a batch of that sangria you enjoyed so much last summer."

I tried not to wince at the sight of the pitcher on the table. I had enjoyed the sangria my dad's assistant had made last summer, but that was before my mom and I spent one evening during Christmas break testing different sangria recipes so she could use one as a staff pick at the liquor store she managed. Unfortunately, the only thing I'd determined was that all sangria tasted awful when it came back up a few hours later.

"Sangria sounds great," I said, trying to sound enthusiastic. "Thanks, Dad."

"So," he said, his tone businesslike as we sat down and Kimberlee filled the glasses waiting there. "Tell me about school, Nellie. Everything is going well?"

I nodded, taking my glass of sangria, but not sipping it. "I had my final interview for that internship I told you about this morning. The Forensic Analysis one."

"Mmm," he said, not bothering to even pretend to be excited.

"I'm pretty sure I'll get accepted. Which would be great. It's pretty competitive."

"Mmm," he said again. "Your marks are high?"

I tried not to react to the obvious snub. "Mostly. But midterms aren't until after reading week."

"High enough for law school, perhaps?"

"I don't want to go to law school."

My dad sipped his sangria. "It's far more lucrative and certainly less gritty, since you still don't seem to have the aptitude to get into investments or finance."

"I want to be a forensic scientist," I said, trying not to let the remark about my *aptitude* get to me the way I knew he wanted it to. "It's what I've always wanted."

"Of course, but what you want and what is best have not always been the same thing, *ma fille ange*." He smiled. "You know I have plenty of contacts within the legal profession that would help you build an illustrious career."

"If it was what I wanted, I'm sure I could find contacts of my own," I said.

The corners of my dad's mouth turned down as if he was humouring me. "Certainly, but a simple conversation with Jean-Luc next door could set you on a path as a corporate lawyer. I believe his son is about to start as a junior associate."

"Is that so," I said flatly.

"One of the youngest associates he's had in years," my dad said. "Jean-Paul positively flew through his bachelor and law degrees."

I tried not to grimace at the sound of his name. "Good for JP."

"And your level of intelligence is comparative to his," he continued. "Should you attempt to meet Jean-Paul's level of motivation as well, you would have a number of connections on that career path."

"I'd say I'm pretty motivated," I said. "I just have no desire to be a lawyer. I want to be a forensic scientist."

"Well, there is still time to change your mind." He looked at the still-full glass of sangria in front of me. "Is there a problem with your drink, *ma fille ange?*"

Fuck.

"Of course not," I said. "I, uh, was chewing gum before we got here. I'm waiting for the mint taste to fade."

He seemed to believe that and nodded. From the corner of my eye, I watched Kimberlee look from me to my dad.

"Well, Nellie," she said in an attempt to change the subject. "I am very much looking forward to getting to know you this summer. I sit on the board for many of the charities and committees scheduling events."

"Uh... okay," I said, semi-distracted as I started lifting my glass and tried to convince myself to take a sip of the sangria. "That's interesting."

Kimberlee looked at my dad.

"Kimberlee is a fundraising consultant and is working on a number of prestigious events," he said. "I informed her she could count on your support for that this summer."

I stared at him, my sangria glass halfway to my mouth. "Why?"

He raised his eyebrows. "Excuse me?"

"Why would you say that?" I set the glass down. "And not ask me first?"

"It does not need to be for every event," Kimberlee said in what was probably meant to be a calming voice. "But for *Lumière Et Amour* and *Mosaic de Montreal* and—"

"—as many as you will be able to attend," my dad finished. "Because my assumption, *ma fille ange*, was that as you had said you weren't taking summer classes this year, you would be available to show your support as a way of expressing your gratitude for the support *I've* provided you throughout your education."

And there it was.

My mom had tried to warn me. I hadn't listened. I'd thought the same thing that Sydney thought: that I could put up with my dad in exchange for tuition and rent. It hadn't seemed unreasonable. All he wanted was some of my time. For me to visit him. That wasn't asking a lot.

Until it was.

Because those asks got bigger. Because soon, it wasn't just wanting me to visit; it was wanting me to go to a gala to make him look good. And then another one.

Which didn't seem that bad, either. Until he started hinting I could make him look better, perhaps, if I chose a more prestigious field to work in than science.

It was the slow realization that my dad didn't understand that children weren't corporations. That he saw himself as not just a stakeholder in my life, but as the primary investor since he'd contributed the most financially. And that as the majority shareholder, he felt he had the right to advise me on what I should do with my future and final say in deciding what direction that future went.

"And, of course, it is beneficial for you as well," my dad said. "These events are a prime way of creating connections and expanding your network so you can push forward in your career."

"I don't imagine there will be a ton of networking opportunities for forensic scientists at the events you attend," I said, trying to keep my voice even.

"You may be surprised," Kimberlee said, trying to smile.

"And I know Jean-Luc Marchand sees value in attending as a representative of his law firm," my dad added.

"I'm sure he does. But there's also the FAI internship," I said. "I'm going to be busy with that all summer."

He looked unimpressed. "Most of these events are on the weekend, *ma fille ange.* I was under the impression this internship is a Monday-to-Friday type of job."

"Sort of," I said. "But it's also very intense. I'll be working extra hours and—"

"It should be simple enough to drive here on the weekends."

"I don't see why I have to come to these."

"I would think showing support for myself and Kimberlee would be reason enough."

"So you want me to work myself to exhaustion this summer, then drive out here to make you look good," I said.

That might have crossed a line. Kimberlee's manicured eyebrows shot up on her forehead and my dad's lips parted for a moment before he pressed them together, severe lines appearing along the edges.

But then he took a breath, let it out, and sipped his sangria.

"Nellie, it would be prudent for you to have an alternate plan in place," he said. "There is no guarantee you will get this internship."

The only thing that stopped my mouth from dropping open was the amount of practice I had at keeping a straight face when my dad said something awful like that. Inside, my heart was pumping anger through my arteries, sending it everywhere from the base of my neck to the tips of my shaking fingers, but my expression stayed neutral. Kimberlee, on the other hand, didn't seem to have the same skill level. Her eyes went round and her hair bounced as she turned to look at my dad.

"I will be," I said. "My interviews went perfectly. I'm just waiting for the official acceptance."

"Yes, but—"

"Mom even already said that she understands if I won't be able to see her this summer because I'll be working so much," I said. "She might come up to Ottawa to visit if she can get the time off work. That's how much *she* believes I can do this."

If the comment about making him look good had crossed the line, that had just obliterated it. Keeping my face steady was one thing; keeping my mouth shut was a very, *very* different thing. My dad stared at me, his expression mirroring my calm one and his eyes reflecting the anger in mine.

"I believe you think you can do this," he said. "All I am saying is that having a backup plan is sensible. For example, if you are not able to get this internship that would further your career, having good enough grades for law school—"

"You know what?" I blurted. "If I don't get it, I'll take the LSAT."

My dad raised his eyebrows. "Pardon?"

"If I don't get this internship, I'll spend the summer going to your events and studying to take the LSAT," I said. "*That's* how sure I am I'm going to get it."

My dad stared at me, then frowned thoughtfully.

"Alright," he said. "It's a deal."

That simple acceptance, more than anything, made me think I should have probably thought things out more before saying them. But the words had left my mouth before the idea had fully formed in my head. "Fine."

"However, you will ensure you are available for *Lumière Et Amour* and *Mosaic de Montreal*," he said. "Kimberlee will give you the dates and additional details for those."

I tried to maintain the calm look on my face. "Fine. I can be here for those two weekends."

"At a minimum," he said. "I would be happy to arrange for you to attend additional events."

"We'll see," I said. "I'll need to make sure I have enough money for gas and such if you want me here more often."

He gave me a *Look*. "I can put a little extra in your account, but if you are having so much difficulty managing your finances that sundry purchases like fuel are worrisome, perhaps you should consider spending some of your limited time this summer looking for a less expensive apartment for next year."

That was what made my face crack.

I knew it made me sound spoiled. I knew it was privileged. I tried not to let it change who I was or affect how I made decisions. But my dad had never outright denied me anything. He'd never so much as hinted that he wouldn't pay for something I needed.

And the moment he saw he'd unsettled me, he smiled and took a sip of his sangria.

Chapter Five
A Friend of Inconvenience

"WE ARE DONE. *C'est fini,* Remy."

Sydney's eyes met mine in the reflection of Anne-Marie's bedroom mirror, her hair half-curled. I shrugged as subtly as I could, trying not to jar my hand as I applied liquid eyeliner and hoping she understood that it meant "That's just how Anne-Marie is."

"I am telling you, Remy," Anne-Marie said into the phone as she bounced back and forth between French and exaggeratedly accented English. "You are too demanding. I am an independent woman who deserves to have fun with *mes chers. J'ai besoin de mon espace...* Well, if I meet someone else tonight, it is none of your business, is it?"

She gestured dramatically, nearly bashing her hand against the straightener Sydney was using to curl her hair. Sydney stepped backwards, her eyes going even rounder.

"Absolutely not!" Anne-Marie snapped into the phone. "I am going out with Nellie to celebrate the completion of her internship interviews and you are not invited." She hung up, mindlessly tossing her phone onto the top of her dresser. "I swear, *les nouilles ne sont pas toutes dans la soupe.*"

"Sounds like you're better off without him," Sydney said.

Anne-Marie plucked a small photo from the frame of her mirror of her and Remy at her last high school prom. Even though she was only sixteen in the photo—in Quebec, high school finished in grade eleven and students went on to pre-university training or technical college—you could tell they had that forever kind of love. Anne-Marie was clad in a form-fitting gown of turquoise and glitter that made her white skin look more tanned than usual, her blonde hair swept to one side in curls that were both elaborate and effortless. Remy wore a black suit with a black shirt and tie, his coiled hair showing off its natural curls instead of the usual twists or braids he kept it in. There was a faint lipstick stain on his dark brown cheek, nearly touching the corner of his mouth, and they were both smiling widely: Anne-Marie at the camera and Remy at her, his arms tucked beneath her protectively and hers thrown around his shoulders as he held her in a princess carry.

"I'm done with him," Anne-Marie said, pretending the bottom right corner of the photo wasn't faded and wrinkled from the amount of times it had been removed and replaced from her bedroom mirror.

"How long were you together?" Sydney asked.

"Not long. Maybe six years."

"Six *years*?" Sydney repeated.

"It's more like six months if you count all the times they 'break up,'" I said.

Anne-Marie rolled her eyes. "We don't 'break up' *that* much. He's just being especially ridiculous right now. He thinks because Jean-Paul offered to put a word in for him at the firm in Quebec City he articled at, he's hot shit now. Despite the fact that Remy won't even be articling for ages yet."

"Who's Jean-Paul?" Sydney asked.

"Nellie's crush," Anne-Marie replied.

I threw the Q-tip I'd been using to dab an errant smudge of mascara off my cheek at Anne-Marie. "I don't have a crush on JP."

"Mmm," Anne-Marie said knowingly. "Sure you don't, *chérie*."

"Just because you wish it was true doesn't mean you're not delusional."

She paused her lipstick application to smirk conspiratorially at me in the mirror. "Well, I can tell you for certain that, as usual, he isn't seeing anyone right now. My brother is the definition of a womanizer and not the fun sex-toy kind. But if you want me to put in a word for you—"

"I really, really don't," I said. "Thanks, though."

"If it's just about getting laid, I can talk to Marc-Andre instead. He's eighteen now."

"Annie, I don't want to sleep with either of your brothers," I said.

"Yes, but I know when you're going without for a long time, it can start making one—" She paused, circling her wrist in the air as though she didn't know exactly how she was going to finish that sentence. "You know. Prone to give in to desperation."

"What, exactly, is your definition of 'a long time'?" Sydney asked incredulously, but I shushed her.

"I don't see myself ever getting desperate enough to hook up with either JP or Marc-Andre," I said, helping myself to an expensive-looking highlighter from Anne-Marie's makeup bag. "Especially if we're going out to see a selection of Montreal's finest asses tonight."

It was the perfect distraction.

"Oooh, are we planning on taking someone home?" Anne-Marie said, abandoning her attempts at making me admit I had a crush on her brother for the much more intriguing topic of getting laid.

"No," Sydney said. "Nellie said we can't bring anyone back to her dad's place. But we might go home with someone. Or, more accurately, multiple someones."

"You wouldn't share a hot French guy with me?" I asked, faking offense.

"You know if I had even a modicum of attraction to women, you'd be top of my list," Syd said. "Unfortunately, the universe saw fit to make me attracted solely to men."

"Sucks to be you," I said.

"Wait," Anne-Marie said slowly. "Are you not, Nellie?"

"Not what?"

"Solely attracted to men?"

Shit.

"Um... no," I said.

"Oh." There was an odd silence, but before I could say anything else, Anne-Marie turned and folded her arms. "Why is it that I am just finding out about this?"

"Because I haven't told you?" I said.

"Yes, but why?" She pouted, sticking her lip out. "First of all, it means you have most certainly been keeping secrets from me about any salacious little adventures you've had, since I do not remember hearing any about women—"

"You can know you're not only attracted to men without having ever been with a woman," Sydney said defensively.

"Well, of course," Anne-Marie said. "But is that true of Nellie?"

I twisted my mouth to the side. "Well... no. I have."

She scoffed. "Exactly! So you are keeping secrets from me!"

"Okay, but—"

"Second of all," Anne-Marie continued, then paused. Unfolding her arms, she walked over to me and took my hands in hers, a pointed but sincere look in her large brown eyes. "Given that you are my best friend, *chérie*, I hope you know I would be supportive of you no matter what."

And even as I hugged her tight and promised her I knew she was supportive and thanked her for being my friend, guilt rushed over me.

Because there were two reasons I wasn't Anne-Marie's best friend.

The first reason was space. Growing up, Anne-Marie and I spent nearly every single day together because we lived beside each other. But after my parents divorced when I was eleven and my mom and I moved to Toronto, I only saw her whenever I visited my dad.

Not that we were friends of convenience. If anything, Anne-Marie was a friend of inconvenience. She was vapid and fickle, with no sense of when she was pushing things too far. But there was far more to her beneath the surface than one thought, given that she looked exactly how one would expect someone like Anne-Marie to look. Her natural hair colour was a dark brown that hadn't seen the light of day since dyed it to a cool-toned blonde when she was twelve. Tall, slim, and perky with white skin that seemed to be naturally tanned all year round, she dressed in trendy designer clothes and never left the house with so much as a chip in her nail polish or an eyebrow hair out of place.

She was also fierce and loyal and bold, never afraid to go after what she wanted. And she was shrewd enough to make a system of materialistic inequality work for her. There was nothing so dangerous as a woman who knew how to use the system against those who had developed it, and Anne-Marie was a fucking *hazard*.

She also made a point of *being* my friend. I was the first to admit I wasn't good at keeping in touch with people. I never had been, and that was probably why I didn't have a lot of close friends. But Anne-Marie refused to let us fall out of touch. Once we were both old enough to have phones, we texted regularly and she kept me updated about all the things happening in her life. She was still there for me when I needed her, and I was there for her when she needed me.

Like best friends are.

The second reason I wasn't her best friend was really only half a reason because Anne-Marie didn't know about it. And since she didn't know about it, she *thought* we were still best friends.

But it still counted as a reason because I'd fucked Anne-Marie's brother and that's not something you do to your best friend.

Especially not in his bedroom while your best friend is in the room next door.

Even if she's been teasing you for practically your whole life about having a crush on JP.

Even if the whole reason you end up in JP's room is because Remy came over because he couldn't wait until you got back from the bar to play their little on-again-off-again jealousy game and you ended up stranded in the hallway with only a towel on.

The point is, you just... you *don't* fuck your best friend's brother. Especially not if it's your first time. And especially not when you know Anne-Marie could be stuck in a swarm of a thousand bugs and *still* wouldn't be able to keep her mouth shut.

Because no one could know I'd had sex with JP.

Especially not my dad.

I didn't want to think about what would happen if he found out. He was the kind of person who married my mom and insisted she'd given birth to a premature baby that weighed nine pounds instead of taking her to get a secret abortion or something.

I, on the other hand, was the kind of person who bought a cake and threw a party to celebrate the day my age and body count lined up, though by the end of the night, those numbers didn't match anymore. And not because it was my birthday.

But unashamed as I was, I couldn't risk my dad finding out about any of this. So over time, I'd kind of... *curated* the things I told Anne-Marie.

Like, she knew about the guy named Jake that I'd hooked up with a few times. She *didn't* know that we'd hooked up in Brandon and Calvin's garage during a party while three guys smoked weed on the other side of the car we were hiding behind.

Or about the threesome I had with Jake and a girl named Veronica a few months after that.

She didn't know about the games of strip beer pong, the dirty Truth or Dare nights, the girl named Tabby who had been my first hookup with another woman, or the fact that there were just as many rumours about me at Ottawa Tech as there had been when I was in high school.

Only now they were true.

And now they didn't bother me.

Now I leaned into them. Now I owned it. And I didn't know if it was because I wasn't ashamed of it or if people were more mature in university or more accepting in Ottawa, but it didn't seem like as much of a big deal. People didn't shun or ostracize me; they still *wanted* to be friends with me.

JP had agreed he wouldn't tell anyone what we did. And if *he* didn't tell anyone, Anne-Marie would never know about it, which significantly lowered the risk of any of this getting back to the last person on Earth I wanted to know about it.

Although he'd still almost ruined everything the very next time I was in Montreal after we'd hooked up.

"I cannot believe you're leaving already, *chérie*," Anne-Marie had whined as we walked out my dad's front door. It was my first trip to see my dad after starting university and I'd spent most of the weekend with him, so Anne-Marie and I hadn't had much time to hang out.

"I'll be back next month," I said. "The week after Thanksgiving, I think."

"Good." She looped her arm through mine. "You better have some exciting stories for me."

"I already tell you any exciting stories I have," I said.

"It's not the same over text and you know that."

"Yeah, but it's better than..."

I trailed off, frowning as I looked at my car and the small yellow square stuck to the driver's side window.

"What is that?" Anne-Marie said, having followed my line of sight because she was apparently concerned that I'd stopped talking.

"I think it's a Post-It note," I said.

"A blank Post-It note?" she said, then gasped. "Ohmigod. Is this one of those sex trafficking things where they tie something to your car door and that's how they mark you? With blank sticky notes?"

"I think they'd use something less likely to fall off," I said, reaching for the note. "Maybe someone was just—"

And I stopped again.

Because the sticky note wasn't blank.

No, the person who stuck it there was just so fucking *clever* that he'd written on the back of the note so when he stuck it to my car, it would face the inside.

Because apparently, someone was both stupid enough to *leave* this note knowing I was having lunch with Anne-Marie, but also smart enough to think of that and attempt to conceal what he'd written.

Which wasn't much. Just his phone number, followed by two lines:

Call me, babe□
xoxo

"What is it?" Anne-Marie asked, reaching for the note.

"Nothing!" I crumpled it in my hand. "It's nothing."

Anne-Marie stared at me, then a disturbingly familiar smirk played on her lips, her hand still outstretched. "If it is nothing, why can't I see it?"

"Because I said so."

That seemed to make her think I was playing hard-to-convince or something, because instead of respecting what I said, Anne-Marie lunged forward, grabbing my forearm with one hand and trying to pry my fingers open with the other. I yelled, yanking my hand away from her.

"What are you *doi*—STOP!" I said, twisting as she tried to grab me again.

"Let me see, then!" she said, giggling as she caught my wrist again.

I got my arm back, but Anne-Marie was unnervingly good at this. She scuttled forward, blocking me between me and my car, and tried to get my arm again.

So I did the only thing I could think of.

Well, sort of. I don't know that I actually *thought* that much about it because then I'd have to admit I did it on purpose. So maybe it was more accurate to say that I did the only thing I could instinctively do.

Which was to put it in my mouth.

The playful look on Anne-Marie's dissolved and a look of semi-disgusted shock replaced it almost immediately after I slapped my hand to my face. "Nellie, *what* the fuck?"

"I th'aid no," I said through my mouthful of Post-It note.

Then, because I was just so fucking smart, I punctuated my statement by chewing.

Anne-Marie stared at me, her mouth-half open. I stared back at her, desperately hoping that the leaver of the note wasn't witnessing this entire thing.

Then Anne-Marie started *howling* with laughter.

"Oh my *God*, Nellie!" she said, doubling over as she cackled. "Did you seriously just *eat* it?!"

While she was bent forward and not looking at me, I spat the paper into my hand and shoved it in my pocket, then belatedly realized that I could've pretended to put the note in my mouth and kept it hidden in my hand. Anne-Marie braced herself against my car, wiping her eyes as she laughed, then called me crazy before hugging me goodbye. I pretended to plug my phone in and fiddle with the music as she walked across the driveway and lawn back to her house, then dug the soggy note JP had stuck to my car from my pocket.

The *bastard*.

Unfortunately, either Anne-Marie regaled her family with the story of me eating a Post-It note off my car or JP had been watching from the Marchands' house. A few visits later in January, I went to start the snowy drive back to Ottawa and froze, then sighed. I was wearing mittens, so it took a few awkward tries for me to pluck the soft pink square off my window.

Tip: put # in your phone before eating
Let me know if the pink ones taste better
xoxo

I read the note again. Then one more time.

He thought I didn't call because his phone number got messed up when I put it in my mouth. Or maybe he thought I legitimately chewed and swallowed the whole thing. Either way, it seemed like JP wasn't aware I didn't call him on purpose.

I didn't *want* to call him.

I didn't want to know why *he* wanted me to call him.

Because if he wanted a repeat, I didn't. I mean, God. It was hard enough still being friends with Anne-Marie as it was.

I couldn't *handle* a repeat.

And if he wanted more...

He couldn't. He couldn't want that. He couldn't *have* that. Part of the reason I'd justified fucking JP was because of all the times Anne-Marie had told me he was a player. A manwhore. A womanizer. Someone who only introduced women to his family when she didn't sneak out fast enough the morning after.

Yet there I stood in the snow, months after we'd had sex, a sticky note with his phone number and an inside joke and a fucking *xoxo* at the bottom pinched clumsily between my fingers.

I didn't want more.

Not with him.

Not with anyone.

Not now, and maybe not ever.

And JP needed to get that through his thick, stupid head sooner rather than later.

Slowly and deliberately, I turned so I was in profile to the Marchands' house. I took off one mitten, then the other, and tucked them beneath my elbow.

Then I ripped the Post-It in half.

Then in quarters.

Then again and again until my cold fingers couldn't tear the bits any smaller.

Then, without looking at the Marchands' house, I let the pieces fall to the snowy ground, got in my car, and drove away.

Chapter Six
Stealing A Cowboy's Panties

WE WERE THREE DRINKS in that night when a man gave Anne-Marie his panties.

He stuck out like a cowboy at a nightclub because that's what he was. And like, an *actual* cowboy. Even from across the bar, I could tell he wasn't just some white college boy who had plopped a cowboy hat on and bought a pair of overpriced embroidered cowboy boots for the *aesthetic*. There was dark hair beneath the worn-in cowboy hat on his head and thick eyebrows that set off the warm tan on his white skin. An easy, friendly smile was spread across his lips and when he was a few feet away from the high-top table we were sitting at, he took off his hat politely.

"Yeehaw, cowboy," I said as Sydney and Anne-Marie looked at him with amusement.

"Evening, ladies," he said, and despite never having been there in my life, I just fucking *knew* that he was an Alberta boy. "My name's Jesse. Enjoying yourselves tonight?"

Anne-Marie flicked her eyes up and down. "It's become more enjoyable in the past thirty seconds, *chérie*. Can my friends and I help you with something?"

"I have a bit of an ulterior motive in coming over to talk to you three lovely ladies tonight." He glanced behind him, then took a step forward. "I'm here for a bachelor party for my buddy Cody. The best man—his other buddy, Olivier—asked me to come up ahead of time 'cause we need a little help."

"What kind of help?" Sydney asked.

Jesse glanced behind him again, then leaned in a little closer. "Look, it's gonna sound weird and I know that, okay? If it's an issue, you say no and I will be on my way, no hard feelings and no disrespect."

"Keep talking like that and we're going to think you want us to give you our panties or something," I said.

Jesse looked at me, something between embarrassment and amusement on his face. "Well, actually..."

"Oh my God," Sydney said. "Are you serious?"

"He's doing a scavenger hunt!" Jesse said. "But hear me out, okay?" He dug a hand into his pocket and, after another look behind him, withdrew it to reveal a scrap of slinky, hot pink fabric. "He doesn't know, of course, but we're settin' it up so he can actually get them *without* making some girl super uncomfortable. I got these brand new—you can still see the tags and everything—and I was hoping one of you might want to put them on. All you gotta do is take 'em. I mean, you can wear 'em over your actual underwear or whatever if you want, but you don't have to. Then once he's here, we'll make sure he gets over to ask you for 'em and you can run to the bathroom or something to 'take them off' and give them to him."

I would've said yes, but Anne-Marie snatched the panties out of Jesse's hand before he'd even finished speaking.

"I am in," she said. "But I expect compensation, *monsieur.*"

"I'd be happy to buy you and your friends a drink," Jesse said.

"Hmm," Anne-Marie said. "It is a kind offer, but I'd much rather have you take me for a dance, cowboy."

"A round of drinks for all of you." He put his cowboy hat back on, then tipped it at Anne-Marie. "And as many dances as you'd like, miss."

"Keep your word and I may even show you *la danse du loup*," she said.

He looked confused as Sydney and I both started laughing. "Is that some kind of Quebec dance?"

"Something like that," Sydney giggled.

Jesse shrugged good-naturedly but didn't ask any further, which was too bad, because Anne-Marie had *definitely* just said she wanted to fuck him.

Now, had I been thinking, I would've realized the flaw in all this long before Anne-Marie went to the bathroom to slip the panties on over top of her other ones. And by flaw, I mean Anne-Marie's plan, because when Remy walked into the bar a while later, I was one *hundred* percent sure she'd done this on purpose.

And if I'd really been thinking, I would've asked her to give us the panties before Remy herded her out of the bar. But I was too busy trying to convince Sydney that no, Anne-Marie was okay and didn't need her to step in and throw hands with the slightly angry, slightly desperate, and definitely horny man who'd found Anne-Marie on the dance floor.

"You're seriously letting him do this to her?!" Sydney shouted over the pounding bass, her eyes wide with disbelief and concern as I subtly danced us away from the spot where Anne-Marie was valiantly arguing with her boyfriend. She brandished a finger in the air angrily, then flipped her long blonde hair over her shoulder. Even from where I stood, I could see Remy's eyes darken, not so much in frustration or rage as it was desire. He brought his hand to her chin, tilting her head back to look at him, and said something no one but Anne-Marie would have been able to hear over the music.

"Trust me," I shouted back. "They're going back to his place to fuck. It's a game for them."

"How do you know that?" She looked at Anne-Marie, then back at me. "What if she doesn't want to?"

"Then he won't make her. They've done this for years, Syd."

Sydney folded her arms and glared at me. "You're telling me she made these plans to come out with us, broke up with him, and is standing there arguing with him because she *wants* to go to his place?"

I was telling her that, but Sydney was being stubborn, so I shrugged. "If you don't believe me, try to step in. I'll come with you."

She gave me another dirty look, then spun on one heel and stomped across the dance floor. By the time I caught up with her, Syd had said something, and Anne-Marie was smiling prettily at her.

"It is okay, Sydney, *chérie*," she shouted. "Thank you for your concern, but I know how to handle Remy." She looked at me, then leaned towards Sydney. "I *do* want to go home with him, I promise you."

"But what about the hot cowboy you were going to give your panties to?" I shouted helpfully.

Remy stood up straighter. "The what?"

Anne-Marie rolled her eyes dramatically. "Oh, it was simply a *game*, Remy. You need to be calm. A cowboy gave me a pair of panties so I could take them off and give them to a man at his bachelor party."

He glanced down, then back up. "Have you?"

"No, he hasn't—*oh!*"

Anne-Marie yelped as Remy's hand shot out and gripped hers, tugging her forward. He used his other hand to grab her hip and press his body against hers, devouring her mouth in a heated, intense kiss.

"You are coming home with me," he growled loud enough that I could hear it. "Now, *ma coquinette*. Before I throw you over my shoulder and everyone in this bar sees the panties this *cowboy*"—he spat the word out like it was dirty—"gave you."

Sydney's mouth dropped open and Anne-Marie let out a breathless giggle as her cheeks turned red. "Fine. I apologize, my dears, but we will need to reschedule our night for another—"

"*Now*," Remy repeated, and Anne-Marie waved gleefully as he tugged her off the dance floor just as a herd of cowboys to descend onto the bar. A confused-looking Jesse watched as Anne-Marie left, then glanced across the dance floor at us.

"Well, shit," Sydney said. "How are we going to tell him she stole his panties?"

"It's okay," I said, then threw a thumb's up at Jesse. "I've got a plan."

"Does the plan involve you giving your panties to a random drunk guy?" she asked.

I smiled and watched as Jesse subtly herded the group of men towards us.

Unlike Jesse, the rest of the group was not made up of real cowboys. Some of them were more cowboy than the others. The groom, Cody, for example, looked at home in his plaid shirt and cowboy hat. That may have had something to do with the fact that Cody's pasty skin was flushed red with liquor and there was a glazed look in his eyes that made me think alcohol wasn't the only thing he'd been overdoing that night. But it seemed more likely that Cody, like Jesse, was probably from Alberta.

But I didn't spend all that much time looking at Cody.

Or Jesse.

That was because there was someone who either didn't get the memo about the party's theme or, more likely, didn't give a shit, and I was into that. I didn't know his name, of course, but he had dark brown hair and scruff on his chin and a leather jacket that seemed to be causing an argument between him and a bouncer. After a moment, he sighed, then shrugged the jacket off to reveal a black V-neck t-shirt, tattooed arms, and a braided leather band around his wrist.

"Dibs," I said immediately.

"On which?" Sydney asked.

"Generic Bad Boy Number One," I said.

"Oh," she said. "That's fine. I'm dibsing Mr. 'Begrudgingly Attending Because This Is What The Groom Wanted But Clearly Uncomfortable With The Theme.'"

The man in question was quite clearly from Montreal. Where Jesse's plaid had various shades of earthy reds and warm browns and cream-toned whites, his was rich purple with black and white accents. The collar was ironed sharply and there was a stiff starchiness to the fabric that made me think he'd bought the shirt, ironed it, and then put it on for the first time that night. Perched on his head was a black felt cowboy hat that looked uncomfortably warm. He was the shortest of the group, probably an inch or two shorter than Sydney was, with broad shoulders but a slim frame.

"Bet you a drink that's Olivier," I said.

"Who?"

"The best man."

"Right." Sydney's eyes lingered on him for another moment. "Think he's single?"

"I don't see a ring."

She gave me an unimpressed look. "Because he's on the other side of the bar."

"Not for long," I said as Jesse leaned over and said something to Cody, then gestured at me and Sydney. It took a moment for the groom's eyes to settle on the two of us, but when they did, I smiled again, and a grin spread across his face as he started towards us.

"Hey, ladies," he slurred when he was close enough. "How's ya doing up?"

I had no idea if that was some kind of weird Alberta phrase or if he was just that drunk, but he was probably just that drunk. "We're doing great. How about you?"

"Oh, I'm fucking *fantastic*." He lifted his left hand up. "I'm getting married!"

Sydney raised her eyebrows as she looked at his hand, which was devoid of all adornment. "Uh... did you lose your ring?"

"Huh?" Cody looked down at his naked finger. "Oh. No. I don't have it yet. It's my *bachelor* party. Which is why I need your help."

"What kind of help?" I asked, trying to sound intrigued.

"I need... panties," he declared.

"Whoa, whoa, wait a moment," said a loud, accented voice, and a moment later Begrudgingly Attending Because This Is What The Groom Wanted But Clearly Uncomfortable With The Theme came up behind Cody, an apologetic look on his face. With him were Jesse and Generic Bad Boy Number One. "*Bonjour.* I'm Olivier, Cody's best man. He may be a little too drunk to, uh, explain what he just said."

"You owe me a drink," I said to Sydney before turning to Olivier. "I think it was pretty straightforward. My understanding is that Cody needs panties."

"Right, but—"

"She seems to *fully* understand the situation," Jesse said, clapping a hand on Olivier's shoulder.

Generic Bad Boy Number One raised an eyebrow. "I thought you said a tall blonde in a pink dress."

Jesse glanced at us nervously. "Well, yeah, but... trust me?"

"What I don't understand is why you need panties," I said. "Did you leave yours at home, Cody?"

Cody made a *pfft*ing noise. "Nah, I got two other pairs. But I need three to win the scaff... scander... scavenderger—"

"He's doing a scavenger hunt," Olivier said. "One of the items *Christian*"—he said the name with a snide sense of scorn as he glanced at Generic Bad Boy Number One—"decided to add was a pair of underwear from a woman in each bar we went to tonight."

"What?" Generic Bad Boy Number One—aka Christian—said innocently. "He's done good so far, hasn't he?"

Olivier's jaw tightened as he pressed his lips together. "It adds a level of classlessness to the party, if that's what you were aiming for."

"Are you saying that women who give up their panties to random men in bars are classless?" I asked.

"What? No," Olivier said. "I meant asking for it is—"

"Look, you know I'm not a classy fucker," Cody said, then looked at Sydney. "Can I have your panties?"

"No," Sydney said.

"Damn." He looked at me. "Can I have *your* panties?"

"Hmm," I said. "I dunno. Why did you ask my friend first?"

"She looked like she might shoot me down so I thought you might feel bad for me and do it," Cody said.

"That's a good reason," I said. "But I'm still not convinced. What's in it for me?"

"Alcohol," he said firmly.

I tilted my head from side to side. "I mean, alcohol's great and all, but do you know how expensive panties are?"

"No offense, darling, but I know for a fact you can get them at the dollar store," Christian said.

"I'm sure you can," I said. "But while some of my *friends* may shop at the dollar store, I *don't*. And *I'm* wearing my very favourite pair tonight."

Jesse blinked in realization. "Oh. *Oh*."

Cody looked confused. "Oh what?"

"I… uh…" Jesse glanced at Christian, then back at me. "We couldn't possibly ask you to part with your absolute favourite pair of panties, miss."

"Don't be too hasty," I said. "I might give them up. For a price. Like maybe if you help me with *my* scavenger hunt…"

Cody's face brightened with breathless excitement. "You're doing a scavenger hunt too?"

"Mm-hmm. But there's a problem." I reached out and took his left hand, tapping the bare spot on his fourth finger. "The things I need to collect can't come from men who are about to get married. But maybe if your friends think they can handle it…"

"We can handle it," Jesse said immediately.

I grinned. "Perfect. Because I need to collect kisses from three different men tonight. So if you give me those, I'll give you my panties."

"Deal," Christian said, and then without so much as a breath of hesitation or enough time for me to drop Cody's hand, he reached forward and kissed me.

I kissed him back, trying not to grin against his lips as a warm rush of adrenaline and desire rushed over me. After a moment, I felt Cody take his hand back and heard the group of them laughing and cheering indistinctly, but that was overshadowed by Christian leaning in closer and slipping his tongue into my mouth, flicking it against mine before drawing back and opening his eyes.

"Did that meet the requirements for your scavenger hunt, darling?" he asked, his voice low and gruff.

"Oh, yes," I said. "I might have to get you to help me with some of the other things on my list."

He flicked an eyebrow up. "What other things?"

"Things that you can't usually do in a crowded bar," I said, then let go of him as I turned to Jesse. "Are you planning to help me too, cowboy?"

Jesse took off his cowboy hat, handed it to Olivier, and elbowed Christian out of the way as he stepped forward. Wordlessly, he reached up, cupping a hand on my cheek before dipping down to kiss me.

And then kiss me again.

And one more time after that until Christian punched him on the arm.

"Damn," Jesse said, quiet enough that his friends couldn't hear over the music. "I was worried when we saw your friend leave, but this might be the best thing that's happened to me all night."

I didn't have a chance to respond before Sydney spoke up.

"Only one more kiss left," she said, looking at me then glancing at Olivier. "Your turn, best man?"

"Uh…" Olivier said, then coughed.

"Oh, ouch," I said, laughing. "Is it because I've made out with two of your friends in front of you? Or am I not your type?"

Olivier's cheeks turned red. "No, it's… well, I… uh… You *are* very pretty, but—"

"Is your type more of a strawberry blonde babe with long legs and a tongue that both speaks and kisses the best French you've ever had?" I asked.

"Nellie!" Sydney said, laughing in shock.

"I mean, that's only fair," Cody slurred. "If *my* friends could earn me the panties, *her* friend can earn her the kiss. Yeah?"

"That makes almost no sense," Christian said. "So yeah, of course. Absolutely."

"But—" Olivier started.

"Come *on*, buzzkill!" Christian said. "Are you the best man or not?"

"If you really don't want to kiss her, you don't have to," I said. "I guess I could share one of the others with her instead of keeping them for myself."

Jesse choked on his drink.

"It is not that," Olivier said, glancing at Sydney. "I... I'm just..."

"Shy?" Sydney guessed.

Olivier's throat flexed as he swallowed and nodded.

"But that's the only thing stopping you?" I asked.

Christian raised his eyebrows. Jesse looked amused. Cody leaned in and nudged Olivier.

"Come on, man," he said. "You've been checking her out since we walked in."

"I... alright," Olivier said. "Fine. Yes, I would like to kiss you, Miss, uh..."

"Sydney," she finished, then stepped forward and plucked the black cowboy hat off Olivier's head, revealing a mussed-up head of light brown curls beneath it. She popped the hat on her own head, grabbed a handful of his pressed shirt, and stooped slightly as she tugged him in for a heated kiss.

"Fuck yeah!" Cody hollered, pumping a fist in the air as Jesse and Christian let out matching cheers. "Atta boy, Olivier."

"'Bout time you loosened up," Christian said.

Olivier and Sydney parted and Olivier's face was pink, but he let out a soft laugh.

"Want your hat back?" Sydney asked.

He shook his head. "It looks much, much better on you."

"Remind me, what was that rule about cowboy hats again?" Sydney asked nonchalantly.

"Wear the hat, ride the cowboy," Cody, Jesse, and Christian all said in unison. Olivier's face went fully red as Sydney adjusted the hat on her head and grinned.

"Well now," Jesse said, looking at me and folding his arms. "We held up our end of the bargain."

"You sure did," I said cheerfully, then handed my empty glass to Christian. "Hold this."

"What are you—" he started, then his mouth dropped open as I hiked my skirt up just enough to keep myself covered while slipping my hands beneath. Shimmying left to right, I slid my panties down my thighs until they were far enough down that I could let them drop to the floor. With a swift movement, I readjusted my skirt and stepped out of the lacy black thong I'd been wearing. Using my right foot to hook them with the pointed toe of my high heel, I kicked my leg out towards Cody.

"There you go," I said.

Cody gleefully took my panties off my shoe and held the scrap of lace up. "These are by far the nicest pair I got tonight."

"You, ma'am, are a fucking *rock star*," Christian said.

"I think that earns our new friend here a few drinks," Jesse said, making a motion that looked like he was adjusting his belt but that was *clearly* him adjusting the front of his pants. "What, uh... what was your name again, sweetheart?"

"Are you asking because you want to add me to your bar tab or because you and your friend want to know what to moan later?" I asked.

Jesse's mouth dropped open and he shared a look with Christian. "Uh—"

"Because either way, it's Nellie," I said. "Now, about those drinks..."

Chapter Seven
A Little Reminder

IT WAS AROUND ONE-THIRTY when I walked out of the nightclub by myself.

Sydney had left half an hour earlier after untangling herself from Olivier. She'd felt bad about leaving without me, but I told her it wasn't a big deal and that I wasn't ready to go yet. That was mostly because Jesse had his hand up my dress at the time, the scene blocked by Christian's body so no one could tell Jesse's fingers were inside me, and I was close enough to coming right there on the dance floor that I couldn't stomach the idea of asking them to stop so we could leave, too.

I'd intended to ask the guys to bring me back to their hotel as soon as I'd finished. But after Christian moved forward and pressed his body to mine so my face was buried in his chest and no one could see my expression as an orgasm ripped through me, the two of them had seemed uncertain. Neither of them had been willing to say why, even though it was *super* clear to me, so I said I was going outside to "cool down" and they could come find me when they were ready.

I mean, I figured it was only fair to give Jesse and Christian some privacy as they furtively discussed if they could actually *do* this, like, with each other there, and like, no touching bro, of course not but what about friendly fire, well I mean that obviously happens I'm not gonna be *mad* about it, yeah me neither, but also no touching on purpose, yeah definitely not on purpose unless she asks us to, wait what, I mean no touching at all haha right 'cause no homo bro, dude that's homophobic you can't say that, sorry I just meant, look it's fine I just, no no you're right and I mean if there's some stuff that is it's not a big deal, wait are you saying like... *some* homo because if you are, maybe we should talk about this another time, holy shit dude wait are you saying—

Or at least, that was how I imagined the conversation went, given the steely resolve and meaningful glances between the two of them over the rest of the night.

And yeah, I could've waited inside or gone to the bathroom or something, but I needed the fresh air and the solitude. Not *total* solitude; it was a well-lit street with plenty of nightclubs and the bouncers weren't far from where I wandered to. But a break from the lights and pounding music and bodies moving here, there, and everywhere wasn't unwelcome.

Though it ended up being a longer break than I'd anticipated.

I was staring at a patch of snow, shivering and wondering if the guys were actually going to come outside or if they'd chickened out completely, when someone walked across my line of sight. I didn't notice them at first, but the same person stopped and took a few steps backwards, blocking my view of the snow patch.

"Ms. Belanger?" he said.

If you looked up the definition of "silver fox" in the dictionary, you'd see words describing what it means, because that's how dictionaries work. But even if it was one of those picture dictionaries that apparently exist, you wouldn't see a photo of Ben Cameron—or as Sydney called him, Professor Sexy. He might've been older than me, but he wasn't old enough to be considered a silver fox.

That being said, he was whatever a man was before becoming a silver fox. I doubted he was even in his forties, but there was a distinctive streak of grey over his left temple. A scattering of salt flicked through the rest of his thick, dark hair that he kept parted on one side. His skin was a warm, light gold colour and there were hints of lines starting around his hazel eyes. And while I knew that professors and teachers of all kinds had lives outside the schools they worked at, he somehow always seemed to *dress* like a professor. That night, he was wearing a thick black peacoat over what seemed to be a turtleneck and jeans.

"Professor Cameron!" I exclaimed, then immediately remembered I'd been drinking and tried to tone my voice down to something approaching sober. "What are you doing here?"

"I was at a midnight book release party for a, ah, former colleague," he said, motioning down the block at a small bookstore.

"That's cool. I didn't know they did release parties for... what, like, self-help or something?"

He laughed and shook his head. "No, a novel. A psychological thriller. She's written a series of them, but I haven't had a chance to read any yet."

"Oh." I blinked, frowning. "When you said colleague, I thought it would be a psychologist or something."

"She is in academia, but writing seems to be her true calling, so I thought I'd come by and show my support," he said. "And what are you doing here? A reading week getaway to Montreal or...?"

I shook my head. "Visiting my dad for the weekend."

He glanced past me, a look of mild concern on his face. "Do you often go out to nightclubs with your dad?"

I slapped a hand to my face, as if that would hold in the laughter that burst out of me as I shook my head. "No, I'm out with my friends right now. I meant in *general*, I'm here to visit my dad. I drove in with my friend Sydney after my interview today so we could go out tonight since tomorrow I have this gala thing to go to. Then we'll go back to Ottawa Monday morning."

He chuckled. "Of course. That makes sense. But—" He paused and frowned, looking around us. "You're out here alone?"

"Yeah," I said.

"Why?"

It wasn't like I could tell him exactly what I was doing, so I just smiled. "I'm waiting for my friends. They'll be out in a few minutes."

His forehead creased even more. "Is that safe?"

"Why wouldn't it be?"

He glanced down the street. "Well, it's... it's night. And you've been, ah, drinking. Presumably. Would you like me to wait with you?"

And honestly, I don't know what it was. Maybe the fact that I *had* been drinking or maybe the fact that he cared enough to show concern at all. Because I could absolutely take care of myself. Nothing was going to happen to me on a well-lit and busy street. Or at least, nothing that didn't have a ton of witnesses or that could have happened to me at literally any other time.

But hearing him worry like that and offering to wait was just...

Nice, I guess.

Nice enough that a sensation of pleasant heat washed over me, so palpable that it almost seemed to warm the tips of my fingers in the cold winter air.

"You don't have to do that," I said, trying not to smile. "But thank you. They really will only be a few minutes."

"Of course," he said, and I thought he'd say good night and head off. But instead, he put his hands in the pockets of his jacket. "Before I go, though, you said you had an interview today. Did that happen to be for the FAI internship?"

"It was," I said. "How'd you know?"

"I've had a number of students apply for it in the past," he said. "They generally do their final round of interviews on the first Saturday of reading week. Congratulations on making it to that level, Ms. Belanger. It's quite an accomplishment given how competitive it is."

I tried not to beam, even as more warmth flooded over me. "Thanks."

"Knowing you, I'm assuming it went extremely well?"

God, apparently I couldn't get enough of the implication that I'd impressed him somehow since that warm feeling only grew. "I'm pretty confident I'll get it. Do you know when they usually contact people? They said any time between March and the beginning of May, but if you've had students get it before..."

"Usually the first round of acceptance letters goes out mid-March, though in some years it's closer to the end of the month. Then if they have anyone who's unable to accept the internship, they'll send out letters to the second round picks in early April."

"Cool," I said, nodding slowly. "So, like, I should know in about a month, hopefully."

"I would say so, yes," he said. "But they also send official rejection letters so they don't leave people guessing. Not that I think you'll get one, but some students have found it comforting to know they'll find out either way."

"Definitely. I hate not knowing things."

"Given what I've seen of you in my classes, that's not surprising."

I laughed, sure my face was turning red, and not from the cold. "Thanks, Professor Cameron."

"It's just the truth. And you can call me Ben. You know that."

"Yeah, but then how would everyone around me know you're a professor?"

"Fair point," he said. "But, ah... why would anyone need to know that?"

I shrugged. "What if someone was watching to make sure a stranger wasn't harassing me? This shows I know you. Or what if they were looking and they were like, 'Damn, who's that fine-ass gentleman that girl over there is talking to?' You want them to live with the weight of that mystery?"

It wasn't until Ben laughed awkwardly that I realized my mouth was moving faster than my brain and I might have pushed things a little too far.

"I, uh... I'm—" he started.

"And clearly, I need a little reminder of, like, who... you are and how I know you," I said. "Otherwise I get too, um... friendly."

He cleared his throat and under the streetlights, I could see a hint of pink tinting his skin. "It's alright. You've been, ah... out at a nightclub. But I am, ah... flattered. Thank you."

"I haven't been drinking that much," I said. "And if I'm supposed to call you Ben, shouldn't you call me Nellie?"

Ben opened his mouth, but hesitated.

And I just...

I couldn't explain why I just *knew* why he hesitated. Maybe because he said he was flattered, which meant that warm feeling was probably rushing through him too, and maybe it *shouldn't* have given that I'd been his student.

I knew Ben wasn't *that* kind of guy. I might not be the type of person to fuck a teacher for an A, but if I was, I could've easily found out which ones would take me up on it. There were always rumours about certain professors with names that came up time and time again. I didn't know how true all those rumours were, but I did know that in my first year, a business professor had been caught hooking up with a grad student and had "retired early" shortly after.

Professor Ben Cameron's name had *never* been part of those rumours. And I sincerely doubted anyone would keep silent about hooking up with the hottest professor on campus.

But I wasn't in any of his classes anymore. He wasn't going to even be at Ottawa Tech next year, and then I'd be graduating. He specialized in forensic psychology and I was more interested in forensic biology. I'd only taken those classes to fill out my schedule and because I thought it was interesting. So while I wasn't sure I *actually* had a teacher/student fantasy like I'd joked about with Sydney, if I did, this was probably the only time I'd be able to do something about it.

So I went for it.

"Or did you need the reminder, too?" I asked.

"The reminder?" he repeated.

"About who I am and how you know me?"

Ben stared at me with the expression of someone whose brain was processing eight million things at once. His lips closed and his jaw twitched before he swallowed, then he took a breath and—

"There you are, Nellie," someone said from behind me.

Of course.

I held Ben's gaze as Jesse and Christian walked up, one on either side of me. A warm hand moved to my lower back.

"You alright?" Christian asked from my left.

"Yeah, of course," I said.

On my right, Jesse stood protectively close. "Already trying to replace us?"

Ben's eyebrows flicked up. I tried not to laugh.

"This is Professor Cameron," I said. "He teaches forensic psychology at Ottawa Tech."

"Mmm," Christian said.

There was a beat of silence.

"I'm getting a forensic science degree," I said. "At Ottawa Tech."

"*Oh*," Jesse said as the realization hit him. "Right. Sorry. Uh... nice to meet you."

"Of course," Ben said, though his voice didn't have that smooth, knowing quality it usually did.

"We can forget this happened," I said.

He nodded, though it seemed half-hearted. "We certainly can. Enjoy your—I mean—" He coughed. "Have a good night... Nellie."

Oh, *fuck* yes.

"Thanks, Ben," I said.

He nodded again, then hesitated for half a second before he walked away. Christian's head turned as he watched him.

"You sure he wasn't trying to poach you away from us?" he asked, his voice low.

"Nah." Jesse put his arm around my shoulders. "She wouldn't give up the two guys she's been teasin' all damn night for one guy in a turtleneck."

I twisted my mouth to the side, looking at the back of Ben's form as he continued down the block. "Well..."

Christian's head snapped towards me and he took his hand off my back. "What?"

"I mean, maybe if he played his cards right."

He let out an incredulous scoff. "You would do that to us?"

I grinned, reaching for his hand. "Maybe. Maybe not. Come prove to me I made the right choice."

Chapter Eight
Donut Talk To Me

"I can't believe you," Sydney said the next morning as we walked towards my car. "There's, like, one circumstance where I could see someone justify giving up a hookup with Professor Sexy, and you managed to find that exact circumstance."

Out of habit, I glanced at the house behind me, but I knew as well as Sydney did that my dad and Kimberlee had left for church, since my dad had huffed loudly when I declined to go with them.

"I don't think you're recognizing what a problem it was," I said.

"Choosing between a threesome and Professor Sexy," she said. "That's a *problem* to you?!"

"Of course. It's like a sexy *Sophie's Choice*," I said. "Although, Ben made the decision for me, so it's not like I actively *chose* the threesome."

I could almost hear her roll her eyes. "What a terrible consolation prize."

"Right? After all that, they didn't even do anything together."

"Are you saying it wasn't hot because they didn't?"

I smirked. "No. It was fabulous."

"Fabulous enough that you didn't want to spend the night in their hotel?"

"Syd," I said, almost patronizingly. "They were sharing a room and I made them both come so hard they passed out before I got back from the bathroom. My options were either squish myself between them on a queen-size bed, sleep by myself on the *other* queen-size bed, or let them wake up this morning sharing a bed with each other."

"One of those is significantly more evil than the others," she said.

"Is it, though?" I tilted my head to the side. "They were literally *cuddling* when I left."

"Wait, really?"

I nodded. "I mean, they didn't do anything together while I was there, but maybe Jesse having his face shoved in my pussy while Christian's dick was inside me was the thing they needed to break down the obvious barrier between them."

"So your pussy's a matchmaker now?"

I shrugged. "Maybe."

She sighed. "I'm almost sad I missed all this."

"And for crappy dick."

She huffed. "It wasn't *crappy*. I had a good time. And he's sweet."

"You said he didn't make you come."

"He tried."

"Syd."

"He did!" She shrugged. "He also felt bad about finishing so fast. And he made out with me while I finished up, so..."

I rolled my eyes. "So he did the bare minimum."

She laughed. "You barely know the guy. What do you have against him?"

"He's from Montreal."

"It's not that far."

"It's less the distance and more the being-from-Montreal." I pressed my key fob and the locks on my car clicked open. "And what about Reid?"

The laughter on Sydney's face faded and she stopped walking to glare at me. "There's nothing going on with me and Reid."

"But—"

"There's not. And there won't ever be." She started around my car, reaching for the handle. "Now, are we going to get these donuts or what?"

Reid—also known as Sydney's roommate and unrequited love interest—was a weird topic between me and Sydney. The two of them had grown up in the same town, though Reid was a few years older than she was and had been friends with her brother. He'd moved to Ottawa to work as a carpenter, and when she'd decided on Ottawa Tech for university, he was the only person she knew in the whole city. Timing-wise, his lease was about to expire, so he asked Syd if she'd want to be roommates.

Having been in love with him since she was a kid, she obviously said no.

And then realized how much rent was in Ottawa and changed her mind, deciding it was far more economical to just never say out loud how she felt about him.

Well, not never. She'd said it exactly once when we were blackout drunk in our second year and I was freaking out because there were tears in her eyes as she heaved everything in her stomach into my toilet.

"Maybe we should go to the hospital," I had said, trying not to sound terrified because I was *way* too drunk to get her there safely.

She'd shaken her head. "Don' need it. Jus' go wake up Reid."

"Reid's not here, Syd. You're at my place."

"Reid'll take care of me," she said, ignoring me. "Reid always takes care of me."

"Okay, but Reid is downstairs at your apartment. I don't want to leave you alone here."

She smiled stupidly at the toilet. "I love him."

"You love Reid?"

"So much," she mumbled.

"Like, as a friend?"

She shook her head, then started crying for real. "Can't, though."

"Can't what?"

But she kept shaking her head, then lurched forward and puked again.

She hadn't remembered that conversation the next morning. And she'd never said anything like that about Reid again, but it had been obvious before that, and it was still obvious that she had feelings for him. I didn't know why they couldn't be more than friends, but I couldn't ask. Syd always shut down the conversation as soon as we even got close to the topic.

"Alright," I said, dropping the subject as Sydney opened my car door. "Donut time. I promise you, these are the best donuts you've ever had in your life."

"They better be. Your dad said they were going to a brunch place with the best eggs Benedict in the city and I might not be a church girl, but I would've sat through mass for eggs Benedict. You know how I feel about hollandaise."

I laughed, but before I could say anything else, the slightly creaky whir of wheels turning interrupted us. I looked over my shoulder as a silver Mercedes Benz turned into the Marchands' driveway. Before the engine even turned off, a far-too-perky blonde bounded out of the passenger seat, still clad in the dress she'd been wearing the previous night, and was halfway across the lawn between our driveways.

"*Bonjour*, ladies!" Anne-Marie called.

"Hi, Anne-Marie," Sydney said. "How was the rest of your night?"

"So, *so* good," she said, a roguish smile spreading on her lips. "I am so happy to announce Remy and I decided to give things another shot."

"You don't say," I said in a monotonous voice. "I am so shocked. Wow."

She stuck her tongue out at me good-naturedly as her now on-again boyfriend walked up to join us.

When they'd first started dating in high school, people had thought they were a strange pairing. Anne-Marie was a bubbly social butterfly, sometimes obnoxiously so, and Remy had always been the quiet, studious type. As the years went past, that strangeness only grew. Anne-Marie had gotten more and more social and perky, while Remy had gotten more stoic and serious.

But even though they seemed to be such opposites and even though they played this whole jealousy-breakup-so-we-can-hate-fuck thing and even though they'd fallen in love as teenagers and so many things could change as they got older, there was no way anyone could argue that Anne-Marie and Remy weren't soulmates. They complemented each other perfectly, and as Anne-Marie's friend, I approved of the fact that Remy was obsessed with her and her alone. I doubt he'd so much as glanced at another girl since he and Anne-Marie had been together.

I mean, glanced at as in checked out. It wasn't like he was some rude guy who refused to look women in the eye or something. He just had no interest in anyone that wasn't Anne-Marie, which was probably why their little jealousy game got so intense.

"Hi, Nellie," Remy said, nodding at me solemnly as he joined the group of us.

"Hey, Remy," I replied. "How's it going?"

"Good, thank you." He looked at Sydney, who, despite Anne-Marie's reassurances the previous night, didn't seem convinced about him. "We haven't officially met."

"I know," Sydney said, her voice guarded. "I'm Sydney."

"Remy." He extended his hand for her to shake. "Could I speak with you privately for a moment?"

Sydney blinked at him in surprise. "Uh..."

"It's nothing bad," he said. "I promise."

She glanced at me, then at Anne-Marie, then shrugged. "Fine."

Anne-Marie pretended not to watch as Sydney walked down my dad's driveway with her boyfriend, but turned to me as soon as Sydney and Remy were out of sight.

"So," she said excitedly. "Tell me. Who did you go home with?"

"No one," I said.

She rolled her eyes. "Nellie."

"He had a hotel."

Anne-Marie snickered. "Who was it?" She clapped her hands together. "Was it the cowboy? What was his name... Jesse! Jesse the cowboy?"

I nodded. It wasn't technically a lie.

"Oh, good. Was he amazing? He looked like he would be amazing. Did you get his number?"

"Why would I have gotten his number?"

"What?!" Anne-Marie crossed her arms, giving me a scolding look. "Eleanor Belanger, you spent the night with a gorgeous cowboy and didn't bother getting his number so you could do it all over again?"

"He was from Alberta," I said. "I'm never going to see him again. But Sydney got the best man's number. He lives here."

She said something. And something else after that. And probably even more after that because Anne-Marie almost never shut up, but I didn't hear a word of it.

I was too busy staring at the Marchands' driveway.

If my life had been one of the bad eighties high school rom-coms my mom and I loved to watch together, Anne-Marie's voice would have been drowned out by some ultra-horny glam metal song. The camera would have panned as the black BMW turned into the driveway and after a quick reaction shot of me staring at it with my lips parted like a fucking idiot, done a slow zoom in as a tall, disgustingly handsome man got out of the driver's seat and ran a hand through his thick blonde hair, pushing it back from the warm light beige skin on his forehead so people could see his startlingly blue eyes before he slammed the car door shut.

Then there would be a flashback, moments of memories that reduced one of the most consequential experiences of my life to flickering glimpses of a story.

Me standing in the hallway, hair dripping, wrapped in a towel.

JP inviting me into his room, intending nothing more than to give me a place to dress.

Wrapping myself in his robe, perching on the edge of the bed facing away from him so he couldn't see me blush as we heard Anne-Marie and Remy in the next room.

His foot nudging me, a half-smirk on his face as he hinted towards something I wasn't catching.

My face when he outright asked if it would be weird for him to hit on me.

His face when I stood up, dropped his robe to the floor, and stood in front of him.

The kisses.

The heat.

The slight tremble as I crawled onto his lap.

The grimace when I sank down onto him and he realized that I'd never done this before.

The way he touched me, soft and comforting, as he asked why I hadn't told him.

His hands on my hips and my nipple between his teeth as I rode him. His arms wrapping around my waist and his body moving beneath me after I came so hard I could barely lift myself.

A breathless moment on his bed, recovering, before someone called my name.

Panic. Fear. A whirlwind of activity as I shrouded myself in his robe again.

And that final look, the way he'd nodded as I begged him not to tell anyone.

"...alone, Nellie," Anne-Marie said, and that's where the music would cut off and the camera would flip back to me, blinking as I looked at Anne-Marie with wide eyes.

Thankfully, my life was not a bad eighties high school rom-com, since if it was, I would have said something like "Huh?" and Anne-Marie would have not only realized that I wasn't listening to her, but also *why* I wasn't listening to her and I would *never* hear the fucking end of it.

"Right," is what I said instead, and Anne-Marie looked pleased with herself before noticing the new arrival on her driveway.

"Oh!" she said, then waved. "Jean-Paul! Look who's home for the weekend!"

For almost three years, I'd avoided seeing him. Three years, aside from those couple of times that he'd left Post-Its on my window, I'd somehow managed to only visit my dad while he was living in residence at school or away doing some lawyer thing or travelling or whatever the fuck else rich wannabe lawyers did. Three *years*—okay, two-and-a-half, but still—since I'd bolted out of his bedroom wrapped in his bathrobe, wetness still dripping down my thighs and the taste of him still in my mouth and the echo of his promise not to tell anyone ringing in my ears.

I'd been so close to never having to see him again.

So of course he had to be a bastard and fuck it up.

"Hi, Anne-Marie," JP called back. "And... is that you, Nellie?"

"Nope," I said, trying to avoid looking in his direction.

He laughed. I hated the sound almost as much as the fact that it was coming closer and I had to—yep.

I was going to have to look at him.

Fuck.

His eyes were on me. I could feel them. And my heart was pounding, thrumming in my chest so fast that I was almost sure everyone else could hear it. They couldn't, of course, because there was no way JP would have heard my heart racing like that at the sight of him and ever let me live it down, but still.

"It's been a while," JP said as he walked up to me and his sister. "What, like... at least a few years now, hey? Two, maybe? Or three?"

"Something like that," I said.

His mouth twisted into a smile. "How's university going?"

"Great," I said. "Graduating next year. How's... whatever you're up to these days?"

"Awesome. I just started as a junior associate at my dad's law firm."

"Says the loser still living at home," Anne-Marie said.

JP rolled his eyes. "As are you, sweet sister."

"Yeah, but I'm still in university."

"And my condo won't be ready to move into until the fall."

"That's what you get for buying in a brand-new building," Remy said, rejoining us with Sydney. I glanced at her, raising an eyebrow, and she gave me a slight nod to say everything was alright.

"It is," JP agreed. "How's it going, man?"

"Good." Remy put an arm around Anne-Marie's shoulder. "She wanted to change clothes before we went to brunch."

"Brunch?" JP said, his eyebrows flicking up as if he was incredibly interested in that fact. "Are all of you going?"

"No," I answered before Anne-Marie could say something stupid about how that was a great idea and we should all go for brunch and hey, JP, you should come with us. "We're going to get donuts."

"Donuts," JP repeated.

"At Trou de Beigne," I said almost defensively. "They're my favourite and you can't get them in Ottawa."

"Of course," JP said. "You and...?"

"My friend," I said, gesturing at Sydney.

"Hi," Sydney said, extending her hand. "I'm Sydney Amhurst."

"JP Marchand." He took his hand in hers, flicking his eyes up and down before smiling an all-too-familiar smile. "It's an absolute delight to meet you."

I swallowed hard, my jaw twitching as I watched him blatantly check her out. Not because I was jealous or something. Because... I mean, he'd just met her and was *blatantly* checking her out.

"Well," I said. "Nice to see you all, but Sydney and I have to go. I'll talk to you later, Anne-Marie."

"It was good to see you, Nellie," JP said. "Maybe we'll run into each other again soon."

God, I hoped not.

Sydney said goodbye to Anne-Marie, then hopped in the passenger seat as the other three turned to walk back to the Marchand's house. They'd barely stepped onto their own driveway when I finished backing out of the driveway and started down the street.

"So," Sydney said, her voice high-pitched. "Was that—"

"I don't have a crush on JP," I snapped.

"...Anne-Marie's brother?" she finished after a pause.

My face burned red. "Yes."

"Who you don't have a crush on, as you've just said."

"Exactly," I said. "Anne-Marie seems to think I do, but I don't, and that's it. What did Remy want to talk to you about?"

"Oh, about last night," she said. "Anne-Marie told him I'd been worried and he wanted to apologize if he'd made me uncomfortable. Which was cool of him, but then when I said I was sorry I'd assumed the worst of him, he was like 'Uh, no, don't fucking apologize that for that' because he knew it looked bad and would've way rather I said something if I thought someone was in trouble than worry about offending him. Then there was the whole typical 'I promise I'll never do anything to hurt her and if I do please don't hesitate to beat my ass for it' and blah-blah-blah sweetness."

"See? I told you."

"You did. I was wrong. Remy's an alright guy. But back to JP—"

"There's nothing to get back to. I don't have a crush on him."

"I mean, I wouldn't blame you. He's gorgeous."

I rolled my eyes. "He's a total bastard. I like to think I have higher standards than that."

"Nell, you know I love you, but you let a guy you just met and who probably didn't wash his hands first finger you in a nightclub while his friend gave you a hickey."

I slapped a hand to my neck. "He did not."

"He almost did," she said, snickering.

"Whatever," I muttered. "That says nothing about my standards."

"Your standards are about a foot off the ground."

"Yeah, and JP Marchand doesn't reach them."

She burst out laughing. "Are you sure about that? You seem pretty adamant that—"

"He's everything I hate," I said. "My dad approves of him, which is strike one. He's an egotistical rich boy, which is strike two. And he... he's..."

"Oh, honey," Sydney said.

"Shut up," I said.

"When did you fuck him?"

I almost crashed.

Not really. There were no vehicles in front of me and it wasn't like I blew a stop sign or something. But I considered wrenching the wheel to the side and slamming my car into a nearby tree to get out of the conversation.

"How could you tell?" I asked instead.

"I've never seen you get so defensive about a guy before," she said. "You're not acting like yourself. And given the way he looked at you... he clearly shakes you, Nell."

"He doesn't *shake* me," I said, scoffing.

"Sure he doesn't. So, what happened with you two?"

"Nothing," I said. "We hooked up the summer before I started university. It was one time almost three years ago. I told him I didn't want anything serious, and he decided he should leave notes on my car asking me to call him. I didn't, and I haven't seen him since."

She was silent for a moment. When I glanced over, she was looking out the windshield, but I could still see a slight frown on the profile of her face.

"Three years ago," she said. "The summer before you started university."

"Yeah."

She nodded slowly. "So he was the first."

I considered crashing again. "How do you know that?"

"You told me about your first time," she said. "And that it was right before you started university with a guy you knew growing up. So—wait." She whirled towards me. "Anne-Marie was the girl in the next room when you were losing your virginity? And it was to her *brother*?!"

"Oh my God, Syd," I muttered. "I don't want to think about this."

"I mean, having seen him now, I'd have done the same," she said. "He's fucking gorgeous."

I wrinkled my nose, but didn't say anything.

"I don't see why you're looking at this like it's such a big deal," she said. "Anne-Marie would be thrilled if you two got together."

I looked at her incredulously. "Syd."

"What? She would. She—"

"That's the *problem*!"

Her mouth was still half-open, ready to continue, but she paused. Closing it, she twisted her lips to the side. "Oh. Right. Is that why she thinks you don't get laid on the regular or...?"

"No," I muttered. "That's because the risk of my dad finding out and subsequently disowning and/or trying to send me to a convent is too high."

She looked thoughtfully out the window, but didn't say anything.

"Still feel like you want to trade places to get your tuition and stuff covered?" I asked.

Sydney half-laughed.

But she didn't say yes.

Chapter Nine
Dump Truck Booty

"I'M IN LOVE WITH you," Bruno said the moment after he walked into the Marchands' foyer and Anne-Marie introduced us.

"Wow," I said. "I mean, I know the dress is good, but—"

"Don't flatter yourself," he said, holding up a hand. "I'm the wrong tree for you to bark at."

"*Bark* at? Are you calling me a bitch?" I asked.

He raised his eyebrows. "Have you heard of a metaphor?"

"No, never. Is that a requirement for people to date you?"

"It is now," he said. "So unfortunately, you don't qualify."

"I thought I didn't qualify because I'm not a dude."

"Well, yes, but it's mainly the metaphor thing."

"Yeesh," I said, turning to Anne-Marie. "You didn't tell me a date with Bruno was such a roller coaster ride."

There was resigned amusement on her face and she glanced at Remy. "I have created a monster, I fear."

Remy shrugged. "I could've told you getting the two of them in the same room would be a whole *thing*."

I bit back a smirk and glanced at Bruno. He was not smirking, but behind the solemn expression that made it look like he took himself way too seriously, laughter sparkled in his eyes.

"It's okay," I said. "He's already fallen in and out of love with me in the course of a thirty-second conversation, so the monster is likely dead."

"I didn't say I'm not in love with you. I'm just not attracted to you in any way, shape, or form."

I fanned myself. "Oh, God yes. You know just what I want to hear."

"*Why*," Anne-Marie said with a pointed look at Bruno, "are you saying you're in love with Nellie, *chérie*?"

He put a hand on each of the lapels of his jacket, flattening them down in a smooth motion. "Because she's wearing black. When you said it was *La Nuit Rose*, I thought we'd be in bubblegum pink and that's not my colour."

"Could've fooled me," I said.

He looked skeptical. "Do I look like someone who wears bubblegum pink?"

I raised my eyebrows and looked down at his outfit. Aside from the whiteness of his skin, Bruno was clad and accessorized in black from head to toe. Well, I guess his hair and eyes were technically more of a dark brown and he had very pretty pinkish-beige lips, but he was dressed in a monochrome black number featuring a black dress shirt, black skinny tie, black slim cut suit, and—much to what I assumed would be my dad's eventual chagrin—black Chuck Taylors.

"*Look* like it?" I repeated. "No. You look like you're one hair straightener accident away from a 2006 Myspace photo. But your sass level reads very On-Wednesdays-We-Wear-Pink to me."

"You know what?" Bruno said. "I'm going to take that as a compliment."

"Good. It was one."

He didn't look like the type of person who had a bright, brilliant smile, since his aesthetic was more along the lines of "life is pain," but he did and he flashed it at me just then. Anne-Marie rolled her eyes and picked up the small pink clutch purse she'd paired with her turquoise cocktail dress.

"If you're done trying to prove who is the snarkiest, *mes chéries,* perhaps we can be on our way?"

Bruno opened the front door and gestured to it chivalrously. "After you, Elvira."

"I am not showing *nearly* enough cleavage to be Elvira," I said as I walked past him. "It's not even enough to be Vampira."

"Her father would not have let her out of the house if it was," Anne-Marie said in a stage-whisper.

I rolled my eyes, even though she was right.

He'd been reluctant to let me out of the house in the dress as it was, but honestly, it was his fault for sending me money and telling me to buy something appropriate for a gala. Not only was it appropriate for a gala, it met all his "preferences that were actually restrictions" he'd told me about.

Givenchy was on his approved list of designer brands.

It covered all the most tempting and provocative bits of skin I had. Not a single trace of my cleavage was showing because it had a high neck. The long sleeves meant that my shoulders, as well as the rest of my arms, were covered. And the hemline stopped below both of my knees, because we all know *that's* the most scandalous part of a woman's body.

It was an approved colour—black—and not even the slightest bit sheer. There was no lace whatsoever and the red three-inch heels I paired with it were closed-toed.

But when I walked down the stairs to go over to the Marchands' just as he and Kimberlee were getting ready to leave, my dad's face turned an interesting shade of candy apple red.

"It's not even low-cut at *all*," I said when he asked if I really thought that was appropriate. "Everything is covered."

"Your entire back is showing," he said. "As is…"

He gestured vaguely at me, then looked at Kimberlee.

"It is quite, um, form-fitted," she said.

"All of them are going to be form-fitted on me," I said. "I'm *just* able to fit into the biggest sizes they have in store, Kim."

"It's Kimberlee," she said.

"I am not especially pleased that I've paid for a dress that leaves nothing to the imagination," my dad said.

"It leaves lots to the imagination," I said. "You can't even see my belly button ring outline or tell I have a big dragon tattoo on my chest."

My dad's face was nearly purple by the time I convinced him I was joking about the tattoo. He knew—and hated—that I had a belly button ring, but the idea of a tattoo was enough to nearly break him.

"I mean, your father does have a point," Anne-Marie had said with a giggle when I finally arrived and told her and Remy what had happened while we were waiting for Bruno. "But you will get no complaints from me, or likely from any man in the world other than your father."

"It's not my fault," I said. "He's the one who has a list of designers he wants me to wear and most of them don't make dresses for people with hips."

"I don't think it is your hips that are the problem," she said. "It's probably your dump-truck booty."

"Anne-Marie!" Remy said, his voice a startled hush from beside her.

I nearly popped the seams of my dress as I keeled over laughing.

"It is not a bad thing!" Anne-Marie said again. "Remy, she looks hot. Even you cannot deny that. And Bruno may not swing that way, but if he did, he'd be sending me a fruit basket for setting you two up."

My dad had initially wanted me to join him and Kimberlee in a town car to go to the event, but I convinced him it would be more appropriate for me to go with Anne-Marie and Remy since my date was meeting them at the Marchands'. Remy had offered to drive since he wasn't much of a drinker, so we all piled into his silver Mercedes Benz, Bruno and I taking over the back seat while Anne-Marie sat in the front.

And honestly, not that I'd ever admit it to *anyone*, but it was kind of... well...

Fun.

Which was ridiculous. It was *ridiculous* that Bruno could make a stuffy event like that even a little bit fun. But he did.

Like yeah, as soon as we arrived and ran into my dad, he glanced down to see the Chuck Taylors on Bruno's feet and his cheek had twitched in annoyance. Then he'd given me a *Look* that said he wouldn't say anything in front of everyone because that would make him look bad, but that we were most definitely going to *discuss this later*.

But Bruno had introduced himself and shaken my dad's hand, then immediately informed him that his father was the CEO of some massive tech company and his mom's family had tons of political connections along the East Coast in the US. My dad still looked annoyed, but the begrudging acceptance on his face made it clear that maybe I wouldn't have to *discuss anything later* with him.

"Sorry," Bruno said after my dad and Kimberlee had walked away. "That probably sounded snobby, but Anne-Marie said we weren't trying to push all of your dad's buttons."

"Well, I might decide to push a few of them," I said. "But thank you."

"No problem. Let me know if you decide to. I've got piña colada flavoured juice loaded up in my vape and for some reason, that scent pisses people off more than a cloud of vape smoke usually does." He glanced around. "Hey, they have a chocolate fountain. Wanna get—"

"Seriously, I'm in love with you," I said. "Let's go."

"—some stuff later and—oh," he finished. "You don't want to, like, socialize and stuff first?"

I snorted and threaded my arm through his so we could start towards the chocolate fountain. "Are you kidding? If you're the only person I talk to tonight, I'll be happy."

I hated events like this. I hated galas and luncheons and dinners and awards ceremonies and all of it. When I was a kid, I'd always wanted to go because getting all dressed up and going out to a fancy party sounded fun. And as an adult, it was. I loved getting dressed up and going out.

The problem was that my dad expected me to pay for my education by being a plastic prop that made him look good in his social circles.

If it had been up to my dad, I would be dressed in custom gowns that were perfectly tailored to preserve my modesty, with long sleeves and flowing fabric and demure pastel colours instead of the jewel tones I preferred. I'd be there with a date he personally selected and would smile and nod as my dad took credit for my accomplishments while bragging about me to his colleagues.

And when Bruno and I wandered away from the chocolate fountain with small porcelain plates loaded with chocolate-dipped everything and I accidentally made eye contact with my dad as he talked to a group of people with their backs to us, I would trot over and smile as he shook his head with what seemed like mock but was actually genuine exasperation.

But it wasn't up to my dad, so I begrudgingly dragged my feet towards him with Bruno trailing behind me.

"I think you will find she is *very* interested in what you have to say," my dad was saying as I joined them.

"Interested in wha—" I started to ask, then cut myself off as two of the men standing with my dad turned to face me.

And fuck.

Fuck.

"Nellie," said Jean-Luc Marchand.

"Hi, Mr. Marchand," I forced myself to say.

Della Kinsley, his wife, was standing beside him wearing a long, red satin dress, and looked over as I spoke. "What a pleasure to see you again, Nellie."

"Good to see you, too, Ms. Kinsley."

She smiled prettily. "You know you can call me Della, *chérie*." She looked at Bruno and smiled. "And who is your friend here?"

"This is, uh, Bruno," I said.

"Bruno," she repeated, extending her hand. "A pleasure. Though, you seem familiar. Have we...?"

"Multiple times," Bruno said, shaking her hand. "I'm friends with Remy. We've hung out at your house before."

Della laughed, the sound high-pitched but smooth. "Oh, of course. My apologies, Bruno. You clean up so well, I hardly recognized you!"

It was awkward.

Of course it was awkward.

And then, because it had to get *more* fucking awkward—

"Hey again, Nellie," JP said from beside his mom. "You look great tonight."

They'd done this on purpose. I was sure of it. I wasn't sure if I meant "they" as in JP and Anne-Marie or if it was just JP or just Anne-Marie, but one or both of them had plotted for him to be here without me knowing. After all, there was no way Anne-Marie had simply *forgotten* to tell me her brother was going to be at this event.

And I knew for a fact that JP's refusal to attend as many social events as his parents wanted him to was a huge point of contention in their family.

So the fact that we'd run into each other this morning and he knew I was in Montreal and I knew he'd been trying to get me to talk to him had *something* to do with this.

It had to.

Although, given that there was a thin woman dressed in pink lace standing beside JP with her hand on his forearm, maybe it didn't. If JP wanted to get together with me or something, he wouldn't have brought a date.

So I was going to have to blame Anne-Marie.

I forced a plastic smile onto my face. "Thank you, JP. You look, uh, nice as well."

He grinned. The woman beside him pressed her lips together and dug her manicured nails into his sleeve, but he ignored her.

"Thanks," he said. "Not too bad for a last-minute outfit. I don't come to a lot of these things anymore."

"Which is why it was so incredibly sweet of you to take me," the woman beside him said.

"Incredibly sweet" were not words I would have associated with JP. Neither would anyone else standing there, apparently, because even his mom tucked a laugh behind her hand.

"Nellie," my dad said, and I'd never been so thankful for him to speak before. "I was just telling Jean-Luc about your intention to take the LSAT."

And just like that, I was extremely *unthankful* that he'd spoken.

"He was," Mr. Marchand said. "And you know, a colleague of mine runs an excellent LSAT prep course in Ottawa. I believe he's accepting new—"

"My dad was mistaken," I said. "I said I would take the LSAT *if* I didn't get the internship I applied for."

JP smiled as I interrupted his dad. He was the only one, unfortunately, although Della looked amused. Mr. Marchand, on the other hand, looked annoyed.

"Hmm," Mr. Marchand said. "Well, my mistake then."

"Eleanor," my dad said. "It would be prudent to at least consider looking into this course."

"Don't you think I'm going to get the internship, Dad?" I asked.

My dad's cheek twitched again as he gave me another *Look*. "I simply mean that since it is such a prestigious course, it would be worth looking into it early, even if you do not end up needing it."

"Though, if you're uncertain about law as a career, perhaps it's not the right course for you," Mr. Marchand said. "It's meant for serious law school applicants. JP did well with it, but frankly, his capabilities stem from the fact that he's intended to attend law school for most of his life."

"Just because she is still exploring career options does not mean she is not serious about this," my dad said, and his tone was even more clipped. "And she is entirely capable of succeeding at the course."

"I'm not saying she's not, Max," Mr. Marchand said. "But I'm not inclined to give people a second chance for a recommendation. If she's not ready to accept it now—"

"I'm not," I said. "I appreciate it, Mr. Marchand, but—"

"She will accept it now."

My dad didn't even look at me as he said it. I was pretty sure everyone else did; it felt like a thousand eyeballs were rolling along my skin as my heart raced. Mr. Marchand looked at me, then at my dad.

"You know," JP said, breaking the silence. "I still have all my course material from when I took it and as my dad said, I did well. If Nellie wants to wait until she knows about her internship and can't get into the other course, I'd be happy to help tutor her over the summer. It might not be a course, but the LSAT is about what you know, not how prestigious the prep course was."

"I don't think that would be the best idea," Mr. Marchand said.

I whole-heartedly agreed, but JP seemed surprised. "You don't think I could tutor someone on the LSAT?"

"I think it's concerning that one of my associates is standing here misrepresenting what the LSAT is," Mr. Marchand replied. "And not considering how badly it would reflect on my firm for that associate to send someone into the LSAT thinking she has to memorize a bunch of facts, only to realize it's about logic, reading comprehension, and analytical thinking."

I hated to give JP credit for anything, but I had to admit it was almost impressive that the easy grin on his face didn't falter for a moment, even as his dad talked down to him.

"That would be a logical response," JP said. "But maybe you need to retake the LSAT, Dad."

Oh, *damn*.

I tried not to react, but there was no way I could stop my eyes from widening. Whether that was in shock or from the sudden entertainment of the implied drama, I didn't know, but given that I heard Bruno take in an excited breath from beside me and the woman on JP's arm made an expression that I assumed matched mine, I figured it was the latter.

Mr. Marchand's jaw tightened. "Pardon me?"

JP's effortless smile widened. "In the context of the conversation and with the preliminary knowledge that the speaker scored a 176 on the LSAT, one could logically and reasonably assume that the implication of the statement referred to knowing how to problem solve, not knowing any explicit or definitive facts."

"It's so hot when you talk like that," JP's date murmured.

I almost gagged. Beside me, Bruno's shoulders shook as he muffled a snort.

"And one would also assume an associate at my firm would understand the importance of unambiguous language," Mr. Marchand replied, his voice cold. "Especially one who wants to move up to managing partner one day."

"Allegedly," said JP.

Had he been anyone else, Mr. Marchand's face would have probably gone red, but he just gave JP a piercing look. For a moment, no one said anything.

"Well," Della finally said, her voice taking on a forced brightness as she tried to salvage the conversation. "All that will be moot since Nellie seems certain about getting this internship."

"I am," I said.

"What kind of internship is it?" she asked. "I don't believe I know what you're taking. Were you following Max's footsteps into finance?"

"No," I said. "I want to be a forensic scientist."

"That is... interesting," Mr. Marchand said. "Certainly a law career would be more lucrative, but if you think you can make a reasonable living off of it... You *can*, can't you?"

"Maybe," I said. "And if not, I can always find some rich sucker of a lawyer to marry."

Mr. Marchand raised his eyebrows, but JP burst out laughing. My dad, meanwhile, turned to me with a wordless sense of disappointment rolling off him in waves, but before he could admonish me for humiliating him in public, Kimberlee saved me.

"There you are, Nellie," she said as she floated up to us, clad in a cream dress that set off a goldish glow on her brown skin. She didn't seem quite oblivious to the tension, but ignored it as she turned to my dad. "Max, may I steal Nellie away for a moment? I have an acquaintance I think would be good for her to meet."

"Certainly," my dad said stiffly, and while I still wasn't a fan of Kimberlee, I could've hugged her just then.

"It was, uh, great to see you all," I said.

Della smiled and Mr. Marchand nodded before turning back to whatever conversation he'd been having with my dad before I was called over, but JP lingered for a moment longer.

"Glad I got to see you again, Nell," he said. "We'll have to catch up sometime."

"Oh my God," Bruno whispered as we were following Kimberlee after we'd walked away. "What *happened* with you two?"

"My dad is an asshole," I whispered back. "It's not that complicated."

He snorted. "Not him. Anne-Marie's brother."

My mouth went dry. "JP? Nothing. Why?"

Bruno gave me a *Look* of his own. "Come on. Don't bullshit me. Either something happened or that man just has it *bad* for you."

"He does not," I muttered. "Trust me."

"He does," Bruno insisted. "And so do you."

"I do not!" I hissed. "You don't even know me."

"Nellie, the tension between you two was so thick, it would have taken a freshly sharpened machete to cut it," he said. "Maybe you have a thing for him and maybe you don't, but he definitely has a thing for you. Trust me."

I rolled my eyes. "You're imagining things."

"Wanna bet?"

"No."

"Look back at him. I bet you *anything* you end up staring straight into his lovey-dovey baby blue eyes."

And of course I didn't believe him. Of course I wasn't going to check. Of *course* I told Bruno he was just imagining things and that JP was like that with everyone, like my friend Sydney, who he met for approximately thirty seconds before hitting on her.

But then I looked over my shoulder, because of course I did.

On the bright side, Bruno was wrong. I didn't look straight into JP's eyes when I looked back at him.

But that was only because he was busy staring at my ass.

Half a second later, he looked up and caught me catching him. And not an ounce of shame showed on his face as he grinned.

Chapter Ten
It Has Been 0 Days Since Nellie Got Kicked Out Of Class

"—AS YOU KNOW, ONE of the only disciplines that regularly requires strictly opinion-based evidence. So who can tell me the issues that may arise if—"

Me

> I'm not. I AM saying it's only been a month since you met Olivier and he doesn't even live in Ottawa, so excusing all these little things about him is sending a breeze through the field of red flags.

Syd

> He doesn't have that many red flags!

Me

> More than one red flag is a red flag.

Syd

> You're infuriating. And you, Miss Anti-Commitment, don't get to say it's "only" been a month. Especially when he's visited me.

Me

> I do when you still refuse to ask Olivier if Jesse and Christian finally got together. The waiting is killing me.

"—being cross-examined because their job is to make you seem uncredible, mistaken, or uneducated. If you aren't able to handle that level of scrutiny, it's beyond me why you're even here because forensic toxicology is—"

Syd

> If you wanna know so bad you can ask them your damn self.

"—speak with Veronica Jackson about the FAI internship. If you didn't apply, seriously question not only why you're in this program but how you got into university in the first place. They'll be sending out acceptance letters shortly, so you've missed the boat for this year, but make sure you apply for it next year. It is among the most prestigious opportunities—"

"—application deadline. Yes, Kevin?"

"I applied this year, but in case I'm not accepted, are you willing to be a reference for interested students?"

"I will only write reference letters for students in the top five percent of each year. So for you, no."

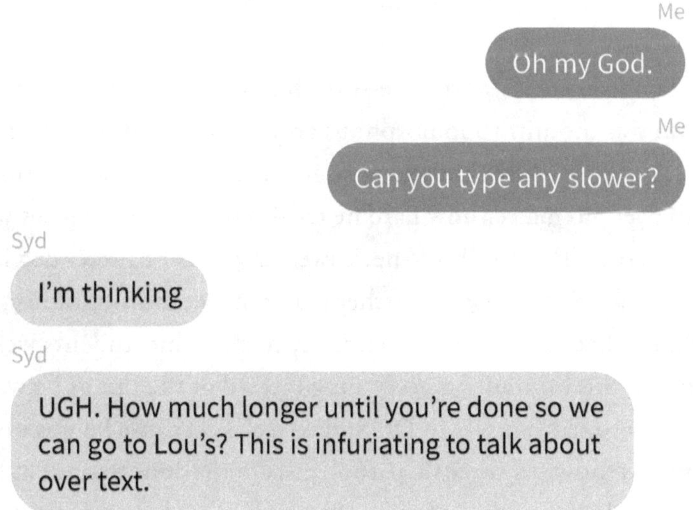

I pressed the volume button on the side of my phone before slipping it into the backpack at my feet and looking at the front of the room. Dr. Spitzki was pacing the lecture hall with his hands behind his back so his chest puffed out to show off his over-inflated sense of importance.

If Ben Cameron was the pre-silver-fox type of professor, Dr. Spitzki was the anthropomorphous grey blob type of professor. He had saggy, pale white skin and wiry grey hair that was far too thin to comb over, no matter how hard he tried. Wire-rimmed glasses were hanging from the V of his V-neck sweater vest as he pretended he wasn't squinting at anyone farther than ten feet in front of him.

He also had an infuriating tendency to think his students were paying for his opinion on everything instead of the things he was supposed to teach. I was in Dr. Spitzki's class because he was one of the most renowned forensic pathologists in the country, but at least once a week, he would drift away from whatever he was lecturing about and into a tangent about...

Well, anything, really.

In other words, Dr. Spitzki's class was worth the time when he made it worth it. The rest of the time, I had better things to do. Positioning my hands on the keyboard of my laptop, I tried to look like I'd been listening the whole time.

"—if you intend to stay in the Ottawa area," he was saying. "Each lab has different processes, procedures, and equipment, so while the FAI internship is useful regardless of your future plans, you should be extra vigilant with your application if—"

And then a horribly out-of-tune recorder rendition of the chorus from *My Heart Will Go On* blared from my feet.

"Ms. *Belanger*," Dr. Spitzki snapped without even looking at me.

"Sorry!" I called, diving to get my backpack.

The people on either side of me burst out laughing.

"Get it before the key change," someone two rows behind me called.

"I'm trying," I said, not trying at all. Still, I knew where my phone was this time, so I only subjected the others to a few more bars of torture before I tapped the decline button. The shrill squeal of the recorder cut off, leaving a scattering of snickers around the room.

"Sorry," I said again. "What were you saying, Dr. Spitzki?"

Silently, he took the wire-rimmed glasses from his sweater vest and slipped them on, since apparently he needed to be able to see me in order to give me a dirty look.

"Ms. Belanger," he said again.

I smiled brightly. "Yes, Dr. Spitzki?"

"You know what I'm going to say."

"Aw, come on," I pleaded. "I didn't mean to. I just—"

"—forgot, yet again, to turn your cellular device off before coming into my lecture hall," he said. "And since this is *how* many times this semester—"

"She's averaging about one call a week," someone called, holding up a crumpled piece of paper that had *It has been 8 days since we've heard Nellie's Titanic ringtone* written on it.

Dr. Spitzki did not look as amused by the handmade sign as I was. "Regardless. Ms. Belanger—"

"Come on," I said. "I don't want to miss the information about the FAI internship."

"You applied already," said someone sitting a few seats away from me. "I saw you at the final interview."

I gave them a dirty look. "That doesn't mean I don't want to hear Dr. Spitzki's acclaimed advice about it."

Dr. Spitzki ignored my blatant sucking up. "Ms. Belanger, leave."

"It's off now," I said.

"Ms. Belanger."

"It was a mistake."

"Ms. *Belanger*."

"I pay good money to be here."

A low murmur of chuckles and *ooo*s circled the room as Dr. Spitzki's dull white skin turned a healthy shade of puce.

"Get out," he said.

"But—"

"Get *out*."

Sighing as reluctantly as I could, I closed my laptop and slipped it into my backpack. Dr. Spitzki glared, his arms folded over his chest. As soon as the door closed behind me, I slung my backpack over my shoulder and half-jogged to the stairway. I got to the first floor just as Sydney put a textbook in her bag and stood up from where she'd been sitting at Starbucks.

"I'm not saying it wasn't a little weird for him to call me that, you're making a bigger deal about it than it is," Sydney said as I walked up to her, continuing our conversation as if there had been no break and also hadn't been over text.

"You've just never struck me as the kind of person who would be into a guy calling her Mommy mid-sex," I said.

She fell in stride beside me as we headed to the exit so we could go to Lou's, the pub across the street from campus. "I'm not saying I liked it, but I didn't *hate* it, either. And I don't think he meant to."

I raised my eyebrows. "It just slipped out?"

"Yeah. He was super embarrassed about it."

I pressed my lips together, trying to hide my laughter. Sydney, being Sydney, caught it anyway.

"Don't kink shame," she said, though a giggle slipped out as she said it.

"I'm *not*," I said. "But picturing it is…"

I snorted, then started laughing uncontrollably. Sydney sighed but joined in with my laughter. "I know. It's a lot."

"I mean, I'm not kink shaming, but I thought he would be more of a handcuffs and yes-miss-there-is-a-way-to-get-out-of-that-ticket roleplay type of kinky, not—"

"Okay, but why would he want to roleplay as his actual job?" she said as we exited the building into the crisp late-March air. "He's a cop. And he doesn't like cops who act like that. Which should be a *green* flag."

"I mean, it might tint the red flag brown," I said. "He's still a cop."

She sighed. "Not this again. I thought you'd be more concerned he's eight years older than me, not with his job."

I rolled my eyes. "You know the age thing doesn't bother me. I'm just saying—"

"*You're* in forensic science. *Forensic*, Nellie."

"I don't want to be a cop, though."

"You'd have to work with them."

"To solve murders and shit! That's different."

She shook her head. "I'm not getting into this."

I held up my hands in surrender. "I'm just looking out for you. But I'll drop it. If he wants to call you Mommy and you're cool with it, you have my full support."

"Thanks. I really do like him. Which is good because…"

She trailed off and I frowned. "Because what?"

But she didn't answer before we reached the entrance to Lou's. I opened the door and glanced around, spotting an empty booth near the middle of the restaurant, and waited until the server came over to take our order before asking again.

"What's going on, Syd?" I asked.

She bit her lip, staring down at the table for a second, then sighed. "Olivier drove back to Montreal yesterday afternoon and a while after that, Reid came home."

"Oh?"

"With that girl again. Alison. She's super nice." She fiddled with the napkin, not looking at me. "But after she left, Reid and I argued."

"What was he wrong about?"

"He wasn't wrong—"

"Syd, you know I'm automatically on your side. You could tell me you farted on his pillow and gave him pink eye and I'd still say you were in the right."

The morose expression on her face disappeared as she started cackling. "Well, I did ask him if he could start dating girls who don't sound like squeaky toys when he fucks them."

"You didn't."

She nodded. "He kept denying it until I pulled up a video from a dog toy company and played it to prove it sounded like her. Then he was just pissed."

There were tears in my eyes as I imagined the look on Reid's face. "I'm still on your side."

"Damn right you are. Especially since his response was to tell me that's what women sound like when they're with a guy who satisfies them and he's sorry I never experience it." She rolled her eyes. "I told him making women scream like they were being stabbed isn't the flex he thinks it is."

"In fairness, he kind of is 'stabbing' them," I said. "With his meat sword."

Sydney gaped at me. "You did *not* call it a meat sword."

"Well, yeah. I figured it made more sense than meat stick. You don't stab with a stick, you beat with it." I twisted my mouth to the side. "Maybe that's why they call it beating off."

"Oh my God." She buried her face in her hands, shoulders shaking with laughter as I cracked up.

"So what did Reid say after you insulted his sword-handling skills?" I asked once we'd calmed down.

The remaining laughter faded from Sydney's face, replaced with an expression that was between melancholy and frustration. "It's stupid."

"Not if it's bothering you."

"Yeah, but I kinda deserved it."

I leaned forward on the table. "Deserved what?"

That was when she admitted she and Reid had a fight. Like, an actual, full-blown, yelling-at-each-other argument about the people they were bringing back to their apartment, culminating with Reid asking why she could make demands about who he dated while expecting him not to say anything about the parade of guys she brought into the place.

"And when I told him that was an asshole thing to say, he said maybe I should stop sleeping around so much," she said. "Then when I gave him shit for slut shaming me, he goes, 'I'm not slut shaming you, but maybe you should try to figure out why you need a new guy every three days instead of finding one that will stick around.'"

"He didn't," I said.

She nodded.

"That *fucker*," I spat. "I will fucking—"

"He tried to apologize right away," she said, her voice soft. "Like, he realized immediately what he'd said."

"That doesn't make it okay!"

"I know." She shrugged. "I told him if he was so set on thinking I was a slut even though I've been seeing Olivier exclusively for a month now, I'd start looking for another place to live. And I went to my room and slammed the door."

"Syd, why didn't you tell me?!" I asked. "I live three floors above you! You could've come over or—"

"Because he tried to get me to come out and then gamed in the living room all night, so if I'd left my room he would've seen that I was crying," she blurted. "And the last thing I want is Reid to know he got to me. So I skipped my Syntax class this morning. That way he'd be at work before I got up. And since I have intramural dodgeball tonight, I brought all my stuff with me so I don't have to go back to his place after class."

"His place?" I asked.

She shrugged. "Trying to get used to it."

"You're actually moving out?"

Another shrug as she stared down at the table. "He's been texting me all day asking if we can talk tonight and if I was serious about moving. I don't think he wants me to. And like, I know I only have one more year of university left. But the way he…"

She trailed off again and I didn't know what to say. My body was torn between rage at Reid for what he'd said and sympathy for Syd, especially knowing about the feelings she had for him that she insisted she didn't have. So I did the only thing I could think of: when the server brought over our order—two craft beers, an order of mozza sticks, and a plate of chicken tenders—I waved Sydney's hand out of the way and handed the server my card.

"You know you don't have to buy my beer," she said after I'd paid.

"Technically my dad bought it," I said, putting the card back in my wallet.

"True." She took a sip of her beer, then plucked one of the mozza sticks out of the basket. "Speaking of your dad, how was your weekend? Any more, um... notes?"

I bit my chicken tender far too aggressively at the reminder of the fucking *notes*. It had been three years since I'd torn up his last Post-It and left the pieces scattered in the snow, and yet, JP fucking Marchand still thought he was so goddamn clever.

"What's that?" Syd had asked the Sunday morning after *La Nuit Rose* as I started my car so we could drive back to Ottawa.

"What's what?"

She pointed at the windshield. Underneath the wiper blade was a small yellow square.

"That *bastard*," I breathed, shoving the door open. Sydney jumped as I got out and snatched the note out from under the wiper blade.

Just like the past two notes, it had his phone number, followed by a note:

For "tutoring" purposes
xoxo

Seriously. Text me.

So of course I had to tell Sydney about the notes JP left on my car three years earlier. She'd laughed as I told her about the one I'd eaten so Anne-Marie wouldn't read it, but didn't understand why I didn't call him after he'd left another note.

"He wants something I don't want to give him," I'd said.

"How do you even know that if you haven't talked to him, though?" she'd asked.

I gestured at the wrinkled Post-It, which I'd balled up and tried to chuck in the back seat wheel well that served as my car's trash can, but Sydney had fished it out and uncrumpled it. "Why else would he be pestering me like this? And offering to 'tutor' me? Like, come on. I get enough of this from his sister. I don't need *him* to think we should date, too."

"Anne-Marie said he's not into dating, though," Sydney said. "Didn't she say he's a manwhore?"

"She called him a womanizer, I think."

She'd shrugged. "Fair. But why can't you call and tell him you're not interested? If he's trying the same thing after three years…"

I grabbed the Post-It off the console where Syd had put it, crumpled it up again, and rolled my window down. Before she could even protest, I chucked the note out, then rolled the window up. "It's not a risk I'm willing to take. And I don't owe him shit."

She'd agreed with me about that, thankfully.

"He didn't leave me another note," I said to Sydney after swallowing my aggressive bite of chicken tender. "I don't want anything to do with him."

She nodded in understanding. "What about the rest of your weekend?"

"Let's see," I said, helping myself to a mozza stick. "My dad hinted that I probably didn't get the internship at least six times a day because I haven't heard back, even though I reminded him at least six times that they might not get sent out until the end of the month or even into April. He also had his assistant look up various LSAT prep courses I could take if Mr. Marchand continued to refuse to suggest me for the one his friend runs. Oh, and he tried to gaslight me into thinking I'd said I would consider going to the First Responders Gala with Clinton

Thibault in April even though I definitely didn't because it's happening the first week of finals and I'd never agree to go with Clinton fucking Thibault."

"Who's Clinton Thibault?" she asked.

"The worst person you can imagine."

Sydney raised her eyebrows. "Worse than Adrian?"

I bristled at the thought of my high school ex-boyfriend. Sydney might not have known me in high school, but I'd told her about him. Adrian had been devastated when I broke up with him, mainly because I did it after finding out the kind of horrendous asshole he could be. And not just a horrendous asshole, but a *stupid* horrendous asshole, which was even worse. I mean, it took a special breed of pure idiocy to say shit about your girlfriend while borrowing her laptop and forgetting to log out of your account.

And then leaving that page open so the next time your girlfriend used her computer, your chat about how she's such a prude and you should just trick her into having sex with you—especially when you're the one who wanted to fucking wait because she's been ready forever—is staring her in the face.

Because that was almost the worst part of it all. If he hadn't been so stupid, I never would have found out. I trusted him completely; I had no reason not to. So even if I'd noticed he'd left his account logged in, I wouldn't have snooped around.

I would've just logged out.

Instead, I got my introduction to what could happen if you told a guy you didn't want to be with him. By the time Adrian was done spreading rumours about me, I literally had teachers calling me "Loose Nell" and implying the entire school had to attend a sexual health seminar because I was such a slut.

So yeah. Adrian was terrible, but Clinton...

"Adrian joked about 'accidentally' making me have sex with him," I said to Sydney. "With Clinton, it's not a joke."

Sydney's mouth dropped. "Wait, what?"

I shrugged. "I mean, they're all rumours, technically. But like, the kind of rumours that stay rumours because someone here or there gets a mysterious payout. Because his family is rich. Like, disgustingly rich. Richer than my dad, for sure. He's had years of tutors and private schools and attempts at teaching him basic human decency, yet somehow he never learned to understand the word 'no.'"

"Oh my God," she said, shocked. "And your dad—"

"Wants me to go with him. Doesn't see the problem with it. Says he's a 'fine young man who was playing the field like young men do and had the misfortune of a jealous woman attempting to ruin his reputation.'" I smiled bitterly. "You know, it happens to everyone, right? Even though you look at someone like JP Marchand who everyone says sleeps around, but no one says stuff like that about *him*."

"Wow," she said.

"Yeah." I took a bite of the mozza stick and chewed. "Oh, and also, my dad made me go shopping with Kimberlee so we could have some 'girl time,' thinking I wouldn't figure out it was literally just a way for him to make me buy new, Max-Belanger-Approved dresses for the next two events. And told me to buy a few extras because even though he 'certainly hopes I will be accepted for my little internship,' he's made plans for which galas he wants me to attend if I don't."

She shook her head. "Jesus."

"Do you see why I hate going there now, though?" I set my mozza stick down. "I asked him to pay my tuition. He offered living expenses, my apartment, all of it, and all he asked was for me to visit him more. Which seems reasonable, right? You'd think, like, oh, that's my dad being a dad. He's helping me out and he wants to see me."

"Well, yeah," she said.

"And then when he wanted you to go to some of these social events and galas and things, that would be fair, right? Like, it's not unreasonable to ask someone to show support and yeah, you think he maybe wants to brag about you a bit because that's what dads do, right?"

"Yeah, but—"

"—but then you realize the person he *wants* to brag about isn't you. He wants to brag about the puppet he wants you to be. He wants you to act like someone you aren't. He wants you to change your career, the fucking thing you've wanted to do for *years*, to something that sounds more impressive and makes him look better." I folded my arms, mirroring Sydney's position. "He acts like he wants what's best for me, but what he wants is what makes him look best. He presents himself as this successful businessman and good Catholic guy and perfect father. But he doesn't care if I think he's a good father. He just wants to look like one to everyone else."

She nodded. "I'm sorry, Nell."

Something about hearing that hurt.

"It doesn't matter." I grabbed my beer but didn't take a sip. "I told my dad I'm not going to the First Responders gala, that Bruno said he'd be my date for the other two galas I committed to, and if he could stop acting like I won't get my internship, I'd appreciate it. I'm going to hear back about it any day now."

"Cheers to that," Sydney said, and we clinked our glasses together.

Chapter Eleven
Dear Ms. Belanger

"Make it make sense, Syd."

"I—"

"Make it make *sense*." I brought both hands to my head, pushing my hair back from my forehead aggressively. "On what fucking *planet*—"

"I know." She shook her head, her forehead creased but eyes wide, something between a frown and a look of bewildered pity as she stared at my phone screen. "I don't know what... like, none of the interviewers—"

"Exactly!" I plucked my phone from her hands and looked at the email again. "What of this is bad? 'Intelligent and driven.' 'Would do well.' '*Ideal fit for this role.*'"

"I don't understand it either. It's like they—"

"Kevin Huang got accepted, Sydney." My voice shook. "Kevin *fucking* Huang, who had to retake Forensic Microscopy and Spectroscopy *twice* and still only passed with a C! I got a goddamn A- in that class and I wrote the final on three hours of sleep."

"Nellie—"

I burst into tears, tucking my head down and hunching forward as all the dams broke at once. A second later, Sydney had her arms around

116

me as I sobbed hot, angry tears, my phone clutched in my hand, my fist tightening as though if I crushed it, the email would go away.

Not that it would matter if the email disappeared. The words were already burned into my brain.

Dear Ms. Belanger,

Thank you for your interest in the FAI Internship Program. Every year, we receive many applications from qualified students interested in this prestigious opportunity.

We are unable to offer you a spot in the program this year.

Don't let this discourage you from reapplying. Our interview panelists have provided the following anonymous feedback for you to take into consideration before next year's application deadline:

Interviewer A: Intelligent and driven. Excellent interpersonal skills.
Interviewer B: Delightful candidate. Resume could use work, but overall would do well in this role.
Interviewer C: References were strong and candidate seems like an ideal fit for this role. There is a lack of previous work experience, however, the outstanding academic achievements speak for themselves.

We hope this will help prepare you for your next application.

Best,

Sheridan Humprey
FAI Internship Program Director

"It's going to be okay," Sydney said. "It's just an internship. There's—"

"I told him I'd take the LSAT," I choked. "I told my dad I'd take the LSAT if I didn't get the internship and I'd go to his events and—*fuck*!" I struggled out of her hug, shoving my hands across my face again. "JP said he'd *tutor* me. I can't—Syd, I *can't*."

"Maybe his dad'll change his mind and suggest you for that course," she said.

I made a noise that was probably some kind of laugh, but it came out high-pitched and accompanied by a snot bubble. I covered my face and turned, one of the billions of tracks in my mind hoping Sydney hadn't seen it, and crossed my kitchen to grab a paper towel off the roll. After taking a sharp, deep breath, I blew my nose, then folded the paper towel and made the redness on my face worse by wiping my cheeks with the rough material before throwing it out. I took another breath, leaning against the counter to force myself to calm down.

"Or maybe it's a mistake," Sydney said after a short pause. "Like... like maybe they accepted you, but filled out the wrong email template or something."

I opened my mouth to respond, but nothing came out, so I shut it again.

"Let me see." Sydney's voice had all the tenderness of someone approaching an injured animal. But not like a big animal. Or a scary animal. Like a ferret or a squirrel or something, where you know the animal is far more likely to bolt away and hurt themselves than they are to attack you. She took my phone carefully from my hand. "Let's re-read this and see if there's anything…"

She trailed off. I thought it was because she was reading, but then she frowned.

"Wait a second," she said, staring at the screen. "Are you sure this is real?"

"How would it not be *real*?"

"Well, isn't… isn't Sheridan Humprey that guy?"

It was my turn to look at her with a bewildered frown. "What?"

"The one you were hooking up with. Or… was his name Simon?"

I stared a second longer. Then a second more. Then a slow, sinking sense of realization grounded me in the worst way.

"Scott," I said.

"Sure," she said. "Isn't it possible he's trying to get payback by sending you a fake letter that—"

"Everyone else got emails today, too," I said. "Kevin Huang posted a screenshot on the class board. But—"

My voice caught as I thought back to that phone call with Scott. He'd known about the internship. I couldn't remember telling him about it, but if he…

"Gimme," I said, holding my hand out for my phone.

Sydney passed it to me cautiously. I tapped on the screen, hesitated for a moment, then texted instead of calling.

After all, you can't screenshot a phone call.

Me

What's your dad's name?

The little checkmarks showed he read it almost immediately after it sent. I stared at the screen, waiting for the little bubbles to appear to show he was typing. When they didn't, I gritted my teeth together.

Me

> I can see you're reading this, Scott.

If it were me, I would've read that from the lock screen, but since I was banking on Scott being less than clever, I was relieved when the checkmarks lit up again.

That time, the bubbles appeared.

Snot

> Oh, so NOW you know my name and how to text me.

Me

> Was this you or wasn't it?

Snot

> I don't know what you could possibly be talking about. Are you trying to add a new name to your slut spreadsheet or something?

Me

> Is your dad Sheridan Humprey, the director of the FAI internship program that you knew I was applying for?

"No way," Sydney breathed, reading over my shoulder. "You don't think...?"

"What else could it be?"

We waited. A few moments later, another response came through.

Snot

> My dad's name is Stephen

Snot

> Wait. No. It's Sylvester.

Snot

> Kidding. My dad's name is Stan.

Me

> Are you sure?

Snot

> Yeah. And he's an accountant. So maybe he'd appreciate your spreadsheet skills.

"Shit," Sydney said.

I twisted my mouth to the side. "Yeah. Or maybe not. I don't know if it's a good or bad thing that—"

And then my phone buzzed again.

Snot

> Funnily enough, though, he's got a twin brother. But what's his name again… Sheldon? Schmitt? Shnorris? Hmm.

I looked at Syd.

She looked back at me.

"It can't be," I said.

She shrugged almost helplessly.

Me

> Does it happen to be Sheridan?

Snot

> It might be. Or it could be Shteven.

"It's his uncle," I said. "Isn't it?"

Sydney nodded reluctantly. "It seems like it, yeah."

Me

> Let me make sure I'm getting this right. I said I didn't want to fuck you anymore because despite telling you multiple times that I didn't want something serious, you thought I'd change my mind or something, so you went running to your uncle and attempted to ruin my future career.

Me

> All because someone didn't want to have sex with you anymore.

Me

> Am I getting that right, Scott? You asked your uncle to reject my internship application to punish me for not wanting to be your girlfriend?

"Do you think he's going to answer?" she asked after we'd waited for a few minutes with no response from Scott, even though the checkmarks had appeared beneath each of my messages.

I half-shrugged. "I mean, maybe. He was stupid enough to answer in the first place. And since it's my only hope to actually fix this..."

"What do you mean, your only hope?"

I looked at her incredulously. "What do *you* mean?"

"There has to be a way to deal with this," she said. "Like, the FAI program must be overseen by something else. You can submit a complaint or—"

"And then what?" I asked. "If I don't have proof, no one's going to believe me and all that'll happen is that I'll get blacklisted from working with them. And since they're one of the biggest employers for forensic scientists in Ottawa..."

"There has to be a way," she said.

"This is the way. Hoping he's narcissistic enough that he won't be able to help owning up to his brilliant plan or something."

She looked skeptical. "I don't know if he's even going to respond, Nell."

I twisted my mouth to the side, staring at my phone before typing another message.

Me

> I guess I'm wrong. Sorry to bother you. I should've known you wouldn't be smart enough think of trying something like that.

"Wait, don't—" Sydney protested as she read over my shoulder, then sighed as I hit send.

"Don't what?"

"Don't say that to him," she said. "It's just going to piss him off and—"

"And hopefully get him to admit he did it."

"Yeah, but—"

My phone vibrated with Scott's response. Sydney and I looked down at the same time.

Snot

Kindly get fucked, Nellie. Have a great summer.

Half a second later, a system message popped up beneath that:

You are no longer able to message Snot.

"He blocked me," I said.

Sydney's eyebrows knitted together as worry turned her lips downward. "What are you gonna do, Nell?"

And God, I wish I knew the answer to that.

Chapter Twelve
Table for One

"You're late," Nigel barked as I burst into the kitchen, juggling my purse with one arm as I tried to tie my black half-apron with the other while.

"Sorry," I said. "I lost track of—"

"Not my fucking problem," Nigel said. "You'd think since you booked off two weekends in a row and left us short staffed, you'd try to be on time for the few shifts you have this week. But I guess princesses think they deserve weekends off even if they've only been working here for a month, despite it feeling like the longest month of my fucking life."

"I told you about this before I even got hired," I said. "I have to go to Montreal for—"

"Nellie, I mean this from the bottom of my heart: I literally, figuratively, metaphorically, rectally *do not fucking care*." He shoved a stack of menus at me. "Drop these off at table three. You're in section five. Table fifteen just got seated. The asparagus appetizer is eighty-sixed and I'm taking it out of your tips if the line has to refire anything because they're too busy flirting with you again."

"How is it my fault if they're the ones flirting with me?" I asked.

"And tie your goddamn hair back. This is a kitchen, not a strip club," he said, ignoring my question as he stormed away.

If it wasn't for the fact that I was a twenty-one-year-old student with no work experience, I would've told Nigel exactly where he could shove those menus.

Not up his ass. That was unhygienic and would probably be too enjoyable for him. But maybe up his dickhole or something.

I had no idea why Nigel hated me so much. Had he been present when I was interviewed, I wouldn't have gotten the job. But Lawrence, the good-looking guy with dark hair and a smooth laugh who had hired me, hadn't been the manager of the restaurant like I'd thought he was. No, he was the regional manager who had taken over doing interviews because Nigel was so repellent as a human being, they were having problems keeping staff for longer than two shifts. He had a rat-like physique and dark circles beneath his eyes, but his skin was so thin I was pretty sure those circles were actually caused by nicotine stains on his skeleton, and a few scraggly hairs on his chin where a beard was supposed to go.

On my first day, I walked in and cheerfully introduced myself. He stared at me, his face blank before it slowly morphed into an expression of disdain and disgust.

"Thanks, Lawrence," he'd groaned. "Just what I need. Another peppy blonde who won't know the difference between sirloin and filet mignon."

"Is that a type of fish?" I'd asked.

I thought it was funny. So did the line cook, who was standing nearby and snorted back a laugh. But Nigel must have lost his sense of humour in a tragic sneezing accident when he first shoved his head up his ass because he'd glared at me, then spent the rest of the night giving me the worst tables and the lowest tippers with close to no training whatsoever.

If the restaurant wasn't the only place I'd found that would hire me, I probably would've left at the end of my shift and never went back. I'd even gone home that night and considered whether it would be worth sucking it up and telling my dad that I didn't get the FAI internship.

Then I pictured having to attend a bunch of galas and luncheons and high society bullshit while going to LSAT tutoring sessions with JP Marchand and put my uniform in the washing machine so it was fresh and clean for the next day.

Because that was what I'd decided to do about the whole situation.

I'd decided to lie.

It was the only option. Spending the summer studying for a test I didn't want to take would have been hell, but it wasn't just that I didn't *want* to take it.

It was that I'd fail.

Not that I *thought* I would fail. Not that I was *afraid* to fail.

Facts were facts, and the fact was that I would fail that fucking test.

Between my mom and twelve years of teachers, I'd heard the whole "You'd be so smart if you just *applied* yourself" thing about a billion times. And I could see why. A graph of my grades in high school would've looked like an ECG, the peaks and valleys intense but expected. English was always low because, according to my mom, I'd always hated reading. And social studies was just as bad because, according to my teachers, I didn't grasp the importance of history and politics unless there was some kind of drama or conspiracy theory surrounding things.

The thing was, I did apply myself. I tried to, at least. I didn't like letting anyone down, especially not my mom. But I just sucked at that kind of stuff. It wasn't that I hated reading. I just wasn't good at it. When it came to books I liked, I could get through them, but Shakespeare? *To Kill A Mockingbird*? All the poems by that one guy that I couldn't remember except the one where the women talk about Michelangelo and an old man rolls up his trousers or whatever? It was almost painful.

But give me a biology experiment or page after page of chemical equations, and my heart would race with excitement.

That was an exaggeration, but not by much. Science was something I could *do*. There was no room for opinion; facts were facts and finding the answers was like putting together a puzzle. There were no intentions to interpret. No hidden meanings. Just a problem and a solution.

For a long time, I didn't know what I was going to do when I "grew up." But a couple of years after my mom and I moved to Toronto, my class had done a career day thing where a bunch of parents came in and talked about their jobs.

It was pretty boring, honestly. Most of the parents had normal jobs. There was a truck driver. An accountant. A hair stylist. A computer programmer. A banker. Stuff that wasn't for me.

And then there was the crime scene investigator.

I couldn't remember whose dad it was, but I don't think I blinked or moved the entire time he was talking, which was significant enough that my teacher had commented on it. I'd been completely enraptured and immediately went home to Google everything I could about crime scene investigation, which led me to forensic science. By the time I went to school the next day, I *knew* I wanted to be a forensic scientist when I grew up.

Forensic science was everything I needed. All sorts of interesting little pieces came together to solve the most complex puzzles anyone could think of. Puzzles that actively worked against you, that tried to trick you, that people took pieces from and hid.

Puzzles that *meant* something.

Even before that, I'd known I was damn good at science of almost any kind. Biology, chemistry, even psychology—all of them were *explanations*. There was reason behind everything. I could be *right*, unequivocally, because there was a set answer.

With the LSAT, there was no set answer.

Everything was open to interpretation when it came to being a fucking lawyer. It was all opinion. Yeah, there was logic involved, but it was a kind of logic I couldn't follow, no matter how much my dad wanted me to or how impressive an LSAT prep course was.

There was no chance I'd do well on LSAT, even if I'd wanted to.

So I hadn't told my dad. I pretended I'd gotten the internship and he'd hmmph'ed before reluctantly congratulating me. After hanging up the phone, I sighed in relief and immediately pulled out my laptop to start job hunting.

Because the only useful feedback in the FAI rejection letter was that I had a lack of work experience. If I fixed that, maybe Scott's goddamn Uncle Sheridan wouldn't be able to justify rejecting my application next year.

Maybe.

It was a long shot, but what else could I fucking *do*?

So I tried to find a job. But given that I had no experience, this stupid restaurant with its asshole manager was the only place that even called me back after a couple of weeks of looking.

So I sighed, swallowing back the response I wanted to snap at Nigel as he told me to put my hair back because apparently only strippers wore their hair down. After tying my apron on, I took a deep breath and went out to the front-of-house, grabbing a stack of menus for table three.

"Hi!" I said cheerfully as I approached a table consisting of two parents and four children far under the age that should be allowed in a neighbourhood pub. "Thanks for waiting. These are for you and your server—"

"Excuse me," said an irritated voice from behind me. Before I could respond, one of the other servers nudged me out of the way with her hip, taking the rest of the menus from my hands.

"Hi," she continued, giving me a dirty look before turning to the family. "I'm Jessica and *I* will be your server tonight. Nellie must have gotten sections two and five confused again. You know, since they're so similar."

I blinked at her, then turned back to the table.

"—and your server tonight will be Jessica, who will be with you in a moment," I finished, my voice flat. "Enjoy your meal."

Jessica scoffed, but I ignored her as I turned and headed towards my section.

Section five was the smallest section and consisted solely of two-top tables. One side of the section was directly next to the bathrooms. The other side was along the entrance to the kitchen and had sweeping panoramic views of the deep fryers to go with the melodic nature sounds of cooks screaming at each other.

In short, Nigel had given me section five because it was the worst section in the restaurant, most likely to be cut first, and had the least potential for decent tips. He'd probably been extra-thrilled to give me the section when he realized that one table was sat with the somewhat rare one-top—a solo diner.

The joke was on him, though. Sure, one-tops generally left lower tips because their bills were smaller, but the customers were among the easiest to deal with. The person usually had a book or a tablet, was exceptionally polite, and didn't need much in the way of attention.

And that night, the universe decided that it had thrown enough shit my way lately and cut me a break by giving me the best one-top in existence.

"Hey, Professor," I said as I approached and set a menu on the table. "I'll be your server tonight."

Ben Cameron jolted, a startled expression on his face as he lifted his bright hazel eyes away from the book he'd been reading and set them on me. He blinked, lips parting, then half-laughed.

"Nellie!" he said. "What a surprise. I didn't know you worked here."

"Sure do." I pulled out my notepad. "Just for the summer."

"Build up the savings," he said, nodding knowingly.

"Something like that, yeah."

He nodded again, but after a moment, a wrinkle appeared between his eyebrows. "Though, didn't you... Didn't you say you applied for the FAI internship? When I saw you in—" He coughed as if suddenly remembering that cold winter night when I'd run into him while on my way to have a threesome.

And that I'd given him the option to forget it happened, which he clearly hadn't.

"In Montreal," I finished. "Yeah, I did."

"Good," he said quickly. "The FAI internship is one of the best in the country. Well, aside from the one at CCFS Labs in Toronto, but I don't believe they take anyone without a bachelor's degree. Most of their interns are already in grad school. But you'll have an edge at getting that one if you're already doing the FAI internship."

I laughed uncomfortably, looking down at the table. "They, um... didn't accept me. For FAI."

A beat of awkward silence passed, long enough that the heat rising up my neck almost certainly stained my cheeks before Ben spoke again.

"I see," he finally said. "That's... unfortunate."

"You're telling me."

The wrinkle between his eyebrows deepened. "It's very surprising, to say the least. What was the reason they gave you?"

And fuck if I knew how to respond to that.

I mean, obviously, I didn't want to badmouth the director of the FAI internship program to someone like Ben, who had actual connections in the community. The last thing I needed was to make Sheridan Humprey even *more* of an enemy.

But admitting the real reason would require me to admit I'd fucked the wrong guy and it had backfired on me.

And I just...

I didn't want to get into that with him.

I didn't want him to judge me.

I didn't want to justify my choice to sleep around.

"I didn't have a strong enough resume," I said, which was sort of true. "Which is why I decided to work here for the summer."

Ben frowned. "Really? Previous work experience has *never* been a requirement for that internship."

Fuck. "Maybe it changed this year?"

"Maybe. But it would be odd."

I dug my fingernail into the side of my thumb, fidgeting nervously. "Well, that was the main thing they said."

"The main thing? What were the other reasons?"

Fuck.

I picked at my thumbnail, not looking at him, heart racing as I tried to think of anything to say. But my mind had gone blank, like I'd never in my life heard any other reason to deny someone a job.

"Well," I said haltingly. "I, um... I also didn't play the Who-You-Know game."

He lifted an eyebrow. "The Who-You-Know game?"

"You know." I shrugged. "'It's not what you know, it's who you know'?"

Ben raised an eyebrow. "I have a hard time believing you didn't have excellent references."

Agh. He wasn't going to let this go.

"I did," I said. "I think someone might have had personal connections that I didn't have and that, um, affected the outcome."

He stared at me for a moment, then shook his head. "Unacceptable."

Oh, thank God he didn't have another question. "It happens."

"It happens to be a massive mistake, you mean." He picked up his menu. "If FAI stops taking the top-of-the-top because of 'personal connections,' it won't be one of the best internships in the country for much longer."

"And then I guess it won't matter so much if I didn't get it," I said, forcing a smile. "How's your summer been so far?"

"Uneventful," he said. "Usually I teach at least one or two summer semester classes, but I'm on sabbatical."

I nodded. "I know. Otherwise I would have taken one of your classes as a summer class instead of overloading my schedule last semester."

He looked up from his menu, eyes almost round. "You overloaded your schedule to take my class?"

"Well, yeah. You're on sabbatical next year."

"Yes, but I'll have a replacement," he said, amusement in his voice. "And unless I'm seriously misremembering, Nellie, you're not even minoring in forensic psychology."

"Nope," I said. "I'm doing forensic biology and anthropology."

"So why on Earth would you overload your semester to take my 400-level psychology class?" he asked.

"Because you're a good teacher," I said.

If I didn't know any better—and I didn't—I'd have said his cheeks flushed pink. "Ah. Well... even still. That must have been a very difficult semester."

"I did it last year, too. My adviser said as long as it was only six classes, I didn't need special permission. My thinking was that between that and a couple of spring and summer classes last year, I could still get a double major and also take this summer off to do the internship. But... well." I shrugged. "Now I just get a summer off. But at least I'm still graduating in four years."

"You could..." His mouth hung open as he trailed off, then he shook his head. "They were crazy not to accept you into that internship."

"I'm flattered," I said, then glanced down at my notepad. "Um, can I get you a drink?"

"Well, normally I don't fraternize with my students," he said, then looked up at me with a careful humour. "Or is this bribery to play the Who-You-Know game for you?"

"Do you think I'm stupid?"

He let out a loud laugh. "I just indicated the opposite."

"Then you know I'm both smart enough to know that a drink wouldn't be nearly enough to bribe you into a favour and dedicated enough to figure out what that thing is."

"And what do you think that thing is, Nellie?" he asked.

And oh, I had an answer to that.

I had a *good* fucking answer.

Well, maybe not good.

But funny. And inappropriate. And maybe kinda sexy. And maybe kind of obvious given the way I pressed my lips together and raised my eyebrows.

The problem was that Ben hadn't meant to imply what he'd implied. There hadn't been a puckish scraping of his teeth over his lip or a flick of his eyes up and down my body before he lowered his voice into a flirty growl.

He had just made the statement, then went wide-eyed as he realized how it sounded.

"Not that I'd—" He stopped and coughed, his face turning a flustered shade of pink. "That may have come out with some, ah... unintended undertones."

"Don't worry," I said, trying not to laugh. "I didn't hear any undertones, intended or otherwise."

He gave me a look. "Do you expect me to believe that?"

"I expect you to pretend to so you can save face."

Despite his embarrassment, he chuckled. "Well, that would mean I couldn't apologize to you And I do want to apologize."

"It's okay."

"It was… I had no intention to—it slipped out."

"Seriously," I said. "It's fine."

"I would never do something like that or—"

"Jeez, Professor Cameron," I said. "You don't have to keep insisting. I didn't think I was that undesirable."

His eyes went wide again. "No, of course not! You *are*."

I pressed my lips together. "You think so?"

"I just—wait. Uh…"

It shouldn't have been so fun. It really, really shouldn't have. I'd never seen Ben get flustered like this, but the confusion on his face was…

I mean, it was kind of endearing.

But there was also panic there, enough of it that I felt a little bad.

"I'm just messing with you," I said. "A bit of payback."

"Right," he said, his voice hoarse. "Of course."

"Unless you're into it."

His eyes widened again. "Nellie—"

"Kidding." I wasn't really, but I tapped my pen to my order-taking notepad anyway. "Now, about that drink?"

He chuckled, the sound both awkward and relieved. "I'll take whatever lager you've got on tap. And a glass of water, please."

"You got it," I said. "And don't worry. I'll put it on your bill."

There was a risk that I might have taken my teasing a little too far, but I heard him chuckle again as I walked away, and when I cleared his dishes and bill away at the end of the night, he'd left me a hefty tip.

Chapter Thirteen
Too Late

"I just miss you, Daughter of Mine."

I knew my mom wasn't trying to guilt-trip me, but she did all the same. Swallowing back that feeling, I stared up at the grey sky as light rain finally fell in a mist on my windshield.

"I know, Mother of Mine," I said. "I miss you too."

She sniffled. "And you're working so hard."

More guilt. I mean, it was true—I was working my ass off at the restaurant—but it was the first time I'd *actually* spent the summer working.

Which was also why she missed me. Because unlike previous summers where I could just "request a few days off" from the restaurant job I'd told my mom I'd had since my first year of university so I could go to Toronto and visit her, this year, I had to *actually* request time off.

And given that if I was dying of dehydration, Nigel would attempt to give himself water poisoning over handing me a drink, the chances of him approving any of my requests were slim. I'd already had to plead for this weekend and the one in a few weeks for the events I told my dad I'd go to, and I'd asked for those off before even signing my hiring paperwork.

Nigel also had a tendency of doing whatever it took to not give me two days off in a row, so it wasn't even like I could tell my mom I'd visit on a random Tuesday or something.

Not that she was asking for a random Tuesday. She'd called just before I pulled into the driveway to ask about a movie festival in June.

"It's all 80s movies," she'd said. "The whole weekend. And you *know* I'm gonna check it out, but it would be a lot more fun with my movie buddy."

I smiled, even though it almost hurt to do so. "That sounds awesome."

"Right? It would be like the old days," she said. "Well, sort of. I doubt they'd let us make a blanket fort in the theater. And I'd probably get in trouble for spiking my root beer with rum like I used to when you were a kid, but—"

"You would spike your root beer?" I said, laughing. "During our movie nights?"

"Oh yeah," she said. "Always. But you and me and a bucket of popcorn, all the classics... I'm sixty-seven percent sure the lineup included *Dirty Dancing* and *Heathers*. And I wanna say *Splash* was on there, too."

"Would we need to dress up all 80s-like?" I asked.

"Daughter of Mine, I'd disown you if you showed up for an 80s movie festival without at least a pair of leg warmers."

I'd laughed at that, too, but then she'd told me the dates and asked if I could stay an extra day or two to visit. And I'd grimaced, awkwardly telling her I didn't know if I'd be able to book the time off.

Which is when she'd started crying and talking about how much she missed me, since I hadn't been to Toronto to visit her since Easter.

"I wish I could make it work," I said to my mom. "The movie festival sounds amazing and you know I miss you too. But the restaurant is just so short-staffed this summer. My boss is... you know. Relying on me."

"I know, sweetie. But your old ma gets lonely."

"You're not old."

"I'm not getting any younger."

"Technically, neither am I."

Her laugh was a warm and crackling sound that conjured up the image of her sitting at the kitchen table in our townhouse in Toronto, throwing her head back and slapping the table. "That's true, I guess. And that makes me want to argue that you should visit me more since we're both getting old. Though"—she let out another laugh—"I guess I shouldn't be one to talk. I think after I turned eighteen, I saw your granny maybe six times before I met the devil."

I sandwiched my thumbnail between my teeth. In front of me, the house of the devil she was talking about loomed, imposing and lonely and cold as the rain picked up.

My mom and I talked for a few more minutes as I sat in the driveway, but I couldn't stall forever. Once we hung up, I took a deep breath, looking out the rain-spattered windshield at the house I'd be spending the weekend at, save for the few hours I'd be at the social event Bruno would be escorting me to that night.

My mom had a list of names for my dad. "The devil" was a popular one when she was feeling dramatic, which was often. But she was also impartial to "that asshole," "your sperm donor," "Maximum Bellender,"—which was the closest she usually got to his actual name, Maximilian Belanger—and "Scrooge McFuckFace." Once in a while, she'd refer to him as my father, though I'm pretty sure she hated calling him that because it was a reminder that she was the one who'd made him a father.

Even with that list of names she had, talking about him in any capacity was a rare occurrence. One might think that we'd talk about him more regularly on account of the whole thing where he was paying for my tuition and all my living expenses.

But that would have required me... you know.

Telling her about it.

Which I hadn't, because apparently lying to my parents was how I handled things.

After three years, my mom still didn't know I'd barely worked a day in my life. She never asked why I seemed to have no issue booking time off work to do the things I wanted to do. She didn't know I'd gone behind her back to maintain a relationship with my dad after I turned eighteen and was no longer obligated by a court order to spend time with him.

I don't know why they'd ever even gotten married. I'd spent a good chunk of my life being described by people as "too much," but those people had obviously never met my mom, because she was *too* much sometimes. The chaos I'd inherited from her had been diluted by my dad, who was…

Well.

My mom's names for him weren't exactly inaccurate.

You would think that one or the other would've realized what a terrible idea it was for them to get married after my dad mistakenly knocked my mom up, but neither did. At least, not right away. Eleven years later, it became a different story.

I don't know if there was anything more to that story than what I'd been told.

I don't know if my dad said or did something that was the last straw.

I don't know if my mom did anything, either. For better or for worse, neither of them would tell me what the final crack in their relationship was that shattered it beyond repair. Which meant it had come as a surprise to me.

But the thing was, not telling me?

That was stupid.

Because it meant I didn't know why my mom took me away from this life. I'd spent nearly every holiday and school break with my dad for the second half of my childhood, not understanding why she'd walked away from all this. From a family I'd never realized was broken from the start. From the pool and the bedroom for a teenager that had an ensuite and a steam shower. From the man who doted on me by giving me anything I could have ever wanted, so long as it had a price tag.

So when I needed money from university and she'd demanded I not ask my dad for help, I hid it from her. I agreed to my dad's terms, which had seemed reasonable.

It wasn't until after my dad started expecting a perfect obedient trophy of a daughter that I realized what my tuition and rent and unlimited credit card were actually costing me. That he was the kind of person who took over things bit by bit, so slowly that you almost couldn't see he was doing it. That he had a vision in mind for who I should be and how I should act and what I should wear.

That he didn't mind using any resource he had available to create the kid he wanted instead of the one he had.

It wasn't until after I'd already taken things from him and built a life that relied on his support that I realized why she left.

But by then, it was too late.

Chapter Fourteen
Call Me

THE GALA THAT WEEKEND was on the Friday night, which meant I could have technically driven back to Ottawa the next day and potentially even worked the evening shift at the restaurant.

But of course, my dad didn't know about the restaurant job, so had assumed I was sticking around the whole weekend. I'd been dreading it, but when I woke up Saturday morning, the almost-summer sun was beaming through my bedroom window, so bright and hot that the air was already taking on a sticky sense of heaviness.

And even I had to begrudgingly admit that was awesome, especially after I went downstairs for breakfast and my dad told me he had to go into the office for a financial emergency or something and said he would take me and Kimberlee for dinner that night to make up for it.

Because that meant I could sit in the pool all day.

My dad put the in-ground pool in when he first built the house. It was large enough for someone to swim laps every morning if they were so inclined, which apparently he had been once upon a time, but I couldn't remember ever seeing him do it. Still, he kept the pool heated and maintained, which was good because it was one of the few things I truly looked forward to when I visited my dad.

After texting Anne-Marie to see if she and maybe Remy wanted to hang out in the pool with me and changing into the spare bikini I left at my dad's—I hadn't thought to pack one of my good ones since it had been pouring rain when I left Ottawa—I went out to the pool house.

Well, my dad called it a pool house. I guess there *was* a set of wicker furniture and a fridge and stuff in it, though I wasn't really sure why. The back door of the house was just off the kitchen and there was a much comfier set of outdoor furniture arranged on the patio. But the pool house was more of a shed where we kept the pool supplies and countless floaties and tubes and air mattresses he'd gotten for me growing up. "Pool house" just sounded fancier.

By the time I finished filling up a couple of the floaties, Anne-Marie sauntered into the yard in a large sunhat. Oversized sunglasses were perched on her nose and she was wrapped in a white kimono-style cover up that was so sheer and insubstantial, I wasn't sure why she'd even bothered putting it over top of her gold bikini.

"*Waouh*, it is a good thing Remy is busy today," she said as she dropped a tote bag on one of the loungers.

"Why's that?" I asked.

"Because I may have ended up jealous," she said, untying her kimono and dropping it on the lounger.

I frowned. "Of what?"

She gave me an amused look. "Did you look in the mirror this morning?"

"Uh... yeah. What's wrong?"

She giggled. "Nothing is *wrong*. I would say it is very, very right. That bikini... *t'es ben chix*. You know I am not into girls, but *damn*. I am almost surprised your dad let you come outside like this."

I looked down at myself. It hadn't been intentional, but I *did* look pretty hot if you were into the whole busting-out-of-a-too-small-top kind of thing. That was what happened when the spare swimsuit you kept at your dad's place was a hot pink bikini you bought in high school when you flitted between a small and medium depending on if it was volleyball season or not and now you're definitely a large. But everything was covered, even if my butt was eating a bit more of the stretchy fabric than it used to.

"My dad isn't home," I said.

Anne-Marie snickered. "That explains it. But I still think Remy would not have been able to keep his eyes off you and the jealous little game we play only works when *he* is the jealous one."

"Remy is madly in love with you," I said, picking up my towel and bringing it over to the lounge chair beside Anne-Marie's.

"Yes, but he's not blind, *chérie*." She smirked, her eyes sparkling behind her sunglasses. "It is a compliment, Nellie. The curves like this? *Parfait*. I know we always want what we don't have, but what I wouldn't give to have a shape like yours."

That was a surprise. Anne-Marie was the kind of girl who looked good in everything because everything was made to fit people shaped like her. But I knew she wasn't being insincere with what she'd said. People always wanted to look different than they did.

We spent all of that Saturday the way we'd spent countless others, floating about the pool and alternating between chatting and a solo activity of our choice: flipping through a magazine or watching videos or scrolling social media on my phone, in my case, and reading in Anne-Marie's.

It was something I really appreciated about Anne-Marie. It was nice to have a friend I could just exist with. Where we could hang out, but not feel obligated to entertain each other. I loved spending time with people, but as an only child—especially one of divorced parents—I was also very used to spending time on my own. So being able to just relax in the presence of someone... it was nice.

"These people are going to fuck," Anne-Marie muttered at one point late in the afternoon.

I looked up from my phone, eyebrows raised. "What?"

"They're going to fuck." She closed her book, stretching and letting out a yawn. "He is her work enemy and they must go on a business trip together. Obviously once they arrive, there will be only one hotel room."

"And you're not going to finish reading the book because you figured it out?"

"Oh, I will." She idly kicked her legs in the water. "But they are about to get on the airplane, so they will be fucking soon. Which is fine, but my family is going to dinner to celebrate Marc-Andre's birthday and I will not get to see Remy until later."

I smirked. "Oh. Of course."

She grinned at me. "So I will save it to read for when I get home. Then I can call Remy and tell him I'm primed and ready and to get his cute little self over asap."

"And he's still going to come over even after you call him both 'cute' and 'little'?" I asked.

The corners of her lips curled up into a sly sort of look. "Of course. I'll need him to show me yet again that he's neither cute nor little. And then of course I'll immediately forget so I'll need him to remind me again... and again..."

"So I guess JP isn't getting any sleep tonight either, then?"

She tilted her head to the side. "What do you mean, *chérie*?"

Oh.

Fuck.

"'Cause... his room is next to yours? Isn't it?" I asked.

She blinked at me before making a noise of realization. "I never thought about that before. Do you think he can hear us do it?"

I knew very well that he could hear them do it, which is why it was extra stupid of me to have made the comment I did. But I shrugged as nonchalantly as I could. "I mean, I would imagine so. You'd have to ask JP."

"Ask me what?"

I fell off my floatie.

It only took me a moment to steady myself, but Anne-Marie started laughing so hard that she nearly choked. Heart still racing, I whirled around and looked up to see JP leaning against the half-railing next to the patio, his arms folded and an amused look on his face.

"What does she need to ask me, Nellie?" he repeated. "It sounds good, whatever it is."

"It's not," I said.

Anne-Marie tried to catch her breath. "She wanted to know if you can hear—"

"*I'm* not the one who wanted to know!" I said, my face burning.

"Know what?" JP pressed.

Anne-Marie stifled another laugh. "When Remy is over, can you hear us? When we... you know? Nellie thinks you can, but I do not think so."

JP raised his eyebrows. Not at Anne-Marie, of course; he was staring straight at me, the amusement still growing on his face. I stared back, sure my face was entirely red, drops of water snaking down my neck from where my hair had gotten wet when I fell into the pool.

"Well," he finally said. "Nellie would be right."

Anne-Marie slapped a hand to her mouth, but her eyes were sparkling. "Oh my *God*. The things you must have heard! Jean-Paul, I am so sorry."

"No you're not," JP said. "There's a reason I have good headphones."

She cackled, shaking her head. I was glad the two of them could laugh about it, because I sure as shit wasn't finding it funny.

"What are you doing out here anyway, Jean-Paul?" Anne-Marie finally asked. "Eavesdropping is not your usual thing."

"I wasn't eavesdropping," JP said. "Mom asked me to come out and tell you we need to get ready for dinner. For some reason, I was included in that, even though I'm probably going to wear far less makeup than you are."

Anne-Marie sighed, some of the sunshine fading off her face. "Already? I was going to start getting ready at five."

"It's five-twenty," JP said.

"Ah, *ciboire!*" Anne-Marie swore, sliding off her floatie and into the water with a splash. "Sorry to end our day so suddenly, *chérie*. I wish you had come earlier, Jean-Paul, so I could help Nellie tidy things up. But I'm going to be late getting ready for dinner."

I knew what he was going to say before he opened his mouth. "Why don't you go home, then, and I can help—"

"I don't have to put anything away," I said. "The floaties go in the pool house and that's it. Then I'm going inside. To get ready. For dinner with my dad."

He held my gaze for a moment. Heated rushed up my cheeks, but I stared back with resolute determination. After a moment, JP nodded, waiting until Anne-Marie slipped her sandals on and grabbed her tote so he could walk home with her.

The next day, when I went to get into my car to drive back to Ottawa, there was a yellow square stuck to the driver's window, because of course there was.

Call me... if you can
Xoxo

Chapter Fifteen
Damn You're Good

"Were you dropped on your head as a baby?" Nigel snapped as I set a rum-and-coke on the bar counter.

"No more than your average baby," I said.

He shoved the rum-and-coke back at me, causing it slosh out of the glass. "This is a rocks glass. Highballs go in—get this, princess—a *highball glass*."

"Ohmigod, so *that's* what a highball glass is for!" I said in a nasally, high-pitched voice. "Thanks, Nigel. Can you go tell the guest that we can't put a rum-and-coke in a rocks glass like they requested because highballs go in the highball glasses?"

Nigel scowled at me. "You're walking on thin ice, Nellie."

"Actually, I'm walking on a sticky coke-covered floor because you keep shoving drinks at me," I shot back. "But if you have such a problem with what I'm doing, maybe you can take over so I can go deal with my tables instead of jumping on bar to help with the fucking backlog."

I should have put a bit more thought into snapping at him like that since Nigel was constantly looking for an excuse to fire me. But he just snarled something under his breath and lifted the counter flap, grabbed a bar towel, and told me to get the fuck back to my section.

I'd only been helping the bartender for a few minutes, but when I got back to section five, I realized the hostess had sat another table and hadn't told me about it. I grimaced, preparing myself to apologize for the wait, but relaxed when I caught sight of a familiar head of salt-and-peppery hair bowed over a book.

Which was surprising, considering how red his face had been the last time he'd been here two weeks earlier. I'd thought it was because he was embarrassed about those "unintended undertones" of what he'd said, but maybe... well.

Maybe they were unintended, but not inaccurate.

"You're on your way to becoming a regular," I said as I walked up.

Ben looked up from his book, his eyes brightening. "Nellie! There you are."

"Sorry about the wait. I was helping the bartender and didn't realize it was my turn to get sat."

He glanced away, then tapped the side of his nose conspiratorially. "It wasn't your turn, actually. But I saw you working and asked the hostess if I could be put in your section."

Something warm spread through my chest and I couldn't help but smile. "You did?"

His throat flexed, something nervous on his face. "I hope you don't mind."

I rested most of my weight on one leg so my hip stuck out. "Mind what? You coming back to see me again?"

"I—"

"Because I can't imagine anyone who would mind that." I smiled at him, then gestured at the closed menu on the table. "Were you ready to order?"

"I am," he said.

I waited, but he didn't say anything. "Are you gonna tell me what you want?"

"Nope." He smiled and a wave of warmth washed over me from the way his eyes sparkled. "I'd like you to bring me whatever your favourite meal from this place is."

I raised my eyebrows. "Are you sure? I'm a chicken-strips-and-fries kind of person. I've talked three different restaurants into letting me order from the kids' menu because they don't make an adult version."

"Are the chicken strips good?"

"I think they are."

"Perfect," he said, holding the menu out. "I trust you."

That was an overall bad decision on his part, but I didn't mention that. "Alright. Do you want sauce? We have honey mustard, ketchup, ranch, barbecue, sweet and sour, hot sauce, or spicy mustard."

"Hmm. Which is the best?"

"None of those," I said. "But the special secret chicken sauce that I invented isn't on the menu."

"Sounds intriguing," he said. "And if one wanted to try said special secret chicken sauce...?"

"The kitchen gets annoyed if I go off-menu," I said. "But I *suppose* I could make an exception for my favourite customer."

"Favourite customer?" he repeated, laughter in his voice.

"Well, you were my favourite professor, but you're not my professor anymore."

His eyes met mine and I held his gaze. I didn't mean to, or at least, I didn't mean for it to last as long as it did. I *definitely* hadn't meant for there to be a flicker of electricity, a hint of chemistry, a whisper of hunger as hazel eyes stared into mine.

Or maybe I did. Maybe I'd meant for that moment to linger until Ben's throat flexed, his Adam's apple bobbing as he swallowed before tearing his eyes away.

"And a lager, right?" I asked.

He cleared his throat. "Yes, please. That would be... delightful."

Had it been up to me, I would've gone back to his table to flirt with him more, since that was way more fun than working. Unfortunately, after I put his order into the computer, I got slammed, and not in the fun way.

Just after I dropped off Ben's lager and the glass of water I knew he wanted but had been too flustered to remember to order, Nigel double-sat me. In the process of trying to juggle that, Jessica threw a fit in the kitchen and stormed off for a break. Despite not at all being responsible for her tables, I got stuck running food for her section. I barely had time to mix up my secret special chicken strip sauce—which was ranch and hot sauce with a splash of sweet-and-sour in it—and bring it to Ben with his meal before the bar got backed up because three of my tables ordered drinks at the same time as a party of eight on the other side of the restaurant, so I jumped in to help again.

By the time I made it back to Ben's table, someone had cleared his plate. He was still reading his book, sipping a coffee I hadn't brought him.

Great. That meant I'd end up splitting any potential tip he left me with whoever had poached my table. Which sucked, but there wasn't much I could do about it now.

"Hey," I said as I approached. "Sorry. It's been a hell of a night."

"It's not a problem at all. I can see you working your ass off," he said.

"Most people don't tell me when they're staring at my ass," I said.

Ben's eyes went wide with a mix of astonishment and embarrassment. "How did you—I mean—" He coughed. "I... I wouldn't—That wasn't what I—"

"I was joking," I said, though I *absolutely* flagged the fact that he'd been about to ask me how I knew he was staring. I hadn't, obviously, since the only thing I'd been doing with my ass was talking out of it.

But damn, that was good to know.

"Sometimes I talk before I think," I said. "But it all works out since now we're kind of even from last time you were here."

He laughed. "Well, that's fair. We'll call it even, then."

I smiled. "Do you want any dessert?"

It wasn't meant to be suggestive, but that hadn't stopped Ben from taking the things I'd said as suggestive before. And honestly, given how shitty my shift was going, if he had come back with something about maybe having me for dessert, there was a good chance I would've said fuck it and spread myself out on the table for him.

That time, though, he held himself together and shook his head. "Great tip on the sauce, though. I don't know that I'll ever be able to eat chicken strips without it again. I'll just get the bill, please."

None of my other tables needed anything right at that moment, so I was back at his table with the bill and the machine a moment later. Which sucked.

I mean, not that he was going to pay or that I was back at his table. But I'd barely gotten to talk to Ben while he was there and I just...

Well.

I didn't want him to leave.

"Well, Nellie," he said as the receipt printed. "I—"

"Hey, before you go," I interrupted. "You're a psychologist."

"I'll be one after I go, too," he said solemnly.

I glanced over my shoulder. Nigel wasn't at the bar anymore and my tables were all still good. Pulling out the empty chair across from Ben, I sat down. "Can I pick your brain about something?"

He nodded, tucked his credit card back in his wallet, and rested his elbows on the table so he could fold his fingers in front of his chin in that serious, stoic, professorly way. "What is up, as the kids say?"

I smirked, checked behind me again, then leaned. "Okay, so my boss here? He hates me. I have no idea why."

"Mmm," Ben said. "That must be difficult."

"It is. So I was wondering if like, psychologically speaking, there's a way to figure it out? Or ideally to get him off my back? I'm tired of him getting on my case for stupid stuff."

As if on cue, Nigel burst out of the kitchen. He stormed through my section, passing me without a second glance, then stopped in his tracks and turned around.

"You're not on break," he said.

"I know," I said. "I'm—"

"And you are *not* to be sitting with the guests." He walked up to the table and looked at Ben. "My apologies, sir."

"Unnecessary," Ben said. "Actually, you have excellent timing. I was about to ask her to get her manager for me."

My eyes went wide. Even though I wasn't looking at him, I could feel Nigel glowering at me.

"I am so sorry for whatever it is she's done," he said in a simpering voice. "How can I fix this for you?"

"Oh, there's nothing to fix," Ben said. "I wanted to pass on my compliments and gratitude for the exceptionally personable service this evening. You see, I'm out on my own because I thought a nice meal would cheer me up after my ex-wife tried to demand I cover the cost of a new vehicle for her, despite getting far more than I did in the divorce. Your very kind server here sat down to listen to my sorrows and commiserate. She has gone out of her way to cheer me up tonight, including bringing me the most fabulous chicken strip sauce I've had in my life."

A myriad of emotions crossed Nigel's face. Suspicion was among them, but if I didn't know better, I would have said his eyes softened a bit.

"I'm sorry to hear about your troubles with your ex-wife," he said. "Thank you for passing that on. Nellie, when you're done, please give Jessica a hand rolling flatware."

With that, he walked away, leaving me gaping after him.

"Is everything alright?" Ben asked.

"He's never said please to me," I said, then looked back at him with wide eyes. "What did you do?"

"He's divorced. Recently divorced, most likely."

"How—"

"His general demeanour paired with the tan line on his finger and the semi-visceral reaction to the words 'ex-wife.' And I would bet my year of sabbatical that his ex is a bubbly blonde woman, potentially with a name that either starts with an N or rhymes with Nellie. Ellie seems like a safe bet, though it could be Kelly. Or maybe Shelley." He tapped his fingers on the table. "If I'm right, try telling him a story about how awful your mother was to your father. It might gain you some sympathy."

"Damn," I said. "You're good."

He smiled, allowing himself briefly to drop his sense of modesty. "I know. You'll have to tell me what the outcome is."

"But how will I get a hold of you to let you know?"

It was another one of those things that was far too flirtatious, but unlike some of the previous things I'd said, Ben didn't stammer or flush a flustered red.

"Well actually, that relates to why I was hoping to catch you here tonight," he said.

I looked up at him, surprised. "Does it?"

He nodded and his voice lowered into something almost business-like. "It is my professional opinion that you should have asked me for a reference letter."

I squinted at him. "You said at the start of every psychology course I took with you that you don't do reference letters."

"For most students, no." He took a sip from his almost-empty coffee. "For students who are actually worth being a reference for, like the ones who take every four-hundred level forensic psychology class I offer despite it overloading their schedule and not being necessary to their final degree?"

"Well, I like the way you teach psychology," I said. "And you're going on sabbatical next year, so I had to do them all this year."

"And you were at the top of the class in every single one of them," he said. "In my time as a professor, I've written reference letters for four forensic science students. Every one of them has been accepted into the FAI internship program."

Beneath the table, I tapped my toes rapidly, hoping he couldn't sense the movement. "What would I have to do to be student number five?"

Ben glanced up, a sparkle in his eyes. "Ask."

"Can you write me a reference letter?"

"On one condition."

And that made me pause.

Because fuck.

Fuck.

Anyone who knew me knew I slept around. I wasn't ashamed of that. Sex was good. Sex was great, actually, and I wanted to have it as much as possible.

So if Ben had wanted to hook up, I wouldn't have said no. It didn't bother me that he was my former professor or that he was at least in his late thirties.

But not if that was the condition for something, especially something that could define my entire career.

That was a line.

And one that I was almost devastated to think someone like him would cross.

"What's the condition?" I asked, my voice tense as I prepared myself to turn him down.

"I want you to apply for the CCFS Labs internship next summer."

Oh.

I blinked at him, then frowned. "The one in Toronto?"

He nodded as if he had no idea what I thought he'd been implying. Which, in fairness, he probably hadn't, given his past inability to think of undertones before he made a statement.

"I mean, I'll try," I said. "But that one is even harder to get into than the FAI one."

"Apply for both, of course," he said. "I'm sure you'll be accepted to both, but I feel like you've learned from this year that it's good to have a backup plan."

I half-laughed. "Yeah, you can say that again."

"CCFS may be more particular, but they would be ridiculous not to accept you," he said. "So apply for both, but when you get offered the CCFS internship, take it."

"Is that part of the condition?" I asked.

He shook his head. "That's simply my advice. The condition is just that you apply. I know you *will* take it because it'll be far more helpful for you, both education wise and career wise. And it also pays far better than the FAI internship. But if I'm wrong—which I'm not—then take the FAI internship."

I nodded slowly. "I mean... yeah. I can do that."

"Excellent." He cleared his throat. "Now, with classes being done for the summer, I know you won't be around campus and with me leaving on sabbatical next year, getting you a reference letter in the fall won't be possible. So if it's okay that I email the letter to you..."

"Sure." I thought for a moment. "Though, I don't check my student email much during the summer. Maybe you could, um, text me once you've sent it?"

Ben looked at me, his eyes almost unreadable. "I'd need your phone number for that, Nellie."

"It just so happens I have this pen and paper to provide you with said phone number." I tore a scrap of paper off my order pad and took a pen from my apron, jotting it down. "Unless you feel that's too forward."

He looked at the piece of paper, but didn't grab it before setting his eyes on mine again. "I would like to clarify that you will receive this letter, regardless of any sort of, uh... attempts at... bribery. With intended *or* unintended undertones."

And there it was.

Proof.

Almost.

Like, a bit of proof. Slight proof. An implication of proof that Ben wasn't quite viewing me as a student anymore.

And yeah, maybe I should've been more worried about the ethical implications of that, considering where my thoughts had gone as soon as he'd brought up the idea of a condition. Maybe it should have concerned me that I really wanted to fuck this man that I also wanted a reference letter from, and he appeared to want something like that, too.

But I had no doubt that Ben was telling the truth.

And even if he was...

Well.

I had to do something to make my summer a little more interesting.

"Understood," I said. "Any and all bribery attempts will be completely unrelated to the reference letter."

"Yes, I—wait."

I smiled innocently. "Yes, Professor Cameron?"

He studied me for another moment, then shook his head, a resigned chuckle coming out as he reached forward and took my phone number.

"Alright," he said. "I'll send you a text once I've emailed your letter."

Chapter Sixteen
Speak of the Devil

"Why does all the cool shit happen to you?" Sydney complained as I told her about Ben's visit over pad thai the following night.

"Cool shit happens to you, too," I said.

"It does not."

"You don't have to pay rent for the next two months with a guarantee that your roommate will do all the chores around the house after cooking dinner for you at least twice a week."

She rolled her eyes, covering her mouth as she finished chewing a large mouthful of noodles so I knew she was about to respond.

"Reid grovelling so I don't move out isn't *cool*," she said once she'd swallowed. "And he's not doing all my chores. Both of us drew a line at laundry."

"I still don't get why *you* drew a line there."

"Because the thought of Reid touching my panties is—" She shuddered and shook her head. "Ick."

I was very proud of myself for not at once rolling my eyes and calling her a liar because I sincerely doubted *ick* was the sound her panties made when they got wet. "Okay, but still. No cleaning for two months, no rent, and home-cooked meals you don't have to make? That's awesome."

"Trade you."

I frowned. "What?"

The corner of Sydney's mouth tugged up. "Trade you. You can have Reid clean your apartment and cook for you while I fuck Professor Sexy."

"Not a chance in hell."

She laughed. "Exactly. So all the cool shit happens to you. I just get grovelling and the occasional late-night sext from a random French guy."

I raised my eyebrows. "You mean Olivier?"

"Uh... yeah. Who else would I be sexting regularly?"

I shrugged. I wasn't Olivier's biggest fan, but I couldn't quite articulate why. There was nothing I specifically *disliked* about him. I mean, he was a bit older than we were, but I was actively hoping to hook up with a literal professor, so it wasn't like I could talk. And Sydney was really into him.

"No one, I guess. Is he sending you dick pics yet?"

"Yep."

I raised my eyebrows, intrigued. "Seriously?"

She nodded, her cheeks flushing pink as she tried to hide a smile.

"Unsolicited?"

"Oh, of course not," she said. "He's way too much of a gentleman for that."

I hmm'ed and tilted my head. "Is he, though?"

"And it's illegal to send unsolicited nudes."

"That doesn't stop most guys."

"Yeah, but he's a police officer."

"Oh yeah. Has he broken out his handcuffs on you yet?"

"No," she said. "I asked if he'd show them to me next time."

I raised my eyebrows. "You're going to see him again?"

"Maybe." She pushed the noodles around on her plate. "I might go back to Montreal to see him. Or he mentioned coming to visit me again."

"Even after the whole Mommy thing?"

She shrugged but couldn't stop a mischievous smile from spreading on her lips. "I mean, remember how I put my finger in Tyler's butt that one time because I said he had to take it in the butt before I would?"

I raised my eyebrows. "Are you saying Olivier wants to take it in the butt?"

"I'm saying that sending links to each other with different strap-on options got me dick pics featuring two different cumshots in the same night."

A laugh hooted out of my throat. "I can't believe you're sitting there saying nothing cool happens to you when you had a one-night-stand with a cop who's now sexting you consensually and wants you to peg him. I mean, you've got the chance to *literally* stick it to the man."

"Yeah, but that's not Professor-Sexy-Is-Gonna-Put-His-Dick-In-My-Butt kind of cool."

I rolled my eyes. "I don't know if he's actually gonna put his dick in my butt. It's not like I'm gonna start the conversation with 'Hey, Ben. Thanks for the reference letter. Do you have any interest in anal?'"

"Why not?"

I opened my mouth, considering what she said, then frowned thoughtfully. "I don't know, actually. It might work."

"It was a joke, but I can see you doing it."

"You can see me doing it any time you wanna watch," I said. "But there's still no guarantee I'm gonna bone him. He said he was gonna text me when he emailed me the letter. It's not like either of us suggested we meet up or something."

"Hmm. That does put a damper on the whole dick-in-butt-ening," Sydney said thoughtfully. "I guess you could always email his Professor Sexy email address and ask."

And I was going to respond, but then my phone rang. Sydney perked up as I grabbed my phone.

"Speak of the devil? Is it him?" she guessed. "*Please* tell me it's speak of the devil."

I grimaced. "I mean, it is, but not in the way you think."

"What do you mean?"

I didn't respond, just put my chopsticks down and tapped the screen.

"Hi, Dad," I said as I stood, intending to wander to the other room to talk to him without having to look at Sydney.

"Eleanor," my dad said.

"It's—"

"Right now, it is Eleanor."

Each word was as clipped and cold as ice cracking against metal. As many times as I'd heard my dad speak in a frigid tone, it had never been like *that*.

Ever.

And I was so stunned by it I froze in place, unable to speak.

"Nell?" Sydney whispered in concern.

"You know, it has been heartbreaking to see Kimberlee try so hard to earn your affection and you to be so unreceptive to it," my dad continued. "I do not expect you to be endeared to someone immediately, but I do expect you to have a modicum of respect for the people who mean something to me."

"What are you—"

"Do not interrupt." Those words were just as terse as the first ones and I fell silent again. "She has been making a concentrated effort to befriend my daughter because as one of the two most important women in my life, she seems to comprehend that it is imperative you learn to co-exist peacefully with each other."

"Okay, but I don't know what's bringing this on," I said, honestly confused.

"Of course you don't," he said. "Because you felt the need to lie to me."

"I did?"

"When were you going to tell me about the internship, Eleanor?"

Oh.

Oh no.

Oh, *no.*

Blood drained from my face, pooling in my palms and making them clammy. "The i-internship?"

"The FAI internship," he said. "The one that you were so certain you would get, you said you would take the LSAT in the fall. The one you said was the reason you could not possibly join us for any additional social gatherings despite my request you do so. The one you said you have been working at since the middle of May. Do you know which *internship* I mean now?"

"I—"

"You know, Kimberlee is so sweet and caring that she was not even going to tell me what happened, but I could see something was bothering her earlier today," he said. "And she finally told me she had hoped to brighten your day by receiving some flowers at work, but when the florist called to tell her the delivery was not accepted, she was *exceptionally* hurt."

My palms seemed to have sucked the moisture out of my mouth, too, because they felt like they were dripping with sweat while my tongue was coated with sand.

"And I nearly called you at once to ask why you would do such a rude and nasty thing, but she asked me not to. Because"—he let out a dry, dramatic little laugh—"she wanted to give you the benefit of the doubt. After all, perhaps the receptionist didn't know who you were and declined the delivery."

"That seems plausible," I forced myself to say.

"It does. So plausible, in fact, that I had my assistant attempt to find your contact information so we could forward it to the florist for redelivery. Imagine my surprise when he informed me he'd called and was told no one by the name of Eleanor Belanger was working there."

I dug my fingernail into the side of my thumb and bit my lip to keep my chin from trembling.

"And you know that Pierre is very thorough. So he informed me he then got in touch with Sheridan Humprey, the director of the internship program, and was told that Eleanor Belanger was not *accepted* as an intern this year," he continued.

"Dad, I can—"

"And on top of that, Mr. Humprey asked to book a call to *personally* apologize for that oversight, as when he declined your application, he wasn't aware *whose* daughter he was rejecting. Since perhaps you do not know, but my company had donated a *significant* amount of money to various first responder programs—including the one in Ottawa."

Fuck.

"I can explain—"

"Explain what?" he asked. "You insisted you would get this internship. You made promises for what would happen if you did not get it. Instead of following through on the very simple request I had for you to attend a few events with myself and Kimberlee or beginning to study for the LSAT so you have a backup plan for when this scientist thing blows up in your face, you have been sitting around doing nothing."

"I haven't been doing nothing! I—"

"All I asked was for you to show some support," he said. "So now that I'm aware you have been lying to me, you understand that I expect you will be at *every single one* of the events Kimberlee has requested you to be at this summer. Otherwise—"

"Dad, I *can't*," I said. "I'm working."

"Working," he repeated.

"The letter said that was why I didn't get the internship." My voice almost shook, but a tight, shallow breath kept it steady. "They said I didn't have enough work experience. So I... I got a job."

"Where?"

I swallowed hard. "A restaurant."

"And you expect that to help you get a science internship?"

His tone was so flat, so skeptical and condescending, so clearly implying that he thought I was a fucking *idiot*, that it felt like a bolt of fabric woven from shame and embarrassment was winding itself around me, tightening around my ribcage and biceps and mouth.

"Eleanor?" my dad repeated. "Please, explain to me how you expect a restaurant job to help you when I could have easily spoken to Mr. Humprey myself. Or perhaps arranged for a different internship opportunity for you here in Montreal. Jean-Luc Marchand's firm accepts—"

"That's a law firm," I said. "I'm not in law. And I don't need you to arrange anything for me. I can do this myself."

"Of course you can," he said, sharp sarcasm cutting through the phone. "But still, I am having trouble understanding the logic behind working in a restaurant instead of something at least tangentially related to your industry or focusing on networking with people who could help you. Do you know how many contacts you could have made at the events Kimberlee is planning this summer?"

"There aren't that many—"

"Frankly, I expect the lack of logic you're displaying had plenty to do with Mr. Humprey's decision."

The words bit at me. Heat rose up my spine, blazing through the shame and guilt that had built up like dry brush on the ground and leaving room for words I shouldn't have said to spill out.

"Maybe if you actually believed in me and you gave me the chance to prove I can manage my own life instead of trying to control everything I do, I wouldn't have had to lie," I said.

And my father went silent.

Completely.

Fucking.

Silent.

Which was understandable. I mean, that pushed buttons I definitely should have left unpressed. I could have phrased it better. I could've not poked a dragon who already had smoke drifting from his nostrils.

I could've, but I didn't.

So I waited. Seconds ticked by and all I could hear was my own breath and the eighteen threads of swirling thoughts in my mind. But he didn't speak. I didn't know if he was speechless or shocked or waiting for me to apologize, but finally, I couldn't take it anymore.

"I thought if I told you I didn't get the internship, you'd tell me I had to change careers when all I have to do is improve my resume," I said. "So I got a job at a restaurant to show I have work experience because that seemed like a better solution than going to a bunch of fancy parties and hoping I meet someone who might have connections that I don't need because I'm *good* at what I do." I swallowed hard. "Just because you don't think I'm smart enough doesn't mean I'm not."

"Fine," he said. "Prove it."

I blinked. "What—"

"You must be making reasonable money at your restaurant job. If you are so smart, *ma fille ange*, you can prove it by using that to pay your way through your last year of school."

I'd lived in my apartment for three years. I knew every inch of the place. It was my home, the first place I'd lived on my own. I'd cooked meals here, though not as many as I'd ordered as takeout. I'd had guys over. Girls. Friends.

And yet, in that moment, even though I was standing in a place I knew intimately with my eyes open and focused on whatever was in front of me, I couldn't have said what I was looking at.

It was erased from my memory. All that existed was the voice in my ear and the sweat on my palms and the sick, heavy feeling collecting in my stomach.

"Dad, I... I can't."

"Certainly you can," he said. "Allow me to *prove* I believe in you."

My voice shook. "No. I... I won't be able to work when school starts. I'm taking too many classes and I-I don't... I mean, I'm a server. I don't make *that* much—"

"Perhaps you should have thought of that before deciding lying to me was preferable to keeping your word," he said.

Then he hung up.

Chapter Seventeen
Negotiations

I spent the rest of the night aimless.

Sydney tried to help. She really did. But after hanging up, it was all I could do to sit down on my couch and stare, trying to figure out what...

Just what.

Just how.

How I was going to pay my tuition. How I was going to make enough money to pay rent. How I was going to take all of my classes. How I was going to look my dad in the eye when I went to Montreal in two days for the fucking gala I was supposed to go to. If I still even *needed* to go.

I didn't know how I was going to do any of it.

"We could go to the club," Sydney suggested. "My treat."

I shook my head.

"Come on. You always say getting laid helps you think more clearly."

I half-laughed. "I do say that."

"So let's go pick someone up."

It was thoughtful of her, but I shook my head again. "I think I... I need to go to bed."

"It's not even eight o'clock, Nell."

"Yeah. You can hang out here until Alison and Reid are done, if you want."

She tried a few more times before giving me a resigned hug and going back to her apartment despite the offer to stay at mine.

Then I went to bed.

But the blankets were too tangled, so I got up and made the bed before getting back into it. Then I was too hot, so I wandered to the kitchen. There were dishes in the sink and I started washing them, got bored, and wandered to my living room.

Over the course of the next hour, I did nothing and everything. I'd put away a few things here and get distracted wiping down something else over there. I put a load of laundry in but didn't turn the machine on. Took my vacuum out, but decided it was too loud and left it abandoned in the second bedroom of my apartment.

I'd just started going through one of the baskets I stuffed things I didn't know what to do with into when my phone rang again.

If I could have, I would've ignored it. But the moment my phone went off, I had an inherent drive to know who was calling me. And even when I had no desire to talk to whoever it was on the other side, a prickling sensation started in the small of my back and travelled up until my shoulders were tense with the unrequited curiosity of needing to know *why* someone was calling.

So even though I tried to ignore it, even though it was the last person on Earth I wanted to talk to just then, even though I was numb with hurt and fear and anger, I answered.

"What?"

"A polite person answers a call with *hello*," my dad said.

I didn't say anything.

Neither did he.

"Why are you calling?" I finally asked.

"So no hello, then?"

My jaw twitched and every nerve, every bone, every capillary in my body screamed at me to tell him there was no reason for me to be polite to him, not after he'd cut me off and called me stupid and hung up on me. But the part of me that hated disappointing people took over and I took a deep, calming breath.

"Hello, Dad," I forced myself to say.

"Hello," he said. "I would like to discuss our conversation earlier."

I wouldn't, but I didn't say that. I didn't say anything and after a moment, he continued.

"After we hung up—"

"You hung up on me."

He paused and when he spoke again, there was an intolerant impatience in his voice. "After our call, I had the opportunity to think of a better way for this to be handled. So here is what will happen. You will come to *Mosaic de Montreal* this weekend as planned."

Of course. He'd probably forgotten that was this weekend while he was busy cutting me off and was now backtracking because he needed me there to make him look good.

Although, that wasn't necessarily a bad thing. Maybe it meant I *wouldn't* get cut off, and then I could—

"You will attend it with Clinton Thibault."

"No," I said.

"Eleanor—"

"It's Nellie, and no," I said. "I already have a date and even if I didn't, Clinton is a creep. And what's the point in me going to your stupid events? I mean, I should just call my boss and tell him I can work this weekend. Since I'm going to need the money to pay for next year."

He waited until I was done, then another long beat, before speaking again.

"You will attend the *Mosaic de Montreal* luncheon with Clinton," he said. "That is the first condition to receive your tuition and your allowance. The second condition is that you will attend any additional events this summer that Kimberlee or I request of you."

"I have a job. I can't ditch it to go to your events."

"And why do you need that job if you're going to get your allowance payments back?"

My jaw twitched. "Because it's not about the money. I need to put experience on my resume."

"Waitressing experience is a pointless thing to put on your resume," he said, his voice full of derision. "Networking at these events will be a far more effective use of your time. Kimberlee has at least four or five people in mind that would be good for you to speak with at this weekend's gala, and that is just one opportunity."

Again, I went silent.

"The final condition is that you will keep your word," he said. "I expect you to sit for—and score at *least* an average grade on—the LSAT."

"No," I said.

The sound he made was as close to a laugh as I thought might be possible for my dad. "No?"

I closed my eyes, mostly so that I didn't start crying. "No. I won't do any of that."

"You will not even keep your word about this weekend?"

"I said I'd go with Bruno," I said. "Not with Clinton."

"Eleanor—"

"You know what he's done, right?" I opened my eyes. "You know who you're asking me to be alone with?"

"Those rumours are greatly exaggerated," my dad said. "I have known the Thibaults for years and spoken with Clinton on many occasions. There was no evidence he had done anything wrong aside from the word of a person who clearly had an agenda against him."

I gritted my teeth. "Well, I guess it doesn't matter either way. I'm not going to *Mosaic de Montreal* with Clinton, which means I guess I'm not going at all, and I'm not quitting my job to go to your stupid events. And I'm *not* taking the LSAT."

And then I hung up on him.

I hung up on my *dad*.

And it felt good. It did. For approximately four seconds before the trembling sense of panic kicked in again and I had to figure out how the fuck I was going to manage any of this. The proverbial clock started ticking and my mind started racing, weighing options that didn't work and doing math that didn't add up until the racing turned to cycling and those cycles turned to spirals.

Despite those spirals, I managed to get a few hours of sleep. Nowhere near enough; Nigel's sole strategy behind his scheduling seemed to be giving me the shittiest schedule possible, I would've thought meant he would've scheduled me to work Friday night since I'd booked the weekend off. But he'd given me the day shift, probably because the tips were worse, so I had to drag my ass out of bed when my alarm went off only a few hours after I finally fell asleep.

Which sucked, of course. Almost as much as the annoyingly insistent knowledge that I had the weekend off for nothing now. There was no chance in hell he'd give me another weekend off. And it was too late for me to schedule a last-minute trip to Toronto to see my mom or something, especially since I was about to be broke. So it was a total fucking waste.

Or, I thought as I stood in front of my bathroom mirror, blearily pulling my hair into a ponytail, maybe it wasn't.

Maybe—just maybe—I could gain a silver lining out of this shit storm of a situation.

It would take a lot of luck. Maybe some skill. A lot of hope that Ben had been right in his assessment of Nigel.

But I had to try.

I sped through my morning routine as quickly as I could so I could get to work early enough to loiter near the office. Just as I'd hoped, the distinctive lurch of Nigel's walk came out of the office not too long after I got there. I was facing away from him, staring dramatically at the schedule posted on the wall across from the office with a perplexed and downcast look on my face. Pretending I didn't know he was there, I sighed heavily.

And thank God, he took the bait.

"What is it now, princess?" Nigel asked snidely.

I jumped, pretending he'd startled me. "Oh! I didn't know you were there."

He rolled his eyes. "Let me guess. Your hours are impeding your thrilling social life and you want me to cover your shifts for you."

I shook my head. "No. Not at all."

"Then what are you doing moping around here when you have opening tasks to do out front?"

"My shift doesn't start for another ten minutes," I said. "I came in early to see if there was anyone who would switch shifts with me because my mom decided to come into town this weekend to visit. Which is bad enough on its own, but I'd booked this weekend off *specifically* to go see my dad. But of course, she's completely against that and my dad's insisting it's okay to change our plans because he hates making her mad. And now the only other weekend he's available, I'm working." I tapped on the schedule, my fingers landing on the weekend of the 80s film festival my mom had mentioned. "I don't think anyone's going to want to switch with me."

"And that's my problem how?" he asked.

"It's not. It's entirely my problem and I'll... I'll be okay." I sighed. "I just worry about him. He's been so sad since she left. Honestly, if I could make her come into town when I was working so I didn't have to be at home half the time, I would. I just can't believe what she did to him. But I'm sure he'll understand. I just… it's my *dad*, you know?"

Nigel stared at me.

Then he stared at me some more.

And as the amount of staring became uncomfortable, his jaw twitched and he looked at the calendar.

"I know you're used to getting special treatment everywhere you go, princess, but that's not how I run my ship," he said. "That being said, Jessica's been asking around for someone to take her shifts this weekend because she wants to go to a music festival and if she has no takers, I'm sure she's gonna come down with a case of the totally-real flu tomorrow. So as long as you know this is the *only* time I'll help you, if you come in for her shifts on Saturday and Sunday, I'll get her to cover yours that weekend."

Holy.

Shit.

It took everything in me not to do a dance of joy before Nigel walked away. As soon as he had, I pulled my phone out and texted my mom to tell her I'd be able to come to Toronto for the film festival. She texted back a gif of a screaming goat almost immediately, which was her favourite way to express her excitement, and I barely had to force the smile on my face for the rest of my shift.

It was almost like a turning point. The rest of the day wasn't great, but it wasn't bad either. Nigel was oddly not-mean to me—I couldn't say he was nice because he still referred to me as a bimbo three times and asked when the last time I shoved crayons up my nose was because clearly there was one still stuck in my brain, but he didn't say it with the same amount of vitriol he usually did—and I made decent tips.

And just before the end of my shift, everything got *exponentially* better.

"Nellie!"

I looked up to see Ben smiling at me. Despite it being a warm almost-summer day, he was wearing dark jeans with a dress shirt and blazer like he always did, and his leather messenger bag was slung over his shoulder.

God, he was so fucking hot.

"Hey, Professor Cameron!" I said brightly. "Welcome back."

"I was hoping you'd be here," he said. "Would it be too much for me to ask to be seated in your section again tonight?"

I grimaced. "I mean, no, not at all, but I don't actually have a section. I'm off in fifteen minutes."

His thick eyebrows creased into a frown. "Well, that won't do. You're the only person who knows how to make the special chicken sauce I liked so much last time."

Now, I could have offered to make it for him before I left. I *could* have said I'd get the server who hadn't cashed out to put his order in right away so it would be ready in the next few minutes, since the dinner rush hadn't started yet. And yeah, maybe I could've offered to stay a couple of minutes late to make sure he got it.

But sometimes in life, there are problems you don't want a logical solution to.

Sometimes, the world collapses around you one day, and the next, you're looking at your former psychology professor that you really want to fuck, and you decide to blink innocently and shrug because you know.

You just fucking *know* what he's going to say if you do.

"I wish there was something I could do," I said.

"I suppose I'll have to go elsewhere for dinner tonight," he said almost sadly.

"That's understandable," I said, then made a show of checking around me. "There's a great little bistro-type place around the corner from here. Their chicken strips are almost as good as the ones here, but they make a *mean* French onion soup if you're into that kind of thing."

"Hmm," he said. "That does sound delightful. Around the corner, you said?"

I nodded. "It's called Cool Eats."

"*Cool Eats*?" he repeated. "Really?"

"It's meant to be ironic, I think. It's a hipster-y kind of place. The food is good, though."

"Sounds intriguing. Thanks for the recommendation."

And then he hesitated.

For a psychologist, Ben didn't have much of a poker face. I could almost match the expressions on his face to the thoughts I knew were running through his head as he battled with what to do next.

Because this wasn't just about chicken sauce.

It wasn't about a reference letter.

It was about the almost gleeful level of certainty I now had that Ben wanted to break some rules, and that I was the person he wanted to break those rules with.

Finally, he cleared his throat.

"Although," he said. "It sounds like you really enjoy this bistro."

"I do," I said.

"Well, since you're off shortly and I wanted to talk to you about that letter, perhaps you'd like to, ah... join me."

Chapter Eighteen
A Psychoanalytical Date... I mean, Dinner

"I HOPE YOU DON'T mind," Ben said when I walked into Cool Eats about twenty minutes later. "But I went ahead and ordered. Chicken strips and fries, correct?"

I grinned as I sat down. "That's exactly what I wanted. Thanks."

"It should be here in a few minutes. I wasn't sure what you'd like to drink, though, so I got water for now."

"Water is perfect," I said, reaching for the condensation-covered glass sitting in front of me. "It's so hot in the kitchen."

"Can't you drink water on your shift?" he asked as I took a huge gulp from the glass.

I swallowed and nodded. "Yeah, but Nigel uses my need to address my basic bodily functions as fodder to yell at me, so sometimes it's easier to wait until I'm done work."

Ben's eyes darkened. "Why do you keep putting up with a terrible boss like him?"

"Because I've never worked a job before in my life and people don't like to hire twenty-one-year-olds with no work experience."

"Twenty-one," he repeated, almost under his breath.

"What?"

"Nothing. Have you had a chance to test my theory?"

I nodded. "It worked perfectly. You're a genius."

He smiled, the corners of his eyes crinkling. "I don't know about genius, but I'm glad it helped."

"It'll make the rest of the summer tolerable, at least."

"And then next summer, you'll be in one of the internship programs and won't have to worry about working for someone like him." He reached into the messenger bag beside him, withdrew a piece of paper, and slid it across the table. "Your letter."

"Thank you," I said, somewhat surprised. "I wasn't expecting a hard copy, but this is perfect."

"I sent you an email version this morning, but I thought you may want the original."

I looked down at the letter. I wasn't going to read the whole thing in front of him, of course, but a quick skim of the contents made a soft wave of pride fill my chest as I saw words like "outgoing, confident, and passionate" and "strong interpersonal skills mixed with a tenacious desire to master everything she can at the highest level possible." When I looked back up at him, I was smiling.

"Thank you," I said. "Seriously. This'll make a huge difference."

"Every bit of it is true," he said, his voice solemnly earnest. "You are going to excel at whatever you choose to do, Nellie. I have full faith in that."

The server picked that moment to bring our meals out, which was good because it meant Ben probably didn't see my cheeks flush pink.

I wasn't lying about how good the food here was. The chicken strips were far better than the ones at my job; they didn't need sauce whatsoever, let alone my special chicken sauce. That didn't mean they didn't come with sauce, of course. I had no idea what they put in theirs, but it was something you could get addicted to. And their fries were phenomenal: crispy on the outside and fluffy on the inside and piled so high on the plate that I'd never finished an order by myself.

Ben had gotten a bowl of the French onion soup like I'd suggested, along with one of their signature sandwiches piled high with pastrami and salami and pepperoni and probably some other deli meats that ended in *ami* or *oni* that I didn't know the names of. Arugula peeked out of the bread, which was baked fresh, and there were at least two kinds of cheese in there.

"Wow," he said as the server set the food in front of him, his eyes wide. "This looks phenomenal."

"I's so good," I said, already having popped a few fries into my mouth.

He glanced up, amusement on his lips. "This was an excellent suggestion, Nellie. Thank you."

Silence fell between us. At first, it seemed natural given the whole eating-our-meals thing, but after a few moments, a strange, disquieted tension seemed to float between us.

It wasn't hard to figure out why. I was certain Ben wanted more than a quiet dinner at a bistro, but I was more than certain that he was far too shy to ask for it even though "shy" wasn't a word I would have previously associated with him. He'd always seemed confident and approachable and passionate. But that was when it came to his work. Past that, he seemed to have as much uncertainty as the rest of us.

And honestly, that made things better.

The student/teacher thing was a fantasy for some and a red flag for others. As it probably should have been. But he wasn't Professor Cameron to me anymore. He had no way of adjusting my grades or holding anything over me. And the fact that he seemed somewhat hesitant to push things into a more personal territory... well.

It made him easy to trust.

But it also meant that if this was going to go anywhere, it was going to be up to me.

"So are you married?" I asked, taking a bite of my chicken strip.

Ben nearly choked on a spoonful of soup. "What—"

"I don't know much about you," I said. "Like, personally. And it's weird not to talk during dinner."

He recovered, his shoulders relaxing slightly. "Fair. Well, no. I'm not married anymore."

I raised my eyebrows. "Wait, the ex-wife thing you told Nigel about was true?"

"Half true," he said. "I have an ex-wife, but she's demanded nothing more from me than what we agreed on during our divorce. Granted, she makes more money than I do. But we've always been on good terms."

"You have?"

He nodded. "She's one of my best friends, actually. I'd say we're closer now than we were when we were married."

"Really?" I asked skeptically.

"Mm-hmm. Getting divorced is never *good*, of course, but ours was fairly drama-free and entirely congenial. We just grew apart and decided it would be best to be friends, not partners."

I nodded slowly, then shook my head. "Nope. That sounds way too unlikely."

He chuckled. "Maybe, but it's true. We were married for eight years, together for four before that. But neither of us had even finished our undergrads when we first got together. I think both of us agree we started wanting different things about three years after our wedding. Priorities and viewpoints and desires change with time. But her being a kind, intelligent person never changed."

"Yeah, but there's still gotta be something else. Like, something had to trigger it."

He used his spoon to separate a piece of bread in his soup, a hidden smile playing on his lips. "Well, yes."

"I knew it. What happened?"

"Isabelle, ah… well." He glanced up at me, the corners of his eyes crinkling. "She realized she was a lesbian."

I stared at him, blinking a few times. "Wait, you were together for twelve *years* before she realized she was a lesbian?"

"It's not uncommon," he said. "From a psychological standpoint, it makes sense. Women go through constant states of flux until they're in their thirties or forties. Men too, of course, but on top of university and careers and relationships and all of that, women have distinct societal pressures and hormonal changes that men don't. Once they reach their thirties and so many of those big changes are done and those goals are met and those pressures—well, they don't go away, but they change—many women realize there are things about them they haven't had the mental space to address."

"That must have been frustrating."

"Of course. But far less for me than for her. She was the one experiencing it, after all."

"Yeah, but still."

He smiled. "It's much easier not to harbour animosity and appreciate that the constant state of flux is a part of the human experience." He lifted a spoonful of soup from the bowl, but didn't eat it immediately. "But I wasn't lying about us growing apart. It just happened to coincide with her understanding her sexuality. And I can't be angry that she was born a certain way. Especially not after seeing how relieved she was after she came out. We were never unhappy together, but you can be satisfied without being truly happy, if that makes sense."

I nodded and he smiled.

"She's happy now, and that's something that makes *me* happy. She and her wife got married last summer in a small ceremony on top of a mountain in the Rockies. It was an incredibly lovely event."

"You went to it?"

"I officiated it, actually."

I nodded, chewing a fry in thoughtful silence. My experience with marriages breaking up was obviously completely different than his, but what he was saying made sense. It was hard to imagine myself in ten or twenty years wanting entirely different things than I wanted now, but I couldn't pinpoint why. It wasn't like I hadn't changed in the past three or five years of my life.

But it was kind of comforting to hear someone say out loud that it was not only okay, but also normal for your mind to change about things.

"What about you, Nellie?" Ben asked after a moment. "I know you're not married, but you must be dating someone."

I shook my head.

He raised his eyebrows skeptically. "No one? I find that hard to believe."

"I'm not dating anyone," I said, picking up a fry. "Emphasis on *dating*. And I guess on *one*."

His lips parted as he stared at me. "I see."

I tried not to smile. "Does that surprise you?"

"A little."

"Does it bother you?"

Ben gave me a strange look. "That you don't date anyone?"

"That I sleep around." I bit my fry as Ben coughed, his cheeks going pink. "Or that I'm not embarrassed telling you about it."

"Of course not." He cleared his throat, shaking his head at the same time. "Being confident in yourself as a, uh, sexual person is nothing to be ashamed of. I believe many people would be much happier if they followed their hearts rather than the opinions of others. But those societal pressures are tough to fight against, so it's always, ah... intriguing to me when someone does."

"I've been called worse things than intriguing," I said. "So why do you think I'm like this?"

He chuckled, which made his shoulder relax. "You're asking me to psychoanalyze you? Most people prefer I don't. Especially on a d—at dinner."

I pretended I didn't catch that he almost misspoke in the best possible way and shrugged. "I'm just curious. It's not every day I get casual access to a psychologist who can tell me what's going on in my brain."

"You understand I can't treat people I have a..." He trailed off, thinking. "People I know on a personal level?"

"I meant in general," I said. "But we can change the subject to something less intriguing, if you want."

He stared across the table for a moment, an amused but contemplative look on his face as he studied me.

"Well," he finally said. "I hate to make assumptions, but given what I know about you, maybe you could tell me more about your father."

I groaned loudly enough that Ben laughed in surprise and the server looked at us from across the restaurant. "Don't tell me it's daddy issues. That's such a cop-out. It's *always* daddy issues."

"Are you saying you have a good relationship with your father?"

"No. I just don't want you to say that's the problem."

He stifled another laugh and shook his head. "Well, if you're not willing to consider that, then I'd say it's probably the exploration of sexuality by someone who has a high level of confidence both in herself and about what she wants."

I ate another fry, mulling over what he said as he picked up his sandwich and took a bite.

"Okay," I said after a moment. "But what if it's an excessive amount of... exploring?"

He swallowed the bite he'd taken. "What do you mean by excessive?"

I looked him in the eye. "Is that a personal question or a general one?"

He didn't look away from me as he considered the question. A thousand things flashed through his eyes, hesitation and excitement, nerves and thrill, curiosity and desire.

"I feel like making it a personal question would be much more interesting," he said, his eyes staying on mine even though his voice went soft.

I couldn't help the smile that crept across my lips. "I don't know if I can answer that without you judging me, Professor."

His jaw twitched when I called him that, but he didn't say anything about it. "It's not my place to judge you. But your question boils down to what you feel is excessive."

"So does, like... eight seem excessive?"

"Eight what?"

"People."

"Not particularly."

"So far. This year. If you don't count the, um, people who sort of watched that one time."

A nervous laugh bubbled up from his chest. "Perhaps the question shouldn't be about the number but about the... content."

"Like what level of freakiness I get up to?"

"Something like that. There would be a lot of considerations, however. The level of freakiness, as you put it, but also the effect on your quality of life, the way you're finding yourself in these situations, the similarities and differences between partners and encounters, the general relationships you're having with these partners..."

"They're not really relationships. I'm not into the whole settling-down thing."

"I mean relationships in the context of how you relate to those people. A one-night stand is still a relationship by definition, though colloquially it wouldn't be a *relationship*, per se."

I dunked another fry in ketchup and considered what he'd said.

"I don't think it's particularly freaky," I said. "It's not like I've been letting people tie me up and put clothespins on my nipples or something."

Ben's face went red, but he kept his expression neutral. "And how would you say you find yourself in these situations? Is it something you plan ahead of time?"

I shrugged. "Like, I'll go out intending to find someone to hook up with, but sometimes the opportunity presents itself and I might end up leaving the bar with two people instead of one, you know?"

His lips pressed together, but he didn't comment on the blatant reference to when I'd seen him in Montreal. "When did you start having sexual encounters with people?"

"*First* started? About four or five years ago," I said. "I had a boyfriend in high school but we never did anything past, like, hand stuff. Well, and... mouth stuff."

"And when did you..." He trailed off, rolling his wrist in the air and letting the gesture finish the sentence for him. "For the first time?"

"Three years ago," I said.

"With the same—"

"No."

He nodded. "Was that a positive or a negative experience?"

Beneath the table, I used my fingernail to pick at the skin around my thumb. I couldn't help it. The way JP had fucked me, the feeling of his cock inside me, the way my legs had gone fucking *numb* because I came so hard—every moment of it was carved into the walls of my brain and no matter how many times I thought back on it, heat rushed through my body the same way. You would think after three years and a ton of other people fucking me, those memories would go dull, that they'd lose their appeal and their sparkle and I'd be able to think of that day without having to press my thighs together.

But you would think wrong.

"It was great," I said.

Ben's eyebrows twitched up, probably because like everyone, he assumed everyone's first time sucked. But he didn't comment or ask for details. "Would you say your need for sexual experiences is influencing your quality of life?"

I shook my head. "I might do it a lot, but it's not like if I don't get laid, I'm going to have a mental breakdown."

"That's, uh... a good sign." He cleared his throat. "Well, I can't speak specifically, of course, but nothing you've said is especially out-of-the-ordinary, at least at surface level. So as for the why—" He paused, pretending to think for a moment. "I'm going to have to stick with my original instinct and go with daddy issues."

I slumped in the chair. He laughed at my display, finishing the last bite of his sandwich as I straightened back up in my seat.

"I don't have daddy issues," I said. "My dad is a dick, and that's an issue, but it's not like... I'm not going out and trying to find someone who will fill a void."

"Thankfully, otherwise this would be even more awkward," he mumbled.

"What would be more awkward, Professor Cameron?" I blinked at him innocently but couldn't stop the grin that spread across my face.

"I believe you know, Nellie, and given that you do, I think calling me 'Professor Cameron' is a bit formal."

I hadn't expected him to outright say it. Neither had he, apparently, because he blinked as a heartbeat of electric tension surged around the table. But before either of us could break it, we were interrupted by the waiter coming by to clear our plates. Ben tore his eyes off me, taking the bill from the server and waving my hand away as he paid for both our meals. Still, I dug in my purse for enough cash to cover roughly the cost of my meal, shoving it towards him after the server walked away. Patiently, Ben slid it back across the table.

"I invited you to dinner," he said. "So I would like to pay for dinner."

I begrudgingly took the cash back and tucked it into my purse. "Okay. Thanks, Prof... Ben."

Once outside the bistro, there was one of *those* moments. A moment when the electricity settled over us again, making the question of what would happen next blossom. There was anticipation and doubt, exhilaration and fear, the knowledge that whatever happened in this moment would change both of us going forward.

And maybe it was just the way everything was. Maybe it was that I was torn up about other things in my life, feeling unsettled and uncertain about how the fuck I was going to handle all the things on the horizon. Maybe it was that I'd expected to be driving to Montreal right now to do something I hated and now I was unexpectedly free, which meant I could do what I wanted.

Whatever it was, I decided I was too impatient for *those* moments.

"So I live close by." I gestured in the general direction of my building. "Wanna come over and fuck?"

Chapter Nineteen
Would You Like Lube With That

I WAS SLIGHTLY WORRIED that Ben might go into actual shock.

He stared at me, a thousand things flashing across his face as his lips parted. I could guess what they were.

Surprise.

Desire.

Lust.

Ethical dilemmas.

Moral obligations.

The worry that I might actually be crazy battling with the hope that what they said about crazy chicks was true and the shame of having stereotypical thoughts like that in the first place.

It was hilarious as it was kind of endearing. I had no shame about going after what I wanted, but people like Ben didn't always think the same way that I did. Some people would be repulsed or horrified by the things I liked to do. Some would be intrigued in a way that was purely educational; they'd love to hear my stories but had no desire to try any of it themselves. And some would meet me at my level. Some would hear me say hey, let's make out while your friend has his hand under my skirt in the middle of a nightclub, and come along for the ride.

Or, well, *on* the ride, I guess.

But Ben wasn't any of those. He was the kind of person who would have listened with fascination as I told him about Jesse fingering me while Christian kissed me, almost embarrassed by how arousing he found the story. He was the kind of person who had never done anything especially deviant when it came to sex, but with the right person and motivation—aka "me" and "getting laid"—he'd try something crazy.

At least, that was what I'd thought. But after the myriad of emotions flashed across his face and reddened the light gold skin beneath the scattered scruff on his jaw, Ben shook his head.

"No," he said.

Oh.

Well then.

Shrugging, I smiled at him in a way I hoped he understood meant there were no hard feelings—because yeah, the rejection stung a little, but I *understood* why he'd say that—and slung my purse over my shoulder.

"Alright," I said. "Thanks for dinner, Ben."

I had barely turned to walk away when warm fingers circled my wrist.

"I mean," he said, his voice stronger than I'd expected. "I don't want to go to your place. And I don't—" He took a breath and when he spoke again, his voice was still strong, but there was a husky hoarseness that hadn't been there before. "'Fucking' doesn't describe what I want to do to you."

I turned my eyes up to his. The things I'd seen on his face before had faded until all that was left was a heavy, urgent desire in his eyes. Without even thinking about it, my eyes flicked down to his lips, lingering for half a moment before meeting his gaze again.

"What do you want to do to me?" I asked.

"Many things I shouldn't," he said.

"And is that going to stop you?"

His cheek twitched and a small smirk appeared on his lips. "I think the opportunity for me to stop myself disappeared when I decided to see if you were at work tonight instead of just texting you like I said I would."

I would've said the opportunity disappeared the moment he half-admitted to staring at my ass the last time he was at the restaurant, but it didn't matter.

What mattered was I didn't want him to stop.

I assumed that Ben not wanting to go to my apartment meant that he was going to take me to his place, but he didn't want to go there, either. Instead, he led me to a hotel a few blocks away from Byward Market. When we entered the lobby, I had to hold back a laugh. I mean, I had been pretty sure that Ben wasn't the kind of guy to bring me to a cheap motel that charged by the hour, but I hadn't expected him to lead me into a ritzy place where my server uniform and lack of luggage made it *very* clear what we were doing there.

"Would you like two queens or a king bed?" the clerk asked in an impassive voice as we checked in.

"Uh—" Ben said.

"A king's fine," I said.

"The only rooms with king beds left have the jacuzzi upgrade," she said, her voice still emotionless. "Is that alright?"

"Perfect," I said. "And do you sell condoms?"

Ben had picked the wrong moment to breathe, apparently, and choked on air. The clerk didn't so much as look up.

"The lobby store is behind you," she said. "If you go grab a pack, I can charge them to your room."

I turned cheerfully and went to the shelf of travel supplies and other various sundries they had in the lobby, grabbed an overpriced three-pack of condoms, and returned to the check-in counter before Ben had even caught his breath.

"These ones, please," I said.

"Would you like lube with that?" the clerk asked.

"Jesus Christ," Ben said under his breath. The clerk glanced up and it was only as she winked that I caught the twinkle hidden behind her practiced stoicism.

As hilarious as it was, it might have pushed things a bit too far for Ben. He second-guessed himself from the moment the clerk handed him the key cards to the moment I had to pluck one from his hand so we could unlock our room on the third floor. It took him a moment to cross the threshold and when the door clicked shut behind us, he stood almost pressed against it, hesitation drawn through every inch of his body.

"Nellie," he said before I even slid my shoes off. "If—"

"I wouldn't have literally asked you to come to my place and fuck if I didn't want to," I said.

"Let me say this to clear my conscience, at least," he said, his voice soft. "Please."

Now, I could be a brat, but I liked to think I wasn't a bad person. Quietly, I looked up at him from a respectable distance away. His eyes flicked up to mine and cleared his throat.

"I have never... I've never even *considered* doing this with a student before," he said. "Former or otherwise. I can sit here and justify all the reasons I shouldn't do this very articulately and yet for some reason, I still..." He sighed, shaking his head. "With you, I've been struggling not to give in and I... well. I am, clearly. Giving in. But I need you to understand that there is no... no *expectation* that you do this. You have received your grades. You've received your reference letter. There is nothing for you to gain by doing this and I do not want you to feel like you need to... to repay me. For that." He cleared his throat again. "If that's why you're here, we need to stop."

"What if I'm here because I literally just want to fu—"

"Please stop saying it like that," he said, his mouth twisting into an uncomfortable grimace. "That's not how I want this to be."

My red flags may have been different from most people's, but I still knew one when I saw one. "I said I'm not into dating anyone, Ben. At all. And last I checked, you counted as some kind of anyone. If you're expecting more than us messing around—"

"No," he said quickly. "Not at all. It's stupid enough for me to be doing *this*, let alone make it something more." He chuckled dryly. "Although, that does answer my next question."

"Which was...?"

"If you were expecting something more than a... a physical, er... experience."

It was a lot of words to say that he wanted to fuck and nothing more, but the wording didn't matter to me if it bothered Ben to think of it that way. I nodded and opened my mouth to say something, but before I could speak, Ben started talking again.

And then he kept talking.

And talking.

And *talking*.

I suppose it was one of those things that people didn't think about when they were coming up with sexy teacher/student fantasies. I sure as hell hadn't. Or maybe the uncertainty and need to justify what we were doing was specific to psychology professors. Either way, Ben had a *lot* to say before he would even consider proceeding.

I let him continue for a few minutes as he talked about what he expected and didn't expect, what I absolutely didn't owe him, how I could tell him to stop, and reassurance after reassurance that I was in complete control. Which was nice. And thoughtful. And comforting, even though I hadn't really needed any sort of comforting. But when he began a rambling justification of the ethics of what we were doing, not as a teacher and former student but as two humans in general, my ears felt like they'd glazed over and I'd had enough.

Not that I could get a word in edgewise. After I opening my mouth three times only for him to start talking again, I patiently put my purse on small desk against the wall, kicked off my shoes, and began unbuttoning my black uniform shirt.

"—which means you consenting *to* consent doesn't mean you can't withdraw said consent in a situation where..." He trailed off, staring at me. "What are you, uh, doing?"

I didn't respond, instead shrugging the shirt off my shoulders. Ben didn't say anything else until I lifted the black undershirt I was wearing over my head.

"Nellie," he breathed.

I wasn't hurrying, but the shirt had barely fallen to the floor when I unbuttoned my black dress pants. I pushed them down, wiggling from side to side so they slid down the curve of my hips and the thickness of my thighs. Once I'd stepped out of them and was left in my bra and panties, I looked up at Ben.

"Yeah, so I'm cool with all of this," I said. "If you can't talk yourself into kissing me, you can leave. I won't be offended. But I'm kinda turned on from, you know, picturing all this and the anticipation and stuff. So I'm gonna go check out that bed now and get myself off if you won't do it. So, uh... yeah. You do whatever you want."

I reached behind me, unhooked my bra, and let it join everything else on the floor. Just as I turned away, Ben stepped forward, fire blossoming in his eyes as he grabbed my shoulders and kissed me.

Fucking *finally*.

God, he was even more delicious than I'd hoped. I kissed him back eagerly, enjoying the softness of his mouth and the heat of his breath, melting against his chest as a hand moved from my shoulder to my chin. He notched it there for a moment, tilting my head up a hint more than it was before brushing his fingers against my cheek. He pushed back my hair, letting his hand trail down to the back of my neck, touching me like he was making sure I was real. As he moved his other hand to my side to pull me closer, I slipped my tongue in his mouth and he made a soft, groaning noise before flicking his against mine.

"Are you always this incorrigible, Nellie?" he murmured.

"Yes, Professor Cameron," I said.

He swore, the hand behind my neck tightening slightly. "Damn it. That... *damn* it. You shouldn't call me that."

"If you don't want me to call you that, then maybe you shouldn't be talking like a professor, Professor Cameron," I said.

His response was to bite down on my bottom lip. I kind of hoped he'd swat my ass playfully or something, but he pulled away and did something far, far better.

"Bed, Ms. Belanger," he demanded in that husky, hoarse voice. "Now."

Chapter Twenty
Are You Calling Me A Liar?

BEN WAS MY FAVOURITE kind of person to corrupt.

Not that I was actively corrupting him. Or at least, not maliciously. It wasn't like I'd gone out of my way to seduce him or something.

At least, not before knowing with an almost utmost certainty that he was hoping to be seduced and corrupted.

And I guess I wasn't really *corrupting* him. If anything, I was coaxing out a thing that had been there all along, helping him dig past the slightly awkward professor who was heavily concerned with the ethics of it all and liberate the semi-feral man beneath.

Because oh *God*, was that semi-feral man begging to be let out in the best possible way.

The point was, Ben was entirely open to being seduced or corrupted or whatever you wanted to call it. And I liked that. Like, yeah, I'd liked him before. He'd been my favourite professor for a reason other than how hot he was.

But I liked some new things about him now. Like the way his breath felt against my skin when he captured my mouth with his. The way he used his hips to guide me towards the bed. The way he stopped and made me get the overpriced condoms out of my purse before we continued, and when I joked that he was going to have to warm me up a little before he could use one of them, he sank his teeth into my lip again.

"I'm very aware of that, Nellie," he murmured, punctuating it with a little tug that made me whimper. "But once I have you begging me to be inside you, I'd like to not have to stop what I'm doing to dig these out."

And like, yeah, I'd already taken the first few steps down the path of being ready for that, but the low rasp of his voice when he said that got me a *lot* closer to being warmed up.

When we finally made it across the room, I put a hand on his chest before he could push me down on the bed. His hands fell away from where they'd been resting on my hips, surrendering control of the situation to me the moment I'd hinted that I wanted it.

And God, I liked that, too.

"Sit," I whispered, nudging him towards the edge of the bed.

He did so, not with any sort of eager-to-please submissiveness but a sort of respectful obedience, his eyes trained up on mine as he waited for me to make the next move.

Which I did. Gladly.

His knees parted so I could stand between them, my hands resting on his shoulders as I dipped down to kiss him again. A contented sigh brushed against my mouth accompanied by feather-light fingertips grazing my thighs and hips. That was the only noise he made, though. A few moments earlier, I wasn't sure that Ben would ever shut up. Now, he was nearly silent as I moved my hands from his shoulders to the front of his blazer and slipped them beneath so I could guide it down his arms.

He stayed quiet and still as I stopped kissing him so I could take off his shirt, watching as I worked the buttons open one by one. But even though I could almost feel the heat of his gaze, I didn't meet his eyes. I was having far too much fun looking over every inch of his body as I revealed it.

And God, was he hot.

Ben's hair might have had a streak of grey and occasional fleck of salt scattered throughout the darkness, but the smattering of hair on his chest was all a lighter shade of brown. His body wasn't especially toned or muscular, but there was strength beneath the delightful softness of his stomach. Once his shirt was unbuttoned, I laid my palm against his chest, indulging in the feel of his skin before trailing my hand down lower and lower.

He still didn't speak as I unbuckled his belt or unbuttoned his jeans. It wasn't until I ran my fingers over the bulge tenting the denim fabric that he made another noise, and only when I carefully undid the zipper that he finally said something.

"Nellie," he said, and his hand circled my wrist, stilling my movements.

"Yes, Professor?"

His hand tightened and his eyes narrowed. I tried to look innocent, but failed as a laugh escaped my lips.

"Yes, Ben?" I said.

"If you don't want to—"

"How many times do I have to say I wouldn't be here if I didn't want to fu—"

"This is the last time I'll ask," he said. "Because if you're not sure, if you—" He shook his head, then cleared his throat. "I'm not going to ask again. I'm not sure I'm going to be able to *stop* to ask again. I want to be sure you will stop if that's what you want."

I twisted my wrist beneath his grip so I could take his hand in mine. Without a word, I put my palm on the back of his hand, pressing it to my stomach and guiding it down my belly. Ben inhaled sharply as I pushed his hand past the waistband of my panties, held it to my mound, then nudged his finger until it was against my slit so he could feel the wetness collecting there.

"Ben," I said, not faking the breathiness in my voice. "I'm really, *really* sure this is what I want."

He made an incomprehensible noise, then cleared his throat.

"Okay," he said hoarsely. "Alright. You may proceed."

"Thank you, Professor Cameron," I said.

He groaned. "You can't—"

"I didn't mean to that time."

"You understand it's a key part of my success as a forensic psychologist that I can tell when people are lying to me, right?"

I smirked as I guided his hand out of my panties. "Are you calling me a liar?"

"Are you lying to me?"

"Yes."

He laughed, but before he could say anything else, I leaned down and kissed him again as I returned to the task at hand, which was to take his pants off so I could see his very hard, very swollen cock.

And I mean *very* hard. And swollen. And *thick*.

There was already pre-cum leaking from his tip, a bead of it glistening on his tip. I licked my lips unconsciously. His cock twitched as I checked him out and when I looked back up at Ben, he was watching me with an almost nervous expression on his face.

"Nice," I said.

He laughed again, but it turned to a groan almost instantly. Probably because I wrapped my fingers around his shaft and stroked, slowly but firmly. His cock throbbed beneath my palm as I squeezed lightly before letting go and placing a hand on each of his thighs.

"What are you—" he started, then let out a soft "*Oh*" as I lowered myself to my knees.

He tried to restrain his hips from jerking forward, but still tensed as I opened my mouth and took the head of his cock into it. A sharp inhale made his chest rise only to fall a moment later as I pushed my head down further on his shaft and he exhaled heavily. With an almost lazy sort of leisure, I took more of him, then more, my eyes still on his until the tip of his cock hit the back of my throat.

Then I took a deep breath, relaxed my throat as much as I could, and proceeded to swallow until I had my nose pressed against the dark curls on his pelvis.

"Oh, *God*," Ben groaned, his thighs clenching beneath my palms.

I pulled back and did it again, moving deliberately and carefully so I could savour the feel of each ridge and bump against my tongue. It was only once I'd bobbed my head a few times that Ben's hand found the back of my head, stopping me while his cock was buried as deep in my throat as I could get it.

"Please," he gasped. "Let me just... you can't imagine how you look with my—" He cut himself off with a gasp. "Give me a moment to commit this to memory."

When his hand left the back of my head, lingering just long enough that I knew he wasn't quite ready to let the image go, I kept bobbing my head. Ben groaned again and let me develop a rhythm, slightly faster, as I swallowed him over and over. Again that hand ended up on my head, just resting this time, and only tightening when he stopped me with that same reluctant linger.

"What's wrong?" I asked after he pulled out of my mouth.

"Overall, the entire morality of this situation," he said.

"Yeah, but why'd you stop me?"

A smile spread across his lips. "Because you have a wonderful mouth and after all the internal struggling I've done about it, I don't intend to let the aforementioned situation end so quickly." He took my hand, pulling me up from my knees. "I have *barely* gotten to touch you yet."

"That seems unfair."

He pulled me in for a kiss. "Horrendously unfair."

Before I even got onto the bed, Ben had explored my breasts and stomach and hips with his hands. Then he gave his lips a turn, nuzzling his face against my breasts and slipping his hands slipped behind me so he could caress my ass. I had a fleeting thought of what Syd and I had talked about, but I didn't say anything about it. I mean, if he did want to fuck me in the ass, that'd be great, but I wanted to at least see what he was like during a semi-normal hookup before asking for that.

Plus, given the hesitancy that had plagued him on and off throughout the entire encounter, I didn't want to risk pushing him too far and having him call the whole thing off. Especially not when he'd just flicked his tongue across my nipple before taking it into his mouth and sucking and oh *God* did that feel good.

Though, I might not have had to worry about the hesitancy thing. Any trace of that seemed to have faded. Or maybe things other than Ben's brain were now in charge of him.

Like his dick.

Or his hands.

They seemed to have a mind of their own, those hands, and that mind was *damn* talented. It was almost surreal how he could pinpoint the most sensitive spots on my body and instinctively know how to touch those spots to make me shiver. One moment, I was squirming as he feathered his fingertips along my lower back; the next, I was gasping as he pushed his hands into the back of my panties so he could cup my squeeze my bare ass. My whole body tingled under his touch, snakes of heated arousal stemming from his fingers through my nerves, all centering on the one part of my body he hadn't touched yet.

"Ben," I finally gasped when I couldn't take it anymore.

"Mmm," came the muffled grunt of a response, my nipple still in his mouth and his nose digging into the soft swell of my breast.

"Ben, please," I asked, squirming in his arms. "I need more."

I felt his lips curl up into a smile. Well, a pseudo-smile. As much of a smile as he could manage with what felt like half my tit in his mouth. He took one hand off my ass and moved it up so he could tug my panties down. He didn't bother taking them all the way off, just let the fabric bunch and gather until he could nestle it beneath my ass cheeks, then moved his hands to the front of my body.

I tensed in anticipation, waiting for him to slip his hand between my legs, but he paused with a hand on each of my hips. When it became clear he wasn't moving them any farther, I whimpered and a puff of laughter vibrated against my breast.

"Come on," I whined.

"Patience," he murmured, pressing a kiss to the tip of my nipple.

I grumbled in frustration. He knew how wet I was. He'd felt it. Wetness had probably already leaked past my panties and started staining my inner thigh. "I think I've been patient enough already."

"Of course you have." He pulled his face away from my breasts, an impish sparkle in his eyes. "Now you need to be a little more patient."

I glared at him for a moment, but only a moment. It was quickly replaced by a smirk of my own.

"Well," I said, pulling away. "I *did* say I'd get myself off if you wouldn't, so—"

My words clipped into a sudden squeal as Ben grabbed me. Before I knew what was happening, he'd stood, twisted out from between me and the bed, and casually pushed me onto it. A laugh burst out as I landed on my back, but before I could so much as sit up, Ben was on top of me, brushing a strand of hair off my face as the rest of it fanned beneath me on the pillow.

"Not. A. Fucking. Chance," he growled, then kissed me hard.

Chapter Twenty-One
Yes, Professor Cameron

Nothing Ben had done so far had scared me, but when his cock pressed against my pussy with only the tangled fabric of my panties between us, I tensed.

"Ben," I gasped. "C-Condom. Please."

Something in my tone must have flagged his attention. The growl in his voice dropped as he brought a hand to my cheek, caressing it and looking into my eyes.

"Of course," he said, his voice soothing. "I would never... I wouldn't do that. I promise."

Some of the nervousness evaporated and I let my shoulders relax. "Okay."

"But we're not there yet."

I blinked at him, stunned. "What? But I said—"

"And I said *patience*, Nellie." He dipped down and kissed me, nipping at my lip. "It's my turn to taste you."

And oh, *God*.

It was almost mesmerizing to watch him. The change from teasing torment to awe-inspired worship was both gradual and not; one moment, I was whimpering and squirming and ready to beg for more *again*. The next, Ben's body was practically prone on the bed, his hands on my hips and his head pressed to my core and his lungs inhaling my scent as he took a deep breath that released into a longing groan.

"Nellie," he murmured. "My God."

"I believe it would be God*dess*, actually," I said.

His chuckle vibrated against my still-covered mound. "My incorrigible goddess."

And that...

That was concerning.

Not because he said anything wrong.

But because I liked hearing him call me *his* a bit more than I should have.

Before I could think about it too much, Ben's hands started moving again. He slid my panties off in one smooth movement, pausing for only a moment once my pussy was revealed to let out another appreciative noise.

"This is lovely," he murmured, and his fingers traced the edges of the trimmed triangle of hair on my mound.

"Not into the bare look?"

"No." He dipped his head down, pressing a kiss against it. "Not that it's ever up to me since it is very much *your* body, but I'm not especially into women who appear to be barely past eighteen. Even if you, ah, somewhat are."

"I am not," I said. "I'm twenty-one."

There was an odd incredulity in the way he shook his head, but he didn't say anything. Instead, he put a hand on either side of my folds, spread them apart, then glanced up at me. His hair was askew, his face stoic, his eyes practically glazed with need. A moment later, he brought his head down again and slid his tongue between my lips. He paused again, groaned, and a moment after that, I was having my pussy eaten in a way I'd never experienced.

At the same time he feasted on it, he savoured it. Each flick of his tongue was intentional; each kiss was purposeful; each deep breath before burying his face as deep as he could was life-changing. There was no question that what he was doing was for my pleasure, but it was beyond clear he was enjoying every second himself, a genuine zeal that manifested as pure adulation towards my body.

I kept my eyes on him until he pushed a finger inside of me, thrusting it deep but at a slow, leisurely pace. That was when my eyes rolled back, followed a few moments later by my head tilting back as the pad of his finger found my g-spot.

"Ben," I whispered. "I'm getting close."

He moaned.

He fucking moaned against my pussy.

My legs started to shake, but as soon as I began chasing that ascent to orgasm, Ben slowed his movements. It wasn't much, barely enough to be perceptible, but both the tongue on my clit and the finger inside me stilled for long enough to make my body tense. As soon as I clenched around him, he moved again, making it clear he wasn't teasing me or denying me or... I don't know.

I don't know what to call what he was doing, but it was fucking phenomenal.

I clutched at his hair, pulling his head close to my core as he held his pace steady, though slow. He had one hand pressed to my hip, holding me down and preventing me from pushing up towards his face, though I was aching to do so.

"Ben," I gasped again. "Ben, I'm gonna come."

The muffled noise he made might have been a moan or it might have been a word; I couldn't tell. More importantly, it didn't fucking matter. Ben slowed his movements again and I cried out in frustration, struggling to writhe under his grip.

He didn't let go of my hip until my breath started to come in quick, desperate bursts that were dangerously close to sobs. As soon as he did, I curled forward without thought, pushing my pussy hard against his face and tightening my thighs like my body was afraid he'd stop what he was doing again.

But he didn't stop, and a second later, my body surrendered completely.

It wasn't like any orgasm I'd ever had. It wasn't a sudden burst of ecstasy or an overwhelming explosion. It was like I *sank* into it, like I felt each and every nerve firing out its share of my pleasure. My toes curled, then pointed; my legs quivered around his head as the dam that had been holding back my orgasm collapsed, drawing out the intensity and letting it build and build and *build* until I was writhing beneath Ben, crying out as he tormented my clit with his tongue.

It wasn't until the writhing turned from uncontrollable into an attempt to escape the movement of his mouth that he stopped, ensuring he'd squeezed out each tiny aftershock of my orgasm before he pulled away. When he looked up, his whole face was shining: his eyes and his smile as he grinned up at me, and his lips and chin from the wetness he hadn't been able to lap up from between my legs.

"How *dare* you?" I panted.

"How dare I what?" he repeated, amused.

"How dare you—" I groaned, resting back on the pillow. "How dare you be so fucking good at that?"

He chuckled. "Years of experience. Isabelle *did* marry me for a reason, you know."

A breathless laugh escaped my lips and I reached for him, urging him forward until he was hovering over me. He stooped his head down so he could plant warm and attentive kisses on my mouth.

For a while, I basked in the cozy protectiveness of his body, my orgasm-hazed mind content to recover in the bubble of his arms and lips.

But it wasn't long before those kisses started deepening again, and not long after that when the achy spot deep in my core started begging for another round of attention.

"Ben," I murmured against his mouth.

"Condom?"

Ben hmm'ed in agreement, sitting back and reaching for the box of condoms we'd set on the nightstand. "How would you like to—"

He didn't even finish before I was on my hands and knees. He chuckled, raising his eyebrows. "Like this?"

"I like it like this." I looked over my shoulder at him and smiled before wiggling my hips suggestively. "Don't you?"

Given the speed at which he ended up behind me, nudging my legs apart so he could line his cock up with my pussy, I imagined he did.

"Nellie," he breathed as the tip of his cock brushed against my entrance. "This is the last chance to—"

"I haven't changed my mind," I interrupted. "Now would you *please* stick your cock in me, Professor Cam—I mean, Ben?"

I hadn't meant to call him it that time.

Really, I hadn't.

But it didn't matter. I doubt he heard me correct myself.

"For *fucks'* sake!" he growled, but it wasn't in anger. It couldn't have been, not when his fingers dug into my hips and a whimper burst out of my lips as he shoved the tip of his cock inside me.

"Fuck," he breathed again. "*Fuck.* I—"

And then he mumbled something not quite loud enough for me to hear.

"What was that, Professor?" I asked innocently.

He groaned again, his hands tightening on my hips. "You—I... you can't *call* me that when I'm..."

"It sounds like you kind of like it."

"It's the hottest thing I've ever heard in my life," he said. "And that... that's not... I'm inside you and this is *already* so wrong and I—"

I rolled my eyes and pushed my ass back, trying to get more of him inside me. "Stop overthinking, Professor. It's okay to like it. *I* like it."

"Nellie—"

"Would you please just fuck me, Professor Cameron? Please just fu—"

I didn't get the rest of the word out. Well, I did, but it wasn't as a word. It was a cry, a moan, a victorious burst of air as Ben finally let out the semi-feral part of him that was desperate for this. He shoved his cock the rest of the way in and held us there for a moment, almost certainly leaving bruises on my hips as he ground his cock as deep inside me as he could. My ass pressed tight against his pelvis and he groaned, then pulled out before spearing himself back in me again.

Hard.

"Oh, *yes*, Professor," I squeaked, and he practically roared.

"God fucking *damn* it," he spat.

His hands left my hips and there was a whirlwind moment of adjustment, but it didn't take long before Ben had positioned me the way he wanted me. His legs ended up outside of mine, his cock stretching me wide open again. One hand had snaked around to my clit and was fingering it mercilessly while the other wrapped around my ribs, gripping my breast hard.

And his lips—fuck.

His lips were right next to my ear.

"Is this what you want, Ms. Belanger?" he growled into my ear. "Is this what you were pushing me to do?"

"Yes," I gasped.

He drove into me hard, his breath hot against me as he pumped his hips forward.

"Say it again," he grunted.

"*Yes*, Professor Cameron," I repeated, and he let out another wild, almost feral noise as his hips slapped against my ass.

And I was grinning.

How could I not? Ben Cameron, the mostly-mild-mannered psychology professor who knew better than anyone why he'd get off on me screaming out for him to "fuck me, Professor, fuck me harder," was currently doing said fucking and he was really, really good at it. He was letting loose on me, using me as much as he was doing this *for* me, indulging in my body as much as he was indulging me in this absolute fantasy.

My next orgasm was going to be the explosive, intense kind. I knew that even as it built up. There was no way Ben was going to slow down, to draw it out of me, to torment me with slow, purposeful movements as I teetered over the edge.

And I wasn't going to be falling over that edge alone.

"I'm close," I whispered. "I'm so close."

"Come for me," he demanded, his breath hot against my neck. "Come *on* me, Ms. Belanger."

"P-Professor Cameron," I gasped. "I'm gonna—"

And we both shattered.

My pussy gripped his cock as I cried out my bliss, but those cries were drowned out by the sound of Ben groaning. His fingers dug into my breast, his cock buried as deep as it could go as he came. A steady stream of nonsense blurted from my mouth, my vision flashing with white stars, and my breath barely within reach as I finished and slumped forward in his arms.

The sound of us panting for breath filled the room for a moment before his grip on me loosened. He gave me time to find my arms beneath me before pulling out and sitting back on his knees, watching wordlessly as I lay on my stomach before rolling to my side and stretching.

"Damn, Ben," I murmured.

He chuckled a bit, face red, still catching his breath. "I, uh... that was..."

"Hot."

"Yes." He sighed and collapsed next to me on the bed. "That was so fucking hot."

Chapter Twenty-Two
Choices

"Oh good, you're not dead."

I dropped my work bag and hurled my keys in the general direction of the voice. They missed their target completely, partly because I threw them without looking and mostly because the voice had come from the couch in my living room on the other side of my apartment. Despite having an open concept, the couch was tucked behind a little three-foot-wide wall that framed the opening of said living room.

So I guess I didn't miss my target completely, since if the wall hadn't been there, my bundle of keys would have nailed Sydney on the forehead instead of clattering to the floor with a loud jangle.

"*What* are you doing in here?" I gasped, my heart in my throat as she started cackling with laughter so uncontrolled, she slid off the couch and onto the living room floor.

"I figured you weren't home from your fuckfest with Professor Sexy yet, so I used your spare key to get in," she said once her giggles subsided enough to speak.

"And why—"

"Because Reid's got Alison over again." There was no humour left in her voice when she said that.

"Ah." I kicked my shoes off and closed the door of my apartment behind me. "Have you tried telling him it bothers you?"

"It doesn't *bother* me."

"Syd."

She glared at me. "She sounds like a mouse got caught in an unoiled door hinge when she comes, Nell. For the sake of my eardrums, I needed to get out of there."

I thought it was probably more for the sake of her unrequited feelings for Reid but didn't say that. Nor did I remind her that earplugs existed or that she owned a set of noise-cancelling headphones. "Fair enough."

She bent down and picked up my keys. "So?"

I yawned. "So what?"

"*So*?!" she repeated. "I want details. I haven't heard from you since Friday when I got a text literally saying 'Guess who just eggplant-emojied-peach-emojied-water-spray-emojied Professor Sexy?'"

"That's not true," I said. "I replied to your reply."

She gave me an unimpressed look. "Your reply was 'Will share details later' because you were spending the night at a hotel with him. And it's now *later*, Nell, and I haven't heard fuck-all yet."

"Yeah, well, I wasn't about to put the details in writing." I yawned again as I started emptying stuff out of my work bag. "Besides, my phone died. It wasn't like I brought a charger to work on Friday thinking I was gonna spend the weekend getting fucked by my former psychology professor."

She squealed in a way I imagined was reminiscent of how Alison sounded when Reid made her come and clapped her hands together. "So you really did it?"

I nodded, taking my dead phone out of my bag and crossing to the kitchen counter so I could plug it in. "I really did it."

"And...?"

"And what?"

Sydney let out an aggravated noise. "How did it come up? Was it good? Did you ask him to put it in your butt? *Did* he put it in your butt? How many times did he put it in your butt?!"

I snorted back a laugh as I turned, leaning back on the counter. "Well, he came into the restaurant on Friday when I was about to leave and we ended up grabbing dinner together at Cool Eats and then I asked if he wanted to fuck. Yes, it was good. Yes, I asked him to put it in my butt." I sighed heavily. "No, he didn't put it in my butt."

"What?!" Sydney asked, offended. "Why not?!"

"He didn't want to."

"He didn't *want*—"

"Apparently anal doesn't do it for him." I shrugged. "Aside from the occasional cheek squeeze, he's not into butt stuff at all."

"Oh." She looked put-out. "Well... I guess no one can be totally perfect."

I smirked. "Maybe not, but when it comes to his tongue... and his fingers... and his *dick*..."

She drummed her hands on her thighs. "Seriously, stop stalling. Tell me *everything*."

I didn't tell her everything.

I told her most things. Like the whole calling him "Professor" thing lost its appeal pretty quickly.

I liked to think it was because that first fuck was so intense that we both knew we couldn't live up to it. I could call him Professor Cameron eighty thousand more times in various states of undress, redress, bent over a desk, perched on the edge of a jacuzzi, leg propped up on his shoulder in the shower as he marvelled at my flexibility, and it would have been hot, yes.

But it wouldn't be the same as the moment it slipped out of my mouth when he first slid inside me. It was like after smashing through that wall of self-control Ben had been valiantly trying to hold up and letting both of us indulge in the forbidden thrill of what we were doing, the novelty of it wore off.

That was only part of it, though. The rest of it was because of how Ben treated me.

Because he didn't treat me like he was my professor.

He wasn't, not anymore, and wouldn't be again. Not for the rest of my undergrad, for sure, and it wasn't like my career plans included much more in the way of forensic psychology.

And yes, that dynamic of him being my teacher could have remained. I had countless other professors or teachers who would never be anything other than Mr. or Mrs. So-and-So or Doctor Whoever or Coach McCoachFace. But they'd only ever be those things because they would never see me as anything but their student.

Ben, on the other hand, made me feel like I was so much more than that.

He didn't talk down to me. He didn't assume he knew better than I did. He listened when I spoke, lips pressed together thoughtfully as he considered what I said. We'd spent hours in the jacuzzi that weekend, talking about anything and everything, and he'd worn that contemplative look countless times as I shared everything from my career plans to my opinions on different professors I'd had during my undergrad to which Olympic sports sounded the most fake.

I told Sydney about all of that. And I told her about how I hadn't put so much as a single sock on my body after I'd undressed Friday night. How we'd fucked again Friday night and then I'd woken up in the bed next to Ben the next morning. How we'd used the last condom in the three-pack, both of us assuming it was the last time before we finished and Ben had unassumingly asked what my plans for the rest of the weekend were.

"Nothing," I said. "I was supposed to go to Montreal to see my dad again but that, uh... fell through."

"Is that so?" he said.

"Mm-hmm."

"So you're not in a rush to, ah, check out or—"

"Nope."

So while I fell back into a light doze, he got dressed and slipped out of the room to extend our stay for another night and go to the drugstore down the street, which apparently sold twelve packs of condoms for the same price as the three-pack they sold in the hotel lobby.

The thing I hadn't told her about was what Ben had said to me that morning.

Because like, yeah, I might have liked Ben as a person. He might have been a god in bed who worshiped my entire body. It might have been one of the most fun weekends of my life.

But even if I did relationships—which I didn't—and even if he'd been interested in making this whole thing something more than physical—which he wasn't—there was no realistic situation where Ben and I could be together romantically.

Oh, sure, books and movies and countless Wattpad romances would say otherwise because there was always that *one* situation that was different. Where he'd get to keep his job as a psychology professor with no questions or qualms because *technically* I wasn't his student anymore. Where all our friends and family members would be unexpectedly cool with him dating a woman who was starting kindergarten when he started dating his ex-wife.

That wasn't the case in reality. Or at least, it wouldn't be the case in our reality. Ben knew damn well there would be fallout if people found out we'd hooked up.

"I might be on sabbatical, but I'm still a university employee," he'd said as we lay in bed that morning before checking out. "And you are an actively enrolled student. And technicalities don't matter when it comes to public image."

"You don't have to worry," I'd said. "I won't tell anyone."

The words had come out nonchalantly. I'd barely noticed myself saying it, not because it was one of those impulsive things that came out because the words had snuck past my thoughts and out my lips, but because it seemed so inconsequential.

But Ben had looked at me, a half-smile on his lips, and shook his head.

"I'm not asking you not to, Nellie," he said.

I frowned. "What?"

"I'm not and will not ever ask you not to tell anyone about this."

"But... I mean, what about...?"

He twisted a lock of my hair between his fingertips. "It was my choice to walk into this room, despite knowing damn well that I shouldn't. And the only way I could let myself do that was by being entirely prepared to accept the consequences of my actions. Because not telling anyone... that is not my choice." His fingertips trailed down my cheek. "It's yours. I may have given in. I may have crossed infinitely too many lines this weekend. But that is one I won't cross. You owe me nothing and I won't hold this over you."

My heartbeat did something weird. Something fluttery. "What about your job, though? Like... you'd get in trouble."

"That's not your concern."

"But it is."

"It isn't. Or at least, it *shouldn't* be, so please don't make it your concern." He smiled. "Do I hope I can continue my career as it is? Yes, of course. But not at the cost of you feeling forced into silence."

I'd kissed him.

Because I just...

I had to.

I wanted to.

But that was something I wanted to keep for myself, at least for now. Which is why I didn't tell Sydney about it.

"God, you are the luckiest person alive," she sighed as I finished reliving the weekend for her. "When are you seeing him again? Like, this is going to be a thing for you, right? Because I swear to God if you say it was a one-weekend thing, I'm going to take you to a different psychologist. Mainly so you're distracted when I go after Professor Sexy myself."

I laughed. "I mean, we talked about being fuck buddies for the summer. Ben prefers the term friends-with-benefits because he has some aversion to calling fucking 'fucking.'"

"Just the summer?" she asked, looking disappointed. "Like yeah, he's on sabbatical next year, but couldn't you just... you know?"

I shook my head. "He's doing a research study at Stanford during his sabbatical, remember? So he's moving to California at the end of August."

"But you *are* going to see him over the summer?"

"He definitely seems—"

And then my phone distracted me by exploding.

With noise, I mean. It started vibrating and chiming incessantly from the counter as the battery charged enough for it to restart. Which shouldn't have been as distracting as it was, but that was a *lot* of notifications, even for me.

"Damn, Ms. Popular," Sydney said as I picked up my phone. "How many people were trying to get a hold of you while Professor Sexy was dicking you down?"

I opened my mouth to respond, then almost choked on the air. "No."

"What?" Sydney asked, alarmed.

"Oh, *no*," I whispered.

Because yeah, a few different people had tried to reach me. There were my mom's nightly messages of *Good night, Daughter of Mine. Love you.* A few emails, a couple of social media comments, and a missed call from my dad.

But that wasn't what was making my stomach crawl.

No, that was caused by the eighteen missed calls from Nigel.

And the single text message.

Nigel Bossy Pants

Unless you've literally been kidnapped by some masochist who wants to deal with a spoiled rotten princess, consider this both your termination notice and a trespass notice. If you set foot in this restaurant again, your ass is getting kicked out.

"Nellie?" Sydney said. "What's wrong?"

And what the hell was I supposed to say?

How the hell was I supposed to say that I told Nigel I'd work this weekend so I could have a different weekend off to go visit my mom?

That I'd been so into my weekend with Ben that I'd forgotten to go to work?

That my dad had called and offered a deal—not a particularly good one, but a deal all the same—and I'd turned it down?

That even though the money I made at the restaurant wouldn't have been anywhere near enough to cover all the things I needed it to, I *needed* the money now?

How was I supposed to tell her I'd done something so embarrassingly fucking stupid?

"Nothing," I said, shaking my head. "My dad called. And I... I don't know if I want to hear whatever it is he has to say."

She nodded sympathetically. "Do you want me to stick around while you call him back?"

I shook my head.

Because even if I'd told her about the second call from my dad or what he'd offered, it wasn't like Sydney would understand. Even having met my dad, she didn't *get* it. No one did, not really. He never seemed as bad to other people as he did to me.

Except my mom, that is.

But it wasn't like I could talk to her about this. I mean, God. I could imagine the look on her face if I admitted I'd let my dad pay for my degree.

"He *owns* that now, Nellie," she'd say. "He owns your education. And you *know* your father is a man who keeps meticulous records of the things he *owns*."

But that was the choice I'd made. I might not have understood what I was choosing back when I asked him for help with school, but I'd made the choice all the same.

Just like I'd made the choice to spend the weekend fucking Ben instead of going to work.

Because it had to be a choice. Who... what kind of shitty person fucking *forgets* to go to work?

I would've rather it been a choice.

After Sydney left a while later, I showered and washed my hair, then toyed with the idea of faking a kidnapping so Nigel would un-fire me a bit more seriously than I probably should have. Once I'd convinced myself that a fake kidnapping would have serious career repercussions when it was inevitably discovered because the downfall of most murderers and serial killers is the narcissistic audacity to think they've covered all their bases when that's literally impossible, I sighed and grabbed my phone.

Slowly wandering to the living room, I replied to every other message I could. I checked each of my social media profiles and sent a bunch of heart emojis to my mom and a short message about how I'd left my phone at a friend's place and had only just been able to pick it up, which she believed because it wouldn't have been the first time that had happened.

Then I brought up my messages and sent one to Ben thanking him for the amazing weekend and telling him I wasn't going to be working at the restaurant anymore.

Once I couldn't procrastinate any longer, I took a deep breath, let it out, and called my dad back.

"Eleanor," he said when he picked up. "I was beginning to worry, *ma fille ange.*"

"It's Nellie, Dad," I said tiredly. "And I was busy working this weekend."

"Working," he repeated. "Despite your original plans to be here for the weekend?"

"I, um, picked up some extra shifts," I said.

"Even when *busy*, you should understand how to prioritize."

"I do," I said, trying not to clench my teeth. "And that was part of why I was calling, actually."

My dad was silent for a moment, like he was recalculating, reprocessing, rebooting like the machine he was, and figuring out how to respond to something he hadn't expected me to say.

"I assumed you were calling in response to my message," he said.

"Uh..."

"You *did* listen to the message."

He said it like it was fact, knowing that it wasn't. I fidgeted, picking at the skin around my thumbnail.

"I didn't," I said. "But only because I wanted to tell you something as soon as possible. So I just... called."

"And what is it you wanted so badly to tell me?"

I took as deep of a breath as I could while keeping it silent.

"So, I was thinking about what you said," I started. "When we last talked."

"Any particular thing I said, or in general?" he asked.

I picked at my thumb again, digging my index fingernail in almost painfully before flicking it up. "A bit of both."

"I see."

Fuck, I was going to puke.

"I was thinking about what you said about... networking," I said. "And how that would be a better use of my time for my career."

His tone took on a hint of amusement as he seemed to realize what I was saying. "Is that so?"

My eyes started to sting and I slammed them shut. "Yeah. You... you're... you were *right*, Dad."

"Thank you, Nellie."

"So I was hoping that maybe you would consider, um, letting me attend some of the events you and Kimberlee are going to this summer."

"I thought you were too busy to attend these events," he said. "Because of your *job*."

"Well, that's, um—" I almost coughed, though it might have been a gag. "I decided that this would be my last weekend working there. Because I wanted to show you how serious I am about this."

"Oh, *ma fille ange*," he said, his voice so warm and pleasant, he almost sounded like he actually cared. "That is wonderful news. Of course we can arrange for you to attend. Happily."

I swallowed hard. "Thank you. And, um... I was hoping..."

"Hoping what?"

The stinging in my eyes turned wet and I squeezed closed even tighter. "Well, since I decided not to work at the restaurant, I... I'm not getting paid anymore."

I think he was waiting for me to outright ask, but I couldn't force the words from my lips. He let me suffer in awkwardness for a few moments before chuckling.

"You know I'll take care of you, darling girl," he said.

"Thank y—"

"However."

Fuck.

"The original conditions for your tuition and allowance payments to resume were that you would attend *Mosaic de Montreal* with Clinton Thibault, attendance at additional events, and to sit for the LSAT," my dad said. "Clearly, the opportunity to attend *Mosaic de Montreal* has passed, but if you'd listened to your voicemail, you would know I thought perhaps you could attend the luncheon the Marchands are hosting this weekend prior to the evening gala for the library. It is sold out, but I am sure I can find an additional ticket for you to attend that as well."

"Okay," I said.

"With Clinton. If that was not clear."

"Yes, it was."

"But I understand that *ma fille ange* is not a fan of Mr. Thibault," he said. "So for the additional events this summer, I will simply ask that if you cannot find your own date, you will attend with Clinton again. Does that seem reasonable?"

I blinked. It was surprisingly reasonable, actually. For my dad, at least. It was almost... almost *human* of him. "Yes. That—"

"Good. And finally, you will sit for the LSAT."

Fuck.

"I really don't want—"

"You can speak to Jean-Luc this weekend about the course his colleague runs," my dad continued.

"But—"

"The most important thing you should take away from this, Nellie, is that you should always have a backup plan," he said, his voice firm. "And if I cannot convince you that law school is a good choice for you, at the very least, you can acknowledge that it is an excellent backup plan."

I thought the most important thing to take away was that lying was wrong, but that was what my mom would've said. Not my dad.

"Dad, please," I asked, hoping my voice was soft enough that he couldn't tell I was about to cry. "I don't want to."

"It is not about what you want, Eleanor. It's about what's best for you."

When I hung up from my dad, I sat there for another few minutes, trying to let my stomach settle. My eyes were closed when my phone vibrated with what I assumed was a notification of my dad transferring me the money he'd promised to send after I agreed to take the LSAT, but when it vibrated again a few moments later, I looked down at it.

Professor Sexy

> Well, that won't do.

Professor Sexy

> Where am I supposed to get the special sauce for my chicken strips if you aren't at the restaurant anymore?

I bit back a smile. Even when texting, I could hear the cadence of Ben's voice, and somehow, that made everything feel just a bit better.

Me

> Well I GUESS you could always come over to my place and I could share the recipe... Tuesday?

Professor Sexy

> I'll pick up some chicken strips on the way.

Chapter Twenty-Three
Might Isn't Good Enough

My mom's advice for not getting kidnapped was unquestionably logical.

However, like many things she said, it was also slightly insane.

"If you can't run, turn around and dance," she told me one day.

"What?" I'd asked, because she'd said it out of nowhere while we were sitting on a bus in Toronto one day when I was twelve or thirteen.

"If you're being kidnapped and you can't get away, dance," she repeated. "All you have to do is convince them you're too crazy to be worth the trouble."

And while I'd never had to dance to avoid a kidnapping, the concept of being too crazy to be worth the trouble had far more applications than I'd expected at the time.

Like having to be a predatorial creep's date to a luncheon, for instance.

"God*da*—I was just touching your back!" Clinton gasped.

"Listen to me," I hissed as I tightened my fist. "If you—"

"*Bonjour*, Ms. Belanger! A pleasure to see you again."

I plastered an unrelated smile on my face and nodded at one of my dad's business partners as if I wasn't twisting Clinton Thibault's wrist as hard as I could. Which wasn't very hard, but to be fair, my arm was bent in a strange angle behind my back so the plastic socialites around us couldn't see what was going on. And it was hard enough that Clinton was wincing, so it was getting the job done.

"*Bonjour,*" I said. "Are you enjoying yourself?"

He let out a hearty laugh. "Of course I am. Della and Jean-Luc would never allow anyone attending one of their soirées not to!"

"Of course," I said. "Have you had a chance to enjoy the grazing table? Anne-Marie said they flew in a charcuterie artist from California to prepare it."

"I have not," he said. "But now I think I must be missing out!"

"You are!" I forced a socially appropriate laugh. It was a foreign and grating sound, like cellophane gift wrap rubbing against itself. "Please, don't let me keep you from enjoying!"

I kept the plastic smile on my face, dropping it only after he walked away and I turned back to Clinton.

His face was only slightly twisted in discomfort, but that was because he was doing his best not to show it. Clinton, like my father, was a man of appearances. He looked exactly how someone would expect a person like him to look: like an asshole.

His hair was the colour of a sweat stain on a mattress, the pale blonde strands cut short on the sides and slightly longer on top to show off the definition of his waves. He had blue eyes that were only called blue because describing them as grey would make it sound like there was something special about him, and there wasn't. His skin was unnaturally tanned, though not quite enough to be orange.

In short, he was unattractive. Of course, that was only because I knew who he was as a person. Someone who didn't know that he was a slimeball of an "upstanding young man" would probably call him hot, mistaking the glint in his eyes as a good-natured, boyish glimmer and the casual way he stood around in his navy-blue sport coat and khaki pants as confidence instead of arrogance.

But deep down, he was as ugly as they come.

"Let *go* of me," he whined, trying to pull his arm away.

"Listen," I continued through clenched teeth. "If you attempt to touch me like that again, I—wait. No." I tightened my grip on his wrist and he let out a shocked scoff. "If you so much as *accidentally brush against me* in a way that feels inappropriate, I will slowly and methodically remove your testicles and replace your eyeballs with them, then make sure that when I put your eyeballs where your balls were, they're facing backwards so you can see what an asshole you are."

His eyes widened, though not with the level of fear I'd been aiming for. "You're fucking sick."

"And since I'm in forensic science, not only do I know *how* to do that"—which was bullshit, but Clinton didn't need to know that—"but I know how to do it without getting caught." I let go of his wrist and nearly fell over as he wrenched his arm back, redness on his face as I caught sight of someone who I *thought* might be Anne-Marie's aunt and waved politely.

"Yeah, right," Clinton scoffed as he rubbed his wrist.

"I can show you how good I am at it if you don't believe me."

"If you're so good at it, why docs your dad want you to be a lawyer so badly?"

The fucking prick.

My dad might have said I had to attend the luncheon with Clinton, but he hadn't said a word about being nice to him. I was thankful for that, since it meant I was mostly free to follow my mom's "dance until they think you're insane" advice so long as it wasn't in a way that made my dad look bad. And also in a way that left no proof whatsoever.

After all, if Clinton complained I was a bitch, I could use one of his own tricks against him and claim I wasn't, and since it was his word against mine, there was no evidence I'd done anything wrong.

So I wouldn't *actually* have broken Clinton's wrist or cut his balls off, but Clinton didn't need to know those things, either. He just needed to believe that I would, which would hopefully convince him I was crazy enough that if my dad ever tried to make him be my date to something again, he'd turn it down.

Although, I may have overestimated the amount of common sense Clinton had. Or uncommon sense. Or... well, I was starting to question what, exactly, was *wrong* with Clinton. I thought smiling and waving as I threatened to insert someone's balls into their eyes would've made that person beeline for the door, but Clinton was still standing there, looking no more than mildly annoyed instead of ditching me to spend time with someone who wasn't threatening a testicle-to-eyeball transplant.

Which was aggravating, since all I wanted was for him to leave me alone.

But my dad had made sure that wouldn't happen. When Clinton arrived that morning to escort me next door, my dad had made sure to mention that I apparently needed supervising.

"You know how easy it is for young ladies to get distracted at these marvellous events," my dad had said in one of those joking tones that only rich businessmen found funny. "If you could be sure *ma fille ange* gets a chance to speak with Jean-Luc, I know she would appreciate it. She's been desperate for more information on the course his colleague teaches."

"Of course, Mr. Belanger," Clinton said in that gracious, civilized tone that convinced rich businessmen he was an upstanding young man. "And I'm sure I can ask my father to put in a good word for Nellie, too. He's been loyal to Jean-Luc's firm for years now."

My dad had given me a *Look* that said "You see, Eleanor? Good things happen when you play the game and this is the team you should *want* to be on."

Then Clinton's fingers had brushed against the side of my left tit as he slipped an arm around me to guide me towards the door, so casually and unobtrusively that my dad didn't notice even though he'd still been giving me his *Look*.

At least, I was telling myself he hadn't noticed.

I hoped he hadn't.

Clinton offered me his elbow as we walked next door, so I'd had no choice but to loop my arm through his. Luckily, as soon as we arrived, Anne-Marie jumped into action.

"*Chérie!*" she exclaimed, her stilettos clicking as she beelined across the foyer with Remy following her. She grabbed my arm, ignoring Clinton as she forced him to let go of me so she could pull me in for a hug while air-kissing each of my cheeks with a loud *muah* sound. "I am so delighted you could come."

She couldn't keep me away from him forever, though. Especially not after her mother waved her over to speak with one of the other guests and she squeezed my hand, promising to catch up with me and Clinton in a bit.

"Wow," Clinton said after Anne-Marie and Remy walked away. "She's a piece of work, huh?"

"Excuse me?" I asked.

"The only way she could be more of a bitch is if she'd actually acknowledge I exist."

"Don't call my friend a bitch," I said.

He rolled his eyes. "Tell your *friend* not to be one, then."

"She knows as well as you do that I don't want to be here with you."

He looked at me, the hurt in his eyes so realistic that I almost felt bad. "You don't? And here I was so thrilled about finally getting to connect with you. Your dad's hounded me for *ages* about taking you out sometime."

"Don't be stupid."

"I'm not. I really thought—"

"And stop acting like *I'm* stupid." I glared at him. "If I'm friends with Anne-Marie, then you know what I've heard. You can't tell me you didn't know I don't like you."

"I didn't expect you to say it."

"It's not my problem you're not used to people saying things to your face." I turned, but Clinton put his arm around me again.

"You didn't say it to my face." He slipped his hand further around me, finding my hip and digging his fingertips in so he could pull me against his body. "You said it from beside me. Which means maybe you're a little more open to hearing what actually happened instead of rumours from your *friend*."

His hand moved lower on my back, and that's when I decided to follow my mom's advice and dance.

And the dance I picked was the twist.

As in, twisting Clinton's arm behind his back.

The Marchands' house was directly behind us, so no one could see what was going on behind my back when I grabbed his wrist. That could have been a bad thing, since it meant no one could see the dark look in his eyes as I threatened to put them in his nutsack, but it didn't end up mattering.

"Well, who do we have over here?" said a familiar voice just as I finished threatening bodily harm to Clinton.

And just...

Ugh.

If I had a nickel for every time JP Marchand inconveniently showed up right when I needed him, I'd have two nickels, which would mean I would be twice as likely to hit him when I threw them at his big, stupid head. And while I was well aware that stepping in to help someone out when they seemed to be in trouble wasn't generally cause for throwing things at people, in this situation, I felt it was justified.

You know. Because I didn't want to see JP fucking Marchand.

And neither did Clinton, apparently. He looked past me, his mouth tightening as JP strolled towards us like he didn't have a care in the world. Considering the type of event it was, he was dressed surprisingly informal, clad in a pair of chinos and a polo. Still, he looked completely put together, his golden blonde hair swept back off his forehead and an easy-going smile on his lips.

"JP," Clinton said, his voice steady.

"Clinton," JP said.

Clinton forced a smile. "I haven't seen you in ages."

"It hasn't been nearly long enough." JP looked at me. "Hey, Nellie. Glad you could make it."

"Hi," I said. "I'm surprised you're here."

"Yeah? Why's that?"

"I thought you hated events like this."

"It's a little hard to avoid one that's happening in your own backyard."

"Maybe you should consider moving out," Clinton said. "Isn't it a little embarrassing to still be living at home when you're, what, twenty-four?"

"Twenty-six," JP said. "And I wouldn't say embarrassing. It's only until they finish building my apartment downtown. I should be moving in by fall at the latest."

"How interesting," Clinton said, though his face said it was anything but. "Well, great catching up, but Nellie and I need to—"

"I need to talk to your dad," I said to JP.

I don't know why I said it. For one, it wasn't like I needed JP to handle Clinton for me. I was doing that perfectly well. But the words came out anyway, surprising JP almost as much as they'd surprised me.

"My dad?" he repeated. "Why—"

"Yeah," I interrupted. "Just wondering if you've seen him."

JP raised his eyebrows, then silently turned his head until he was looking over his shoulder. Less than twenty feet away and well within my line of sight, Mr. Marchand and Della were talking to my dad, because of course they were. JP paused, then looked back at me.

"He's right there," JP said.

"Great," I said, and then because I had no other way of stalling: "Well, I'm going over there now. Excuse me."

I hadn't planned on talking to Mr. Marchand while my dad was around, but as I walked those twenty feet, I figured it was for the best. At least he'd see me holding up my end of the deal.

"*Ma fille ange,*" my dad said as I joined him, Della, and Mr. Marchand. "Are you having fun?"

"Yep," I said, then turned to Della. "Thank you for hosting this lovely event."

"Thank you for attending," Della said pleasantly. "It is so lovely to see you around again, Nellie."

"Thanks," I said.

Then my mouth went dry.

Around me, I could hear countless other conversations, indistinct voices discussing indistinct things in low rumbles punctuated by the occasional laugh. Soft music played and the sound of glasses being set on tables filled the spaces between the words I couldn't hear. But in front of me, there was silence.

"Nellie?" my dad finally said. "Was there something that brought you over?"

"Yes," I forced myself to say, then looked at Mr. Marchand. "When I was here for *La Nuit Rose*, you mentioned you have a colleague in Ottawa who runs an LSAT prep course."

"I did," Mr. Marchand said. "And I believe you very firmly stated you were getting a forensic science situation and if that career didn't pan out, you would find—what was it? Oh, right—a rich sucker of a lawyer to marry."

"Right," I said. "And what better way to make sure that plan would work than to take an LSAT prep course so I can scout out some potential future husbands?"

I thought it was funny, as did Della, who put her hand to her mouth to cover a laugh, but neither my dad nor Mr. Marchand seemed to agree.

"Eleanor," my dad said, his voice low.

"I respect my colleague far too much to waste his time by recommending potential students who are not serious about their futures," Mr. Marchand said.

Shit.

"I was only joking," I said. "Lightening the mood, you know? But I am serious about wanting to take the LSAT."

"Hmm," Mr. Marchand said. "I'm not entirely convinced that recommending you is worth risking my reputation and relationship with this colleague. The law is no joke, Ms. Belanger."

"Right," I said. "I didn't mean to make it sound like I thought it was. But I also wasn't asking you to recommend me."

From the corner of my eye, I could see my dad's face taking on a practiced, blank expression that hid the cloudiness I knew was brewing beneath the surface, but I did my best to ignore it.

"No?" Mr. Marchand said.

I shook my head. "You were very clear when we spoke that you wouldn't give me a second chance to accept your recommendation and I respect that. If that's still the case, I was hoping you would provide me with your colleague's information so I can apply for the course like anyone else would. And then you won't need to worry about me risking your reputation."

Mr. Marchand studied me for a moment, the look on his face unreadable. Then he folded his arms. "Why the change of heart?"

My dad's eyes were still on me, but I didn't look at him. "I did some thinking and realized my dad made some good points about things. So I thought looking into the LSAT would be a good place to start when I decided I might be interested in switching to law."

"*Might* isn't good enough," he said.

Well, shit.

I wasn't expecting that.

"Darling," Della said, accompanying it with an uncomfortable laugh as she put a hand on her husband's arm. "Be kind, please."

"There's nothing unkind about it," Mr. Marchand said, then lifted his chin as his eyes focused on something behind me. "What kind of lawyers do I hire at my firm?"

"The best of the best and who have the drive and dedication to stay in this for the long haul," JP said promptly as he walked up beside me. "Why?"

Mr. Marchand ignored him and looked at me. "I have never considered hiring someone who had law as a backup plan."

God, if my dad stared at me any harder, I was going to disintegrate into powder. I forced a smile onto my face. "I'm not sure that every firm would agree. I imagine there would be a shortage of lawyers if no one hired people who thought they would do something else for a living."

"And that's why most lawyers aren't as successful as the ones who work for me." He folded his arms. "Also why your plan to marry rich is laughable."

I refrained from bringing up the fact that I was joking, since Mr. Marchand apparently had absolutely no sense of humour.

"I would be good at it, though," I said. "If that's what I decided to do."

"You're certainly argumentative enough," Mr. Marchand said. "But being good at it doesn't matter if you don't want to be there. And it's certainly no reason to take a high-level, exclusive LSAT prep class that plenty of potential law students would sell their souls to get into.

My colleague considers it a poor year if doesn't have at least one of his 'graduates' accepted to Yale, Stanford, *and* Harvard."

"What if three of his students got into Yale instead?" I asked.

"That would actually be more impressive," JP said.

Mr. Marchand didn't seem to think so if the look he gave me was any indication. "Regardless, I don't think taking the LSAT is something you should pursue, Ms. Belanger."

"I think there's something to be said for being supportive of Nellie instead of tearing her down," Della said diplomatically. "What's the harm in providing her with the course information, *chérie*?"

"I'm not tearing her down," Mr. Marchand said. "But my colleague does not accept applications without a recommendation attached." He looked at my dad. "My apologies, Max. But I can't stake my reputation on 'might.' You understand."

"Of course," my dad said, his voice so pleasant that I almost believed it. "It would be a poor decision, business-wise, to not consider your reputation when making recommendations. It is part of why so many of my accounts end up retaining your firm as legal counsel."

No one reacted to the unstated but obvious implications of his statement. Not because no one caught that my dad was subtly reminding Mr. Marchand that he'd sent a *lot* of business his way over the years and implying he'd remember this when recommending law firms in the future. We all fucking knew that.

But it was a social event. Etiquette reigned supreme. So Mr. Marchand nodded brusquely and placed a hand on the small of Della's back.

"Perhaps if her LSAT score is appropriately high, we can consider an internship arrangement once she is accepted to law school," he said.

"I know Nellie would be especially appreciative of that," my dad said before I could blurt out something like "Oh fuck no." He turned to JP. "Which would make you an ideal tutor, would it not?"

Oh, *fuck* no.

I guess it had been too much to hope that both of them would forget about JP's offer. Or even that JP had forgotten and when my dad reminded him, had to express his regrets that he couldn't provide any tutoring because he'd decided to move to Reykjavík and, oh would you look at that, he had to leave right this second to make his flight.

Or something.

But no. JP had to plaster one of his stupid shit-eating grins on his face, barely able to conceal his fucking *delight* at being asked to tutor me.

"Of course, Mr. Belanger," he said. "I'd be more than happy to help Nellie study for the LSAT."

Then he looked at me, his eyes flicking down to my lips for a moment so brief I wasn't entirely sure that was what happened, and his grin widened even more.

"Don't worry," he said. "By the time I'm done with you, the courtrooms won't know what hit them."

Chapter Twenty-Four
Don't Call Me Babe

BY SOME FUCKING MIRACLE, my dad couldn't find an extra ticket to the library gala or whatever the hell was going on that night.

"The Marchands are all attending," he said as we returned to his house after the luncheon. "So I will see if Jean-Luc has reconsidered his position on recommending you for the course. If not, I will tell JP to arrange a regular time for you to study with him."

"Dad, I—"

"You will ensure I have a moment to speak with Jean-Luc privately," he said to Kimberlee, then turned and started walking towards the back of the house. "Nellie, I expect we will be back after you have turned in for the night, so I will give you Jean-Luc's answer tomorrow morning. You are not leaving until after lunch."

"I was planning to leave after breakfast," I said. "Although, if I don't have to go to the thing tonight—"

"It will not kill you to spend a bit of extra time with your father," he said over me, his words crisp and clipped. "I will see you in the morning."

Fucking great.

At least I'd have his house to myself for the night, I guess.

As soon as my dad and Kimberlee left for the gala, I ordered delivery from my favourite Thai restaurant in Montreal before going up to my room and changing into a pair of leggings and a baggy t-shirt. Once my pad thai arrived, I brought it to the coffee table in front of my dad's gigantic TV and settled on the couch, flipping on a true crime docuseries I'd been wanting to watch, and dug in.

I'd just shovelled a gigantic helping of noodles in my mouth when the doorbell rang. I froze with my chopsticks mid-air and cheeks bulging with food.

Ignore it, I told myself.

Just ignore it.

Whoever it is isn't here for you.

Ignore it. Ignore it. Ignore—

"Fumpfh," I said, which was what "Fuck" sounded like through a mouth stuffed full of pad thai.

Doorbells were worse versions of phone calls. I could never bring myself to ignore a phone call because I wanted to know who was on the other end of the line and why. With doorbells, it became a compulsion. Maybe it was because someone being at the door was less common than getting a phone call. Or maybe it was knowing someone was actually *there* and whatever they wanted was so important, they had to see you in person.

So instead of ignoring it, I started chewing frantically.

I'd barely swallowed my mouthful of food before I reached the front door. The door itself was solid wood, but it was surrounded by windows to let in plenty of natural light. My dad had sheer curtains over all of them for privacy, so I went to the peephole and stepped up on my tiptoes so I could peer through it, then immediately dropped back on my feet.

Don't answer it, I told myself.

Don't answer it.

You know why he's here and you don't want to deal with it and if you just go back to the couch right now you can—

"You know I can see you through the window, right?" came a muffled voice through the door.

"No you can't," I said.

A muted laugh. "I can see the shape of you."

I hesitated, then gently banged my head against the door in defeat before opening it.

"What do you want?" I asked.

"Hello to you, too," JP said as he straightened up from where he was leaning against the stone wall beside the door.

He looked good. Because of course he did. Because of course JP fucking Marchand was standing at my dad's front door having changed into well-fitting jeans and a short-sleeved, slim-cut blue button down. Of course that shade of blue made his stupid blue eyes look even bluer and his stupid thick blonde hair was brushed back casually. Of course his stupid smile showed off his stupid teeth that were straight except for the one crooked one on the left side and his white skin was tanned and his shoulders seemed a little broader than they had been when I'd lost my virginity to him because he'd probably been working out or something.

The bastard.

"You didn't want to go to the super exclusive library gala?" I asked. "I hear that's the place to be tonight."

"Turns out I had a terrible headache and couldn't make it. Too bad I didn't know earlier, since I heard Kimberlee was trying to find an extra ticket for you."

"Sounds rough. You should go home and go to bed so you feel better."

"Wouldn't you know it, though, almost as soon as my family turned out of the driveway, it went away."

"So you came over here to... what? See if my dad would give you a ride to join them?" I motioned behind me. "I can ask him if you want."

"Liar," he said. "Your dad's not here."

I opened my mouth to deny it, then shut it. "How did you know that?"

"Your dad would rather chew on glass than be late for a social event."

"Oh, so you wanted to see if I'd give you a ride to the event?" I asked. "Sorry, no. You can get an Uber in like, two minutes."

"If I didn't know better, I'd say you're trying to avoid me, Nell."

"Then you're an idiot. I *am* avoiding you."

"Hmm. Any particular reason?"

I stared at him.

He stared back, then flicked an eyebrow up as though it was a silent repetition of the question.

"Seriously?" I asked.

"Yeah." His mouth twitched. "I mean, I guess I should've taken the hint when you literally *ate* the first note I left for you, but—"

And I snapped.

I just fucking snapped.

"Yes, you should have!" I said, my voice pitching up. "You should have absolutely taken the fucking hint. Instead, you left me another note, and then *another* one, like you think if you stick enough Post-Its to my car I'll eventually want to date you. For someone who thinks he's so damn smart, I can't believe I have to spell it out like this, but I'm not interested, JP. Okay? I don't want whatever it is you think you want from me. I've *never* wanted that and that's why I did it with *you* in the first place. Because *you* were supposed to be this total non-committal player who didn't do relationships either. Instead, you think you're being all cute with your sticky notes and volunteering to trap me into tutoring sessions for a test I have never and won't ever want to take so my dad doesn't—"

Something cut me off before I finished. Myself, I guess, but it wasn't a conscious decision. It was something deep in my chest that ordered me to stop, that pulled me back and let those words plummet like rockfall, leaving a sheer cliff of silence between me and JP. I swallowed hard, my breathing steady even though my lungs were screaming breathlessness, and glared at JP.

He'd refolded his arms while I was ranting. His eyebrows were still raised, but they were joined by an odd expression on his face, something that almost seemed like vague amusement.

"Do you feel better now?" he asked.

My mouth dropped open. JP's face cracked and, infuriatingly, he laughed as he shook his head.

"Jeez, Nellie," he said. "You had this whole story in your head about what was happening here, eh?"

"I... what?" I asked.

"Did you ever think that maybe I just wanted to talk to you?"

"Talk," I repeated. "The multiple flirty sticky notes because you wanted to *talk*?"

"Yes," he said.

"The notes with your phone number and X-O-X-Os on them that you kept leaving even though I didn't call you a single time."

"Well, I figured you'd need a way to get in touch with me." His mouth twitched into a smirk. "And I figured the X-O-X-Os would make it clear it wasn't because I was mad or something."

"And I'm supposed to believe that."

"Yes. It's the truth."

I scoffed as convincingly as I could. "Yeah, well... maybe I didn't want to talk to you."

"Trust me, I got that after a couple of notes."

"It took a *couple* of notes?!"

"I mean, the first time I figured you couldn't call because the number was unreadable after digesting it—"

"I didn't *eat* it. I spit it out."

"—and it wasn't like I was going to ask Anne-Marie for your number. I know you didn't want her to know. So when you didn't call after the second note—"

"You didn't get it from me ripping it up?"

He raised his eyebrows. "What?"

My face felt warm. "I ripped it up. The second I saw it. I assumed you got the hint from that."

"Damn," he said, faking a dramatic sigh. "I guess I'll never know if the pink Post-Its taste different than the yellow ones." I rolled my eyes and he laughed. "No, Nellie. I wasn't pining out the window watching for you to discover the note."

I curled my hand into a fist so I could subtly pick at skin around my thumbnail. "Well, either way. If you figured it out after that, why the hell did you leave me *another* note after *La Nuit Rose*?"

"Well, it was just kinda funny at that point," he said.

I glared at him. "I'm so glad you thought so."

"Thanks."

"No problem. So what was so damn important to talk about that you've been harassing me via sticky note?"

"I figured we should talk about that whole thing where we hooked up that one time and you didn't tell me you were a virgin, then you asked me not to tell anyone about it before rushing out of my room."

"That was three years ago. What is there to *talk* about?"

"Just because it was three years ago doesn't mean I stopped wanting to know if you were okay after," he said.

That made something flutter in my stomach. Something as warm as it was unwelcome. "Well... I was. I am."

"Yeah, see, I dunno about that," he said, tilting his head to the side and making the gold-blonde piece of hair at the front flop over his forehead. "Like you said, it's been three years and you seem to scurry away every time we run into each other."

"I do not *scurry*," I said, insulted. "*You're* the one who acted all clingy. And you and I aren't friends. I don't even know why you wondered if I was okay, let alone got to a point where you faked a headache to skip an event so you could get me alone to ask."

"Don't flatter yourself too much," he said. "I'll try nearly anything to get out of going to these socialite events."

"So that's what this is about. You wanted to stay home without feeling guilty."

"I wanted to make sure you didn't regret it."

I paused, partly the suddenness of his words and partly at the way his tone shifted from light to serious. "Regret... what we did?"

He nodded. "I never want to do something that makes people regret hooking up with me."

That made me raise my eyebrows. "You don't think anyone who's slept with you regrets it?"

"I'm sure some of them do," he said. "But if someone's going to regret it, I'd rather it not be because of something I could've done differently."

"Oh. You're asking me to give you a performance review."

An arrogant smirk broke the solemnity on his face. "You came so hard your legs went numb. I know exactly how well I *performed*, babe."

Heat started to crawl up my neck again. "Don't call me babe."

"You got it, babe," he said.

"You're such a bastard," I muttered.

He laughed again. "Look, it was your first time. I didn't have time to make sure you were okay or that you weren't upset or whatever. And that bothered me. So yeah, I wanted to check in. And then after a while, it kinda turned into a game because it was so fucking funny how hard you tried to avoid me." He shrugged shamelessly. "If you thought I'd stop giving you a hard time about things just because we hooked up once, I'm sorry to tell you that you're delusional, Nell."

Despite being called delusional, another warm flutter quivered its way through my stomach. This wasn't what I'd expected. I mean, JP was an asshole. He was a lawyer. He was, to use Anne-Marie's phrasing, a womanizer.

There was no reason for him to *care* this much.

I swallowed, hoping the action would digest any of those butterflies that were in my stomach. "I don't regret what we did." I fidgeted and twisted my mouth to the side. "I don't regret it being with you, either."

The way his shoulders relaxed was almost imperceptible, but I still caught it. "Alright. And we're cool? I don't want to worry I'm making you uncomfortable every time we run into each other."

"Yes, JP," I said. "We're okay."

"Awesome. So no more scurrying away when you see me or—"

"Oh, shut up," I huffed. "So is that it? This is all you skipped an event and came over for?"

"Well, sort of," he said. "That was the worst-case scenario."

"What was the best-case scenario?"

And oh, fuck.

I shouldn't have asked.

He held my gaze for a moment, then folded his arms over his chest. Leaning against the stone wall next to the door again, he let his eyes trail down my body, then flick back up before cocking an eyebrow at me.

And I just...

I snorted. Because there was no *way* I was going to let the fucking butterflies in my stomach rear up again. There was no way I was going to let that look flatter me.

There was no way.

No fucking way.

"Are you serious?" I asked. "What makes you think I'd want to hook up with you again?"

He smirked. "Do I need to remind you about the whole 'numb legs from coming so hard' thing again?"

I ignored the question. "And why would *you* even want this?"

"Uh, have you *seen* you, Nellie? You've always been hot, but like..." He trailed off with a puff of air and shook his head slowly.

It wasn't just a fluttering feeling in my stomach anymore. My whole body was going warm. I swallowed hard and tried not to look half as flustered as I felt. "Yeah, I know."

"I'm only human, babe." He shrugged. "We both know we can have a good time together. So if you're interested in a repeat..."

My mouth felt dry. "I don't know if that would be a good idea."

Now, I expected him to say something else.

Like "Aw, come on."

Or "Here's all the reasons I thought of that make this a good idea because I'm a try-hard lawyer who overthinks everything."

I didn't expect him to stop leaning on the wall and nod politely. "Okay."

I blinked at him. "Okay?"

"I'm not gonna pressure you to hook up with me if you're not into it."

"O...kay," I said. "Good. Because I don't hook up with people at my dad's house."

His head tilted to the side almost imperceptibly. "Is that so?"

"Well, yeah. The last thing I need is him discovering the boy next door deflowered me."

He threw his head back, laughing so hard that he had to put a hand to his stomach like he was holding himself together.

"*Deflowered* you?" he repeated, almost choking on the word. "Jeez, Nellie. Who calls it—" He stopped and shook his head, trying to catch his breath. "Have you even *gotten* laid since we hooked up?"

It was my turn to burst out laughing, which seemed to surprise him as much as his sudden laughter had surprised me.

"What?" he asked. "What's so funny?"

"Have *I* gotten laid?" I repeated, snorting as I shook my head. "Has Anne-Marie stopped telling you everyone else's business or something?"

"I mean, I know you two still hit up the bars and stuff, but it's not like I get a breakdown of each time she goes out like she used to when she was eighteen. I guess some of the novelty has worn off."

"Well, trust me. I've gotten laid."

"Yeah?" He grinned, his eyes sparkling. "You've fucked around a little since then?"

"No."

"Oh. I thought you—"

"I've fucked around a *lot* since then."

JP looked intrigued, almost subconsciously leaning towards me as he lowered his voice a bit. "Yeah? With who?"

"No one you know," I said.

"Well, duh. But that doesn't mean I don't want to know what kinda shit you've gotten up to," he said.

"Yeah, well, maybe you should find out for yourself."

I hadn't quite meant to say it. I think both of us knew that. The words spilled out naturally, the part of me that had been screaming at me to let JP in taking control of my mouth.

But just because I hadn't meant to say it didn't mean that I didn't *mean* it.

"Should I?" JP said, his voice going low. "I thought you said it was a terrible idea for us to hook up."

"Just because it's a terrible idea doesn't mean it wouldn't be any fun," I replied.

He didn't say anything, studying me for a quiet moment before letting his eyes trail down my body. When they got back to my face, the playful glimmer that was usually there was gone, replaced by something serious for the second time that night.

"If you want this, Nell, you need to invite me in," he said, his voice quiet. "I have to know you mean that."

I told myself to shut the door.

To slam it.

I told myself I couldn't do this with him again. That I shouldn't have done it the first time. That just because I didn't regret it didn't mean I should go for a fucking *repeat* just because he was amazing in bed and set me down a path of trying to find sex as good as it had been with him.

Because that was it, wasn't it? This, right here, with him looking at me with a calm confidence and a glimmer hidden in his eyes.

One look at him and I felt like I was that eighteen-year-old girl again.

One look at him and I could almost convince myself he was worth the risks.

One look at him and it was like that afternoon we'd spent together hadn't changed me at all, even though it had.

And I liked the woman it had changed me into. I *liked* being open and loud and confident. I liked being joyfully promiscuous. I liked being in charge.

But I wasn't entirely sure I didn't also like the way my breath felt a little shallower and my heart raced a little faster whenever I saw JP.

I wasn't entirely sure I'd be up to the challenge of him.

And I wasn't entirely sure I didn't want to try.

"Come here, then," I said, and held the door open as I stepped out of the way.

Chapter Twenty-Five
You Picked The Wrong Girl

I HAD NEVER HAD a guy in my bedroom before.

Adrian, my high school boyfriend, had *seen* my bedroom at my mom's house, but we'd never messed around in there. I don't really know why. My mom probably wouldn't have thought it was a big deal. Even though it wasn't something we talked about much, she was the kind of mom who made sure I was on the pill and had easy access to condoms. It might have been awkward, but if I'd ever need advice or help, I would've been able to talk to her.

Like, I could almost imagine what would have happened if I ever *had* brought Adrian to my bedroom and got caught by my mom. She wouldn't have said anything until he left, and then she would pointedly ask me if he'd been good to me. Not if we'd been safe—on the few occasions we had broached the topic of sex, she'd always said she knew I was smart enough to be safe, which was ironic considering the first *goddamn* time I'd done it, I hadn't made JP bother with a condom—but if he had treated me right.

If he'd respected me.

And if I said he had, she'd nod, then make an awkward joke about it that would make both of us blush a little and that would be that.

But if I said he hadn't, well... I mean, the next conversation I had with her would've occurred through a glass pane and an old corded phone during visiting hours at the nearest prison. If they ever discovered the guy's body, that is.

But if my dad caught me hooking up with someone?

The thought of it was enough to make me consider abstinence. I mean, not that I'd consider it any more than "I wonder if abstinence would be worth it in that situation" followed by internal laughter and a resounding "No," but still.

With my dad, there would be no slightly awkward conversations. No giggling and blushing. No casual mentions of where in the house I could find a secret stash of condoms should I ever have need of them.

There would just be hell to pay from a man who had nearly cut me off once already.

A man who only gave me a second chance when I agreed to be his perfect, socially acceptable little daughter.

A man who made it clear I was only worth something when I was the person he wanted me to be.

And yet, there was JP, trying not to snicker as he closed my bedroom door behind him because even though both of us knew no one was home, I'd ordered him to be quiet as he followed me up the stairs.

"And lock it," I said.

The deadbolt clicked obediently, then JP looked at me.

"So," he said.

"Are we doing this or what?" I asked.

The corners of his eyes crinkled as he smirked. "I dunno. I thought we were, but you're all the way over there and I'm all the way over here."

"Do you forget how to walk across a room when your dick gets hard or something?" I asked.

He laughed. "Come here."

"You want me to come over there," I said flatly. "To you. When you're standing next to the door and I'm standing next to the bed."

"Maybe I like it when a girl chases me a little."

"Then you picked the wrong girl."

I turned, walking towards the small seating area near the window. There was a small accent chair there that I couldn't remember ever sitting on because there was usually a stack of clothes on it, but I hadn't unpacked many clothes this time around. I perched on it, folding one leg over the other, and pulled my phone out.

The screen wasn't even unlocked when his fingers plucked the phone from my hand. I glared through my eyelashes at JP.

"Point made, babe," he said, fighting back the permanent laughter that seemed to be in his voice whenever we were in the same room as he set the phone on the trendy end table beside the accent chair.

"Don't call me that," I said. "I'm not your babe."

"I didn't say you were mine," he said. "But you are a *total* babe, so it's accurate."

"You don't hear me calling you 'bastard' even though you are one," I said.

He laughed, holding his hand out as if to help me stand. "Another point made. How about you come here so we can kiss and make up?"

I looked at his hand, then up at him. Playfulness sparkled in his eyes, but I refused to let it make me smile. Instead, I sighed, then faked reluctance as I put my hand in his.

"That's it, babe," he whispered.

"Oh, for fuck's sa—" I started, but was cut off as pulled me up from the chair. Before I was even steady on my feet, he stooped down and pressed his lips to mine.

And just...

Fuck.

He tasted so good. Familiar in a way, but as new as anyone I'd ever kissed for the first time. Not that it was the first time we'd kissed, but it was like sinking into a memory you'd forgotten, where you're relieving all those little details that had been misplaced somewhere in the back of your mind and there's only a hint of awareness that you've experienced this before. His lips made parts of me light up that plenty of other people had made light up before.

Just not quite the way he did.

He brought my hand to his body, guiding me to rest it against his side before letting go and skimming his palm all the way up my arm and to my cheek. His other hand moved to my hip, pulling me into his body, and I could feel him still fighting back that stupid laugh as he smiled against my mouth.

"Keep laughing at me and I'm gonna think this whole thing is a joke," I whispered, my lips brushing his as I spoke.

"I'm not laughing at you."

"Yes, you are."

"Well, maybe a little." He nipped at my lip. "But only because I need to distract myself."

I frowned. "From what?"

A soft huff of breath brushed against me. "From how badly I want to pin you to your bed and take all of you at once."

"I don't think you could handle me all at once," I said.

"Questionable," he said. "Pretty sure I handled you all at once when you decided to sit on my dick without even pausing."

"You barely handled it," I said, then had to fight back a laugh of my own as I sank my teeth into his bottom lip and made him gasp. "*Pretty* sure you lost control and shoved your cock down my throat when you came."

"Mmm," he said, the noise coming out along with a sigh. "I'm still sorry for that, you know."

"Why? I told you it was fine."

His tongue traced my lip but darted away before I could meet it with mine. "Mostly I'm sorry for how many times I've thought about it while jacking off."

A shiver ran through me. "How often has that been?"

"You're asking me how many times I've come while thinking about the girl who impaled herself on my cock, rode me like a mechanical bull on ladies' night, choked after taking the entire length of my dick down her throat, and then told me how *hot* the whole thing was?"

"Isn't that what I said?"

He smirked. "At least once."

"Oh. And here I was about to be flattered."

"A month. Maybe twice if I've been working extra overtime and haven't picked anyone up for a while."

"For a lawyer, you're not doing a very good job convincing me," I said as he started using his hips to direct me to the bed.

"Convincing you of what?"

"That you can handle me. Especially"—I reached up and grabbed a handful of his shirt, making him gasp in surprise—"when I've got a lot more to handle now."

I meant it like I was more experienced than I had been, but JP didn't take it that way. He groaned as I pulled him in for another kiss, then ran his hands along my sides and to my hips.

"That you do," he murmured, slipping a hand behind me and squeezing my ass, his palm warm through the thin fabric of my leggings. "And that's why it's so fucking hard."

"Your dick?"

"Yes, but not what I meant," he said, then urged me back towards the bed a few more steps. "That's why it's so hard trying not to take you all at once. Because I can't decide if I want to suffocate myself with your tits or spank your ass and watch it ripple or taste every inch of you before seeing if that sassy mouth of yours can still handle my cock."

I knew JP was a smooth talker. I probably wasn't even the first woman this *weekend* he was talking to like he was so desperate for her body, he had to restrain himself from giving into the urge to just *take* her.

And the fact that he was talking about taking me, like I was the kind of person who would just allow him to help himself to me, should have probably bothered me, at least a little.

But it was one of those *things* that was so fucking hot in the moment that I couldn't even be annoyed by it.

"Oh," I breathed, then stumbled as the back of my thighs hit the edge of my mattress.

JP steadied me before I fell. He was already hard, the bulge in his jeans firm against my stomach as he pressed his body to mine. He gave my ass one more firm squeeze, his fingers digging in almost too hard before he let go and slipped his hand beneath my shirt.

"I thought you were hot before, but now?" He shook his head as he lifted my top off, then made a soft noise as he realized I didn't have a bra on. "It's fucking unfair, Nellie. Every time I see you, I want to see what's underneath. Do you know how *indecent* it was of you to wear that goddamn black dress at that gala a while back? Did you even see how irresistible you looked?"

Heat rushed through me, almost certainly staining the skin on my chest pink, but JP didn't comment on it if it did. "I may have checked a mirror or two before going out."

"Your ass was a work of art." He slipped his hands behind me, pressing a kiss to my neck and sighing as my breasts pushed against his chest. "If Chantel hadn't been digging her nails into my arm because she was so jealous, I would've probably gotten hard right there in the middle of the fucking event."

"Chantel was your date?"

"Mm-hmm." He nibbled on my neck. "Not that we were together. I owed her a favour and that's what she wanted to cash it in on."

"What did you owe her a favour for?"

"She gives an *insane* blowjob."

I rolled my eyes and felt JP snicker before he kissed my neck again.

"And that day you and Anne-Marie were in the pool? That fucking bikini? I couldn't tell if I was being rewarded or punished."

"Probably punished," I said.

"Probably," he agreed, reaching for the waistband of my leggings and tugging them down. "The reward would've been if I could've been magically transformed into your bikini bottoms so I could spend my day caught between your ass cheeks."

I snorted. JP's eyes flicked up, letting me see the amusement in them before he focused his attention back to my leggings, which he'd pulled down to about mid-thigh. He made a soft *hmm*ing noise and before I could say anything, he dropped to his knees in front of me so he could peel them the rest of the way down.

"Although," he said casually once my legs were bare and his hands had travelled back up to trace the edge of my thong. "I wouldn't say no to being reincarnated as this, either."

"For someone who was so insistent he could take all of me at once, you sure are obsessed with my ass," I said.

He traced a finger along a spot on my hip that I knew had stretch marks beneath it, then leaned in and pressed a kiss to the same spot. "It's a great ass."

I started to say something else. It was clever. Or at least, I was pretty sure it was clever. It might have been something stupid like telling him he was a great ass. It didn't matter either way. Before I could say it, JP slipped his hand between my thighs and nudged my legs apart so he could kiss my pussy through my panties.

And every thought I had was ripped from my mind, barely a shadow left behind to prove anything had been there in the first place.

"Oh," I breathed.

I half-expected JP to say something snarky. To fight back a laugh again, to tease me for the way my breath sighed out of my body. But there seemed to be a limit on his sass, a line he stepped over where he went from clever quips to steadfast dedication.

And of course, that line existed in sex. Of *course* the thing that JP took more seriously than anything else in the world was sex.

So he didn't comment on the noise I made. Instead, he kept his eyes on mine as he pressed his mouth to the fabric covering my mound. He held that gaze as he placed another kiss lower, and lower, and then to a spot I knew had to be wet with arousal. His nose nudged against my clit, just hard enough to tease relief but not actually give it, and he brought his hands up to the waistband of my thong.

His face moved away for the half-second it took for him to tug my panties down. Once they were off, his lips pressed against my mound again, right at the bottom point of the triangle of hair there, and he brought his hands back up my legs, feathering his fingertips along my calves and knees and thighs until he reached my hips.

"Glad as I am that you didn't have any regrets about giving me your first time, I do have one," he said, his lips brushing against my pussy as he spoke.

My heart jumped so high into my throat that I almost worried it would come out my parted lips. I hadn't even... I didn't even think to ask if *he*—

"I've always regretted not getting to taste you," he continued.

Oh.

Oh.

It took everything in me not to tremble in excitement or react to the shiver skittering across my skin. "Is that so?"

Sitting back on his knees, he nudged my hips, a mischievous look in his eyes.

"Sit on the edge of the bed, babe," he said.

And without a fucking word, I did.

Chapter Twenty-Six
Do It Like You Mean It

JP MADE ME THINK of Ben.

I tried not to think of other people when I was in bed with someone. It wasn't like they'd ever *know*, but it just felt rude or something.

But me thinking of Ben wasn't a bad thing. Not for either of them. I was only thinking of him because I'd been a little worried no one would ever live up to the way he ate me out.

And then unfortunately, JP went and proved I had nothing to worry about except that *he* was the one who could live up to Ben's talents.

But where Ben had developed his technique with one woman over the course of twelve or so years, JP had probably developed his with twelve or so women over the course of a few months.

Then practiced it on twelve more women before perfecting it with twelve after that.

As soon as I sat on the bed, JP's hands were between my thighs, parting them to reveal my pussy. I had no choice but to lean back, resting on my hand to give him full access to my body. He traced his fingers along my inner thigh and up to my folds, casually spreading me open and taking in the sight of me before he leaned in and got to work.

Every touch was confident. Every movement was skilled. He looked up at me, listening and watching as he tested different actions to figure out which ones made me gasp and which ones made me squirm. Fingers traced my pussy lips, teasing around my entrance as he sucked on my clit. A moment later, his tongue took the place of his fingers, dipping inside me just enough to make me desperate for more. And a moment after that, he flattened his tongue and slowly licked up my slit, glancing up to see me biting my lip and the duvet balled up in my fists. But no matter how hard I clutched that duvet, I couldn't stop my legs from quivering on either side of JP's head as his tongue dragged along my clit.

So then he did it again.

And again.

And each fucking time, my body trembled around him, a reflex I couldn't control as much as I didn't *want* to control it.

"Fuck," I whispered, almost not recognizing my voice from the headiness. "Why are you making me do that?"

"Mmm," came the reply, followed by a peppering of kisses along either side of my pussy. "Because you like it, babe."

Which was true. I couldn't deny that. "Yeah, but like... how?"

"You want the technical instructions or...?"

"You know, I like you better when you use your mouth for the things you're actually good at."

He laughed, his breath warm on my pussy, then turned his head and sank his teeth into my thigh. I gasped, jerking back instinctively, but his hands held me in place as he kissed the spot he'd just bitten.

"*How* I'm doing it is paying attention to what your body is telling me," he said. "Since most people won't outright tell a person what they like."

"What do you mean?"

He pressed more kisses against my thigh. "If I asked you, right now, how you liked getting your pussy eaten, what would you tell me?"

I opened my mouth, then closed it. "Well, I—"

"Exactly." Another kiss landed near my groin. "Women are all self-conscious about telling you what they want in bed. So instead I ask them in... other ways."

Oh, *hell* no.

He went to lick me again, but looked up in surprise when I put a hand on his big, stupid forehead and held him back.

"First of all," I said, the headiness in my voice gone and replaced with a firmness that made his eyes widen. "It's not just women who get self-conscious, and it's not all of them. You don't need to be sexist about it."

"I just meant—"

"Second," I continued. "Don't interrupt me."

He fell silent, looking up at me with something like intrigue in his eyes.

"Third, I was *going* to reluctantly admit you were right. I wouldn't necessarily know how to spell out what I want. At best, I'd have to direct you as you were doing it."

A slow grin spread on his face. "I never thought—"

"Refer to point two, JP."

He closed his mouth, pressing his lips together as if to hold both his words and laughter in, then nodded.

"Fourth." I let my hand slide up, weaving his blonde hair through my fingers. "Do it like you mean it."

"What?"

"Stop fucking around and teasing me while you try to figure out what's going to make me come. Eat my pussy like you mean it or I'll get myself off instead, and *maybe* if you're lucky, I'll use your face to do it."

His lips parted, but before any more of his annoying ass words could come out, I pulled his head forward and shoved it against my pussy. I'd expected to hear a noise of surprise, but all that came out was a low, thrilling groan, and then his tongue was inside me.

JP might have been a bastard most of the time, but he was a bastard who could take instruction when it mattered. Gone were the long, lazy licks from the bottom of my slit to the top. Instead, after teasing my entrance with his tongue, he moved his mouth back to my clit, circling his tongue around it before sucking. I moaned, my head tilting back as he increased the pressure. He flicked his tongue across my clit before sucking on it again. The trembling in my legs returned, stronger than before as he alternated the two actions, and I felt the low rumble of his appreciation again as my fingers tightened in his hair.

"Right there," I whispered. "Right fucking *there*, JP."

A muffled noise responded to me, but I had no idea what it meant. Nor did I really care. JP kept doing what he was doing, creating a rhythmic pattern where he shifted between sucking and flicking in one smooth motion. My hand fell to the back of his head, not quite holding him in place anymore, but he kept his face pressed tight against me as he brought a hand up to each of my legs. His tongue kept moving, torturing my clit as he lifted my legs over his shoulders so he could bury his face between them even harder.

"Fuck," I whimpered. A moment later one of his hands moved between my thighs. "Oh, fu-*uh*—"

I squeezed my eyes shut as he pushed a finger inside of me. It was nowhere near enough, which he realized when I whimpered and tried to tighten my pussy around him as he pulled it out. The next thrust had two fingers, which was much more satisfying to that hungry pool of arousal deep in my core. A moan slipped from my mouth and JP sucked my clit eagerly, his fingers moving in and out of me at a steady pace.

"Right there," I said again. "Right there and don't stop, don't stop, don't *fucking* s-s-st—"

The rest of the word never made it out. It turned into a cry as a quick buildup of ecstasy flooded my body. I gasped for breath, every inhale pushing me higher and every exhale causing the intensity to grow until I was panting at the edge of bliss.

And that was when he could've fucked everything up.

Because rule one—rule fucking *one*—of eating pussy, is that when she says "Don't stop," you don't stop. You keep doing what you're doing at the pace you're doing it and don't change *anything* unless you know what you're fucking doing.

And JP...

Well.

JP knew what he was fucking doing.

He *didn't* know how I'd react to it.

But he knew what he was doing when his fingertip slid between my ass cheeks and pressed against the tight hole there. He knew *exactly* what he was doing when he slipped the tip of his finger in and I made a noise that, in my mind, was an erotic moan but in actuality sounded like a pterodactyl shriek.

Luckily, JP seemed to understand it was a positive pterodactyl shriek as that finger of his pushed me past the edge. Or maybe he didn't and my legs just tightened so much he couldn't get his hand out from under me, so had no choice but to leave it where it was as I came against his face. It didn't matter, not when I was clinging to his hair for dear life, my body tensing and releasing until my nerves were stinging from the overstimulation.

When those waves of pleasure faded, I loosened my grip on his hair and let my legs fall away from JP's ears. He pulled his fingers out of me, looking up with a semi-dazed and almost desperate expression on his face.

"Babe," he said, his voice hoarse with awe.

"Fuck me," I panted.

"You want a minute to—"

"*Fuck* me, JP," I demanded. "*Now.*"

He was on his feet in an instant, undoing his jeans and shoving them down. My arms were shaky as I pulled myself backwards on the bed. The moment I was back far enough, JP joined me, one dexterous hand working the buttons of his shirt open as he steadied himself on my open thighs. I reached down, grabbing his thick, throbbing cock as he finished unbuttoning his shirt and tore it off.

The tip of it was inside me before, nearly in unison, we froze.

"Nell," he whispered.

"Oh," I exhaled.

Wide blue eyes met mine as we stopped long enough to let our brains catch up.

"Condom?" he said.

"Everyone I've been with," I said.

"Same." He glanced down between our bodies. "Except you."

"Same," I whispered.

His throat flexed as he swallowed. "Pill?"

"Yes."

A beat of silence.

"Do you want to?" I asked.

His laugh was dry. "Babe, as previously mentioned, I am *definitely* only human. Do I want my dick to feel the hot, wet little pussy that my tongue just got to taste? You know how I'm going to answer that. So it's up to you."

I should have thought about it more.

Or at all.

Or at least hesitated for a moment or something.

But I just let go of his cock and looked up at him.

"Do it," I said.

The noise he made would live rent-free in my mind almost every time I fired up my vibrator for the next little while. It wasn't a moan or a groan. It was too heavy to be a whimper and too desperate to be a growl. And I was pretty sure—not entirely sure, but pretty sure—part of it included my name.

Whatever it was, it echoed in my ears as JP sank his cock inside me. I closed my eyes, basking in the relief of the sensation of *full* and the heat of his lips on the base of my neck.

"Fuck," he said. "This pussy is so good."

"You're welcome," I said.

He was already pulling out, but his cock jostled as he laughed and I made a soft noise of surprise at the rush of pleasure that ran through me.

"So fucking good," he repeated, his voice already strained. "So wet for me. So fucking *hot* for me. So... *ungh*."

His words fell off into a moan, his pelvis meeting mine as he filled me again. I opened my eyes, looking up at the lock of hair that was falling messily over his forehead and the haze of arousal clouding his eyes.

"Keep going," I whispered.

He half-laughed again. "This is going to be over in about thirty seconds if I go harder right now."

"Not that, idiot," I said. "Keep talking."

I half-expected him to make some smart-ass remark about me asking him to talk after shutting him up with my pussy earlier, but he didn't. He paused for a moment to readjust, then leaned in so his body was tight against mine and his breath brushed my ear.

"You know what I was thinking of while you were talking to everyone else at the event today?" he murmured.

"My pussy?" I asked.

He chuckled, pushing his cock deep and grinding his body against mine. "I was wondering what you had on underneath that cute little pink dress."

I rolled my eyes, trying not to gasp as his pelvis pressed against my clit. "I assume you wonder that about ninety percent of the women you meet."

"Of course not. It's seventy-five percent, tops."

"So you're trying to make me feel special by saying I was in the three-quarters of women you saw today that you pictured half-naked?"

"I can pretend you were the only one if that'll make you feel better."

I made an offended noise and he dipped his head down, pressing a hard kiss against my lips.

"You were the only one I pictured completely naked, though," he said, his voice low as he thrust inside me again.

"Lucky me."

"Very lucky you." He nipped at my lip. "I pictured your pretty pink nipples. Standing there, watching you, wondering if you still like it when someone bites them the way I did when you were stuffing my cock in this fucking *phenomenal* pussy."

A wave of heat washed over me and I tightened my hands on his back.

"I was remembering how you tried to keep quiet so my sister wouldn't hear you." He started moving faster inside of me. "And wondering—no. Not wondering. Fucking *praying* that you like having that perfect ass of yours played with." He chuckled, though the sound was strained. "Which I guess I know now. Because you loved that, didn't you?"

"Yes," I gasped.

He swore. "I knew it. I knew you'd love having my finger pressed into your tight little hole."

JP didn't have much of a Quebecois accent. On the surface it made sense, since he'd moved in next door when he was nine. But from growing up with Anne-Marie as a friend, I knew that she and JP were both born in Quebec and their family had moved to Toronto when she was a baby. But where Anne-Marie leaned into the Quebecois accent she'd developed after living here for a while, JP covered up the hint of the accent left from when he learned to talk.

But apparently when he got overwhelmed, it came out.

Apparently, when someone asked him to whisper things in their ear while he was fucking them, he couldn't help the slight changes in pronunciation he worked so hard to hide when he spoke in English.

"You take it so good," he said a while later. "Your sweet little pussy was made to be fucked like this, wasn't it, Nellie?"

He said my name the way most French people did, emphasizing the "Lee" part instead of the "Nell," and I murmured something incoherently pleased in his ear. He nipped at my neck, a hand moving up to my breast and gripping it as he kept thrusting into me.

"And it's *so* fucking sweet," he whispered. "But you know that, don't you? You've known it from the very first time you got fucked because you tasted yourself on my cock while I was coming down your throat. All this time, you've known how goddamn good your pussy tastes and I didn't. Haven't you?"

"Yes," I whimpered as the sparks of another orgasm flared inside me.

"Fuck." He buried his face against my neck. "I'm not gonna last much longer, babe."

"Just a bit more." I pushed my hips up to meet his body as he fucked me. "I'm close."

"Oh, God." His hand tightened on my breast. "How close?"

Not close enough, but I didn't say that. "Really close."

"Come on, then." His next thrust was deeper. "Fucking come for me, Nellie."

"Trying," I gasped, pushing a hand between us so I could rub my clit frantically. "Just a little longer. Please."

He made a choked noise, his hips slapping against me as he both chased his orgasm and tried to hold back. I played with myself, the sparks beginning to catch, my release so close I could almost see it and my legs starting to shake again.

"Babe," he said a few moments later, his tone both firm and desperate. "I have to pull out *now*."

"No," I gasped.

"Nellie, I can't hold—"

"Stay in."

His eyes went wide.

"Come in me," I whispered. "Just come inside me. Don't stop moving."

I wasn't entirely sure if he heard me, but either way, he didn't stop. His head bowed and a second later, the entirely new sensation of his cock pulsing inside me and the warmth of his cum coating the walls of my pussy pushed me over the edge.

I didn't mean to dig my nails into his back or to lock my legs around him so tightly. Just like I didn't mean to arch my back so much and didn't mean to moan in his ear and didn't mean to fuck him in the first place. But I did, and JP held me as I shattered beneath him, clutching me tight to his body as we came together.

When the pleasure subsided again and my legs loosened, JP reached up and brushed my hair off my forehead, his eyebrows furrowed. "Are you okay?"

I nodded.

"I'll buy you a Plan B if you want it."

I shook my head. "I'm on the pill."

"Yeah, but last time—"

"I was eighteen and was scared I'd get pregnant as soon as I started having sex. I'm a little smarter now." There was still uncertainty in his eye when I looked up at him. "But I mean, if it'll make you feel better…"

A small smile played across his lips. "Nah. I trust you, babe."

And as I sighed in exasperation, he laughed again.

Chapter Twenty-Seven
Inquiring Minds

"So when are you coming back?" JP asked.

I frowned at the question, but he didn't see it, since he'd asked while I was in the middle of pulling my t-shirt over my head. "Huh?"

He was smirking when I looked at him, halfway through buttoning up his shirt. "I said 'When are you coming back?' You know, here? To Montreal?"

"I heard you," I said. "Why are you asking?"

"Inquiring minds want to know."

My spine prickled and I turned away, pretending to fix my hair in the mirror so I didn't have to look at him. "I don't understand why the minds are inquiring."

He chuckled, walking up behind me and making eye contact with my reflection. "I just want to know the next time you'll be in town, Nell."

"You remember that whole thing where I told you I fuck around a lot?" I asked.

"Babe, you're good in bed, but the phrase 'fuck my brains out' is a metaphor," he said. "You didn't make me come so hard that I have short-term amnesia."

"And you didn't make me come hard enough that I'd consider being in a relationship with you, so I don't see why you care when I'm back in Montreal."

"Whoa, now," JP said. His voice dropped so much that I looked up at him, prepared to glare at him for his overdramatic antics, but the reservation on his face seemed far more genuine than I'd expected. "Who said anything about a relationship?"

"No one," I said, though I was secretly relieved by his reaction. "I'm just making sure that you're aware of that fact for completely unrelated reasons."

He came up beside me, turning so his back was to the vanity and leaning against it. "Listen, I don't know where you got it in your head that I'm pining after you or something, but I promise, I'm not trying to trick you into a relationship here. I don't have time for that."

"Good," I said. "Because I have some great casual things lined up right now that I'm not willing to give up for one guy's dick."

"What if it's a really good dick?" he asked.

"Unlikely," I said. "So you and your mostly acceptable dick have nothing to worry about."

He laughed. "*Acceptable*?!"

"Mostly."

"Mmm. Right. Your legs still numb or...?"

"Shut up."

"Nah." He laughed again as I glared at him. "I think you should tell me what other casual things you have lined up."

"Why do you want to know?" I asked.

"Just making conversation. Remember that whole thing where you told me you fuck around a lot and I was like damn, I want to know the details of the crazy shit Nellie's been up to because that's so different from the virgin she was the last time I saw her?"

"I wasn't a virgin the last time you saw me," I said. "Not even the last few times."

"You know what I mean," he said. "Tell me about your casual things."

"If I do, will you stop bothering me?"

"Maybe. At least until the next time you're in town."

"Because you're doing such a good job of convincing me to tell you when that is."

"I don't think it matters how well I convince you. You'll have to tell me anyway so we can figure out this whole LSAT tutoring thing."

Fuck.

He was right, which I refused to admit out loud. Not that it mattered, since both of us knew he was right, but still.

"Although," he said. "Seeing as you couldn't make it any clearer that you don't want to take the LSAT if you tried, I have a proposal for you that could be mutually beneficial."

Of course he did.

"Let me guess," I said. "If I have sex with you whenever I'm in Montreal, you'll pretend to tutor me all summer and tell my dad me taking the LSAT is a terrible idea so he'll get off my back?"

"Jesus Christ, Nellie," he said. "You think I'd ask for sex in exchange for that?"

There was so much offense in his voice that I almost felt bad. "I just meant—"

"I was *going* to say I'd pretend to tutor you all summer and then tell your dad you aren't cut out for being a lawyer in exchange for the occasional hand job and maybe a BJ if you wanted me to throw in an endorsement for whatever it is you're actually wanting to do with your life." He shook his head. "Your negotiating skills need work. You offered way too high right out of the gate."

"You're so funny," I said flatly.

His shoulders shook as he snickered. "I know. But seriously, no. I don't actually have time to tutor you and I'm also not into teaching in general."

"So why did you even offer in the first place?"

"Because I didn't think you'd end up needing to take it," he said, his voice so matter-of-fact that it made my chest ache about the fact that JP, for no discernible reason, had believed I'd get the internship more than my dad had. "It was an easy way to end the conversation without causing any drama."

I twisted my mouth to the side. "Alright, but that doesn't explain why you agreed today when my dad asked you."

He shrugged. "I'm not gonna pretend I know what the whole situation is with you and your dad, but something's obviously going on. I mean, my dad wouldn't ever make Anne-Marie go to an event with someone like Clinton or take the LSAT when she wasn't interested. So I figured I'd throw you a rope."

I rolled my eyes. "Bullshit."

He laughed. "Bullshit? How?"

"Because you get nothing out of this."

"And you think I'd only do this if I got something out of it?"

"Yes."

He raked his teeth across his lower lip. "I mean, we were still in the middle of the whole cat-and-mouse thing, so I figured it would be a good way to finally talk to you." I huffed and he chuckled again. "Look, it's not that hard to tell your dad I'm tutoring you and after a while, letting him know my professional opinion is that you shouldn't waste your time doing the exam because if you do eventually want to go to law school one day, your previous LSAT scores can affect your application. If that's what you want. And since it gives us a pretty good excuse to get together and fuck around every once in a while..."

"So that's what this is really about?" I said. "You want to fuck around again?"

"I'm saying you have the unique opportunity to spend your summer living out your very own student/teacher fantasy with an actual 'teacher' of sorts."

"I'm doing that."

The corners of his mouth turned down into a semi-impressed frown. "Damn. I thought I'd have to work harder to convince you. Alright, when's our first—"

"No, I mean I'm *already* doing that," I said.

His forehead creased. "Wait, like… for real?"

I half-shrugged, setting my lip balm down. "Technically he's my former professor, but yeah."

"You're banging a professor?" JP repeated incredulously.

My shoulders tensed. "*Former* professor."

"Ugh." He looked up at the ceiling. "Jealous."

My shoulders relaxed as I realized he wasn't about to get all judgy. "Sorry. I don't think you're his type."

"I meant the prof thing." He sighed. "All these years of school and I never hooked up with any of my teachers."

"Hmm. Well, guess you better consider going back to school. Maybe you could find something more useful to do with your life than being a lawyer."

He grinned. "Or maybe you could let me live vicariously through you next time you're in Montreal."

I sighed. "Don't you have a home to get to or something?"

He laughed, but dutifully finished buttoning his shirt without further comment. I didn't say anything either, following him down the stairs as he made his way to the door so I could lock it behind him.

Once he was gone, I wandered back to the living room. My pad thai was stone cold, of course, but that was nothing the microwave couldn't fix. As it reheated, I helped myself to one of the beers in my dad's fridge, bringing it to the living room along with my very late dinner and unpausing the docuseries I'd started before JP so rudely interrupted me.

I then proceeded not to absorb a single moment of what happened over the next two and a half episodes.

Because for some reason, I couldn't shake this odd, unsettled feeling that had started when JP had offered to pretend to tutor me.

For some reason, the idea of him faking a summer of tutoring made my stomach crawl in a way I couldn't quite describe.

For some reason, I couldn't get the echo of him telling me his dad would never make Anne-Marie do something like this out of my head.

Chapter Twenty-Eight
The Green Ones Are My Favourite

"I'm not taking the LSAT," I said.

My dad's eyes were like stone, his lips pressed together as he stared across the table.

"You agreed to," my dad said.

"I did." I dragged my spoon through the half-eaten bowl of fruit and yogurt in front of me. "But I've been thinking and—"

"If you were thinking, you would take the LSAT," he said. "Do I need to remind you *why*, exactly, you agreed to this?"

"Because you're holding money over my head."

Kimberlee's eyes went round. My dad's didn't, but I knew he was taken aback all the same from the way his hand tensed on the table, the skin around his knuckles fading to white.

"Am I misremembering, then?" he asked. "I thought it was because you lied to me about getting your internship."

"Yeah, and I explained why I did that." I put the spoonful of yogurt in my mouth. "I *also* apologized for it. I *also* agreed to go to a luncheon with a person I despise and don't feel safe around to make up for it. And I said I would give up a lot of time this summer to go to events with you and Kim...berlee."

"And you said you would take the LSAT, which was the other condition for having your tuition and expenses covered."

I nodded. "But Mr. Marchand made a good point yesterday. 'Might' isn't good enough to be a *good* lawyer. I'm not passionate about law and I probably won't ever be. No matter how hard I try, if I go into law, I'm always going to be mediocre and miserable."

"No daughter of mine will be *mediocre*," he said.

"But it's okay if I'm miserable?"

My dad had a pretty good poker face. He wouldn't have made a ruthlessly successful businessman if he didn't. But that was when he was at work. He was a different person there and on top of that, I'd had a lifetime of learning exactly what annoyed my dad and how it showed on his face. Sometimes he went red, like when I joked about having a dragon tattoo on my chest. Other times he clenched his jaw and it made his cheek twitch. And that was when he wasn't just giving a look that was a mix of exasperation and condescension.

But as much as I lived for doing stupid little things to annoy my dad because it was the only way I could rebel against his expectations, I also knew when he wasn't just annoyed.

That was when his face went stony. There were no muscle twitches, no heated blood rising beneath his skin to redden his cheeks, no pressing of his lips together as he gave me a patronizing look. A veil would come down, hiding the anger and disdain I knew was surging through him. The only thing that would truly change were his eyes. They were cold and grey as a default, but he had a way of darkening them even more by furrowing his eyebrows almost imperceptibly.

That was when he started to get *really* pissed off.

And that was what he looked like just then.

"You know the terms," he said. "No LSAT. No tuition. No allowance."

My hands were shaking, but I dug my spoon into my yogurt again, hoping no one would notice. "You remember yesterday how you said it wouldn't kill me to spend a bit of extra time with you?"

"I do," my dad said.

"Well, here I am." I pushed a raspberry around in my yogurt. "Because yeah, it doesn't kill me to do some things when the only reason is that you're my father. But taking the LSAT isn't one of those things. So while I can sit here and hope that you'll still help me out with school, I get it if you say no. Because the only reason for you to do it if I don't take the LSAT is that I'm your daughter."

I punctuated the sentence by putting the spoonful of yogurt and raspberry in my mouth, which meant that there wasn't even the sound of my spoon scraping against a bowl to break the awful silence in the kitchen. My dad's eyes were on me, as were Kimberlee's, but I didn't look at either of them.

"So that is it. You will not take the LSAT," my dad said.

"I'm not going to take it, no."

I wasn't sure if he was upset or proud that I called him out. The tension in the kitchen was too thick to tell either way. It was also hopefully too thick for my dad to hear how fast my heart was racing because the last thing I needed was for him to tell how fucking scared I was.

Because this might be it.

This might be the last time I sat at this table.

I was certain he was going to tell me it would be a snowy day in hell before he gave me another penny. That if I didn't take the LSAT, I wouldn't be worth his money anymore. And not just his money. I wouldn't be worth his approval. His pride. His support. And if I wasn't worth any of that to him, then it wasn't a stretch to think I wouldn't be worth his time.

Not that it mattered, since if I wasn't worth anything to him, he wouldn't be worth mine, either.

So there would be no reason for me to come back.

No reason for me to see him again.

No reason to keep up this charade that I'd been hiding from my mom.

It was as relieving as it was painful. A sense of peace had settled somewhere in my stomach at the knowledge that I'd be able to cut ties here, even if next to it sat a sense of heartache from the knowledge that I never had been and never would be worth it to him.

And yeah, terror was there, too. Fear. Anxiety. I'd have to figure out how to pay my own way for the first time in my life. As much as it embarrassed me to be a grown-ass woman whose only work experience ended in her getting fired because she forgot she had to work one weekend, that was what I was.

I'd have to learn a lot. And fast.

And that would be okay.

It would suck, but it would be okay.

So I waited. I waited for him to tell me this was it. For his dismissal and his derision.

I waited, and I braced myself.

And then my dad looked at Kimberlee and apparently, hell had a cold snap.

"Alright," my dad said.

"Alright?" I repeated.

His jaw twitched as he turned back to me. "You do not need to take the LSAT."

"I... don't," I said.

His lips pressed into a line. "I will have your tuition transferred next week and have my assistant resume your allowance payments."

Holy fuck.

"Thank you," I said instead of screaming, crying, and/or throwing up. "I appreciate it, Dad."

His cheek twitched and he nodded, the motion a sharp, businesslike staccato. "Kimberlee will send you additional details for events this summer you will be attending. We have a commitment to go to shortly, so you should begin your trip back to Ottawa early."

For the sake of peace, I pretended to be disappointed about that.

I finished eating my yogurt and went up to my room as quickly as I could without it being obvious that I was desperate to get out of there. By the time I'd packed my bag and went back downstairs, my dad and Kimberlee had already left.

Which seemed kind of like a dick move, but at least it avoided some kind of tense, awkward goodbye.

It didn't take me long to collect my stuff and take it out to my car. I glanced at the Marchands' driveway, where JP's BMW was parked, so I knew he was home, but there was no little yellow sticky note on my window this time.

Thankfully.

Popping the trunk of my Civic open, I tossed my bag in. Then I went back inside to get the couple of things I hadn't grabbed on the first trip.

When I got back to the driveway, JP was leaning against my car.

"Not worried someone's going to see you here?" I asked.

"Don't worry. My parents left for church and Anne-Marie stayed at Remy's last night. No one's around."

"That doesn't explain what you're doing here."

He shrugged. "I saw you heading out. Figured I'd say goodbye so I didn't have to wait another three years between fucking you and talking to you."

I rolled my eyes. "Move so I can leave."

He stepped back but didn't walk away. I got in the car, closed the door, and turned the engine on before buckling my seatbelt.

Then I rolled down the window.

"I'm going to be back the weekend after next," I said. "For another event."

JP nodded. "Is Clinton going with you again?"

I shook my head. "I only had to go to one event with him. Bruno said he'd be my date for anything else I needed this summer."

"Good."

I pressed my lips together, but didn't look at him. "You'll be around?"

There was amusement in his response. "I mean, when I'm not working, yeah. Why? Looking for some, uh... 'tutoring'?"

I shook my head. "I told my dad I'm not taking the LSAT."

JP's eyebrows arched up in surprise. "How'd he take that?"

"Well, I'm still stuck coming to a bunch of shitty events this summer, but he didn't outright disown me, so I'll call it a win."

He smiled. "Glad I'm off the hook."

"Because this is all about you, of course."

"Always. So if you don't need tutoring when you're back, should I assume you're promoting me to fuck buddy?"

"Shut up," I said. "No. You're just conveniently located."

"Right. Of course." He stepped forward, resting one arm on the roof of my car and bending so his body filled the rolled-down window. "You want to spend the summer hooking up with me whenever you get dragged to Montreal?"

"Maybe."

"And it would have to be a secret, I'm assuming."

"Of course. Why would I want anyone to know I'm into you?"

His smirk grew. "So you are into me?"

I gave him an unimpressed look. "I'm into your dick."

The smirk turned into an irritating grin that spread across his face. "Well, I'm glad to hear my mostly acceptable dick is worth sneaking around for."

"Are you interested or not, JP? Because if not, I'll find someone else to fuck."

"I might be interested."

"'Might' isn't good enough," I said, putting my car in reverse.

JP burst out laughing. "I'm kidding, babe. Yeah, I'm for it. Did you ever take my number off any of the notes I left or do I have to give it to you so you can let me know when you're around?"

I didn't respond. Instead, I reached over to the passenger seat to pluck a green sticky note off the back of my phone, stuck my arm out the window, and smacked it against JP's forehead.

"Now you have my number," I said, then rolled up the window as JP took the Post-It off his forehead. He stepped back from the car as I put my arm on the back of the passenger seat and looked out the back window while I backed down the driveway. When I reached the end of the driveway and glanced forward again, JP's shoulders were shaking with laughter I couldn't hear as he read the note, which consisted of my phone number and one line:

Let me know how the green ones taste

He shook his head, then blew me a kiss before turning to head back to his house. And as I watched him stroll back across the driveway and the stretch of yard between his house and my dad's, I bit my lip, partly out of nerves, but mostly so the huge grin I felt brewing inside me didn't spread across my face.

I had a feeling I was in for one hell of a summer.

The story continues in Hold Me If You Can, book 2 of the If You Can series, coming summer 2024!
Preorder your copy here: bit.ly/iycbook2

The Story Continues...

Find out what was going through JP's head in Chapter 8 with this exclusive bonus chapter!

Find it here: **geni.us/kmiycbonus**

Then grab your copy of Hold Me If You Can, the first book in the If You Can series: **geni.us/hmiyc**

Acknowledgments

I never know how to start these things. It feels like I should intro it but really, I just want to say thank you to a bunch of people. So here are those people.

Nora, Jason, Charlie, Lisa, and Kristi: thank you for your feedback, encouragement, and help in cleaning up this draft!

Nazarea Andrews from Inkslinger PR is amazing and keeps me sane.

Paul M, Kevin Matheny, PM, KJ, MidNyt, RP, Alex, and GW, and all my incredible supporters on Patreon and in my Cheryl's Terrors group are amazing. Thank you all so much for joining me on this journey!

The vast insanity that is all the family and friends who have been amazing supporters this whole time means I will almost certainly miss someone important if I try to list them all. Please just know I'm so grateful for your support and all that you do. For everyone who has asked for a bookmark or suggested my book to a friend or listened to me blab about something writing related - you make such a difference to me. Thank a million times over.

To my parents, thank you for being there for me and for all your encouragement. By the time this book is published, it will be 18 days until you retire (which is 12 working days). You're amazing and congratulations.

Becca and Rachel are amazing cheerleaders and supporters. Love you both and thank you for always being there for me!

Cheddar and Pumpkin: woof woof. bark bark. Good girls.

My husband is last on the list because I get all weepy and sniffly every time I think about how awesome he is and if I wrote his thank you first, I wouldn't be able to write the rest of them. So thank you for being my everything and all that you do for me. Love you more.

Xoxo, Cheryl

En Francais, S'il Vous Plait

Or, a List of Quebecois Words and Phrases In This Book

As the If You Can series is set partially in Montreal, there are several Francophone and bilingual characters. For practicality's sake, the book is mainly written in one language and it may be noted in the text whether a character was speaking French or English. However, there are points where specific words or phrases are kept in French. For those who would like a translation, they are listed on the following page.

Roche-papier-ciseaux - rock paper scissors

Ma fille ange - my angel girl or my angel daughter

Ce n'est Eleanor pas - It's not Eleanor

Mon nom est Nellie, s'il vous plait - My name is Nellie, please/Call me Nellie, please (intended to spoken "badly")

C'est fini - it's over/it is finished

Mes chers - my dears/my friends

J'ai besoin de mon espace - I need my space

Les nouilles ne sont pas toutes dans la soupe - the noodles are not all in the soup. Phrase to suggest someone is stupid, similar to "the crayons are not all in the box" or "not the sharpest knife in the drawer."

Cherie - dear, a term of endearment

La danse du loup - the wolf's dance. French euphemism for having sex

Ma coquinette - literally "my naughty," implication when used for adults (especially women) in a flirtatious or sexual situation. Similar to saying something like "naughty girl" or implying she's a tease. Like "naughty" in English, *coquine* or *coquinette* is sometimes used for mischievous children as well.

Bonjour - hello

La Nuit Rose - pink night

Lumière Et Amour - light and love

Waouh - expression of disbelief, like "wow"

T'es ben chix - you are hot/attractive

Parfait - perfect

Ciboire - a *sacre*, Quebec-specific religious themed profanity. Literally, the container hosts are kept in for Eucharist. Expression would be similar to exclaiming "Christ!"

Character List
Who's Who In Nellie's World

Nellie Belanger: Justified main character syndrome on account of being the main character. Rosy white skin, slightly chubby, blonde hair, brown eyes, 21 years old. Forensic science student attending Ottawa Tech, currently living in Ottawa. Known for being joyfully promiscuous and unapologetically against commitment.

Maximillian Belanger: Nellie's father. Mid-50s hedge fund manager who places a high level of importance on appearances. Greyish blue eyes, straight nose, light olive-toned skin, thick black hair, shorter than average. Lives in Montreal.

Kimberlee Dunn: Max's current girlfriend. Appears to be in her mid-thirties, light brown skin, dark brown hair, large eyes, and about the same height as Max. Involved with a number of charities and associations. Lives in Montreal.

Vicki McCauley: Nellie's mother. Mid-40s, manages an LCBO liquor store. Left Max 10 years ago. Brown eyes, long, frizzy blonde hair, rosy white skin, taller than Max. Flighty and impulsive, doesn't drive. Lives in Toronto.

Anne-Marie Marchand: Nellie's childhood best friend and next door neighbour. Tanned medium white skin, dyed blonde hair, brown eyes, tall and thin. Flighty and slightly out of touch at times but loyal AF. Lives in Montreal and speaks with a distinct Quebecois accent, peppering her dialogue with both French and English phrases.

Remy Tremblay: Anne-Marie's boyfriend. Tall, dark brown skin, coiled hair usually kept in twists or braids, brown eyes. Stoic and serious.

JP Marchand: Disgustingly good-looking and aggravatingly smart lawyer who is the older brother of Anne-Marie Marchand. Grew up next door to Nellie's dad. Tall, tanned light beige skin, thick wavy blonde hair, blue eyes, wide smile with one crooked tooth. Confident, snarky, and in Anne-Marie's words, a manwhore.

Marc-Andre Marchand: The youngest Marchand child. He exists.

Jean-Luc Marchand: JP and Anne-Marie's father. Looks similar to JP, overly serious. Highly successful lawyer who has his own practice.

Della Kinsley: JP and Anne-Marie's mother. Very involved in the charities, associations, and events.

Sydney Amhurst: Nellie's best friend. Tall-ish, pale skin, reddish-blonde hair, hazel eyes, athletic build. Currently lives in Ottawa and also attends Ottawa Tech.

Ben Cameron: Forensic psychologist and professor at Ottawa Tech. Medium gold-beige skin, thick brown hair with a grey streak above the left temple, hazel eyes, average height. Sydney calls him Professor Sexy.

Olivier: a police officer Sydney went home with after they met during a bachelor party Olivier was attending. Light brown hair, an inch or two shorter than Sydney. Lives in Montreal.

Christian: Generic Bad Boy Number One from the same bachelor party as Olivier. From Alberta.

Jesse: Cowboy who asked Nellie to help out with a scavenger hunt during the bachelor party.

Reid: Sydney's roommate and childhood friend. Lives in Ottawa.

Scott Humprey: Frat boy who wants more from Nellie even though she told him she was only after a casual fling. Lives in Ottawa and attends Ottawa Tech.

Bruno Lemaire: Friend of Remy's who agrees to be Nellie's date for social obligations over the summer. Lives in Montreal. White skin, dark brown hair and eyes. In Nellie's words, looks like he's one hair straightener accident away from a 2006 Myspace photo.

Adrian: Nellie's high school boyfriend who started rumours about the status of Nellie's vagina after she broke up with him for making horrible jokes about her. Lives in Toronto.

Clinton Thibault: Son of one of Max's business associates that Max would like to see Nellie foster a relationship with. Lives in Montreal. Wavy blonde hair, pale blue eyes, and a distinct lack of understanding of the word "No."

Join The Chaos

Every hot mess deserves a happy ending.

Get exclusive bonus scenes, short stories, novellas, and more by joining my newsletter: **cherylterra.com/newsletter**
Find even more bonus content, early access to new work, and weekly updates that I sometimes actually do post every week on my Patreon (free tier available!): **patreon.com/cherylterra**

Also By Cheryl Terra

Also By Cheryl Terra

Find all of Cheryl's books at cherylterra.com/stories

Aurora Flats Series

Fate and Fried Chicken

If You Can Series

The Boy Next Door
Kiss Me If You Can
Hold Me If You Can
Keep Me If You Can
Sleigh Me If You Can

Unicorn Confessions Series

The Unicorn Confessions
Unicorn For Sale
Death of a Unicorn

Love Across Canada Series

Get Over It
The Devil Made Me
Runaway
Finding Home

Standalones

When It Rains
Hearts at Play: Special Edition
One Little Question
What Happens In Vegas
Selfish Love
Another Last Call